TRANSCENDENT

INDESTRUCTIBLE TRILOGY: BOOK THREE

EMMA L. ADAMS

The world is ending. Again.

It's been four hours since a second divide tore through the earth, directly through the centre of the Pyros' base. Four hours since our escape. At a safe distance, behind a hill rise, I watch my home burn for the second time. Yesterday, this part of the country was green fields and rivers like a photograph of the world before, if not for the red sky. Now, the ugly jagged line of the divide mars the countryside, dividing the mountain down the middle and turning the green fields into burned, lifeless ground. Though the tremors have stopped, a red haze hangs above like smoke.

The sky's already burned-red, less impressive than the first time, two years ago, when the divide tore through the country. This time, once again, we had no warning. We barely made it out.

We've lost almost everything. There was no time to gather supplies. Even Murray's research labs are gone. We don't even have shelter, food or water. Pyros might be stronger than normal people, but we can only survive for so long outside. Especially with the fiends roaming the countryside. I'm reminded of the two years living on the road before the Pyros took me in. Two years of hiding. When I came into my powers as a Pyro, and again as Transcendent, I hoped against hope I'd be able to stop anything like the fiends' first invasion. But even though I as good as returned from the dead a few hours ago, I was powerless to stop them as they destroyed my new home.

It's a couple of hours until sunset, and although we have the advantage of numbers, we're far too close to the divide for my liking. But only a handful of fiends came through and attacked the base, fewer than I'd have expected if the second invasion has really begun. We can't see through to the fiends' world even close to the divide—the transparent barrier between our world and the twisted dimension the fiends call home. So what's their game? The silence is suspicious. I thought the fiends had a plan.

Unless they were setting the stage for the real invasion.

"Leah," says Elle, sidling up to me and wrapping an arm around my shoulder. I stiffen automatically, though I saw her coming. Her heart-shaped face is concerned, her blue eyes huge. "I don't think you should go back."

Here we go. "I'm all right," I say. "Besides, if the fiends come back, I'm the person with the most likely chance of making it out alive. Apart from Murray." The mountain's a no-go area even for regular Pyros now the divide's sitting right in the centre. But I'm no normal Pyro.

Elle winces. I didn't sugar-coat my words like I might have done before. Murray's fifteen-year-old daughter has had to do a ton of growing up the past few days. Since Jared, Murray's crazy brother and her own uncle, tried to kill her. And me. There's no denying we're desperate, waiting for the go-ahead for a small group of us to go back and try salvaging anything we can from our former home. While risking another attack if the fiends decide to appear again.

"You'll have the others," I say. "Safety in numbers, right?"

I don't voice my worries that a hundred and fifty of us make so much noise, it'll draw every fiend in the area. Most of us are more than capable of taking down one of the monsters. Some of us, more than one. But an army? And the Fiordans? I'm suspicious none of the fiends' twisted leaders showed up. If this were a real invasion, the Fiordans would have been leading the army, burning everything in their path. Sure, I killed one of them before, but there aren't enough of us to protect the whole planet.

The divide looms ahead. Mocking. Warning. I glare at it, wishing anger would burn away the fear twisting inside me. I might be more than human, but the last time the fiends invaded, over half the Pyros died—even the supposedly-invincible Transcendent.

I'm not sure I'll get a second miracle.

"How many are there?" Elle asks in a small voice. She's watching the divide, too.

I shake my head. "I don't know." It's the truth. I didn't see the army close up during my brief time in the fiends' world. Cas and I only had a distant glimpse. Most of the images in my head of the fiend army aren't from the present, but from visions I had of the first invasion, thanks to the blood-link I used to have with Cas.

Cas has been walking around the perimeter of the camp ever since we arrived, chasing after every suspicious sound. Only Murray's insistence stopped him wandering over to the divide itself. Probably to see if he could stick his blade in a fiend from this side. But that's impossible even for the almost-invincible Cas.

I'd join him, but he pretty much bit my head off when I suggested we each take one side of the camp to watch out from. Cas is not a team player. And now the fiends have made another play, the Cas I talked to back at the base has disappeared, leaving a soldier in his place.

I should be prepared, too. But despite having spent most of the past day unconscious, I feel mentally exhausted. In the last few days, I've been Jared's prisoner and experiment. I've been beaten to the point of near death, more than once. I've come so close to losing everyone I care about. And finally, Cas and I survived a trip to the fiends' world, where I killed Jared for the last time. As if that wasn't enough reason for a rest, I almost died from the blood-link connection Cas and I had. But it's been over twelve hours since I was injected with the cure Cas took from Jared's lab, and since then, I haven't had as much as a hint of a vision.

Let's hope it stays that way. There are no upsides to a freakish mental connection with someone who can't stand you, especially when it's actively *killing* you. I can't even complain that the cure was actually blood from the fiends' leaders, the Fiordans. The blood of the monsters that attacked Earth runs in my veins.

Cas walks past, weapon in hand though there isn't a hint of an enemy around. He doesn't look at me, and I can't deny the sting. I can't get the look on his face when he thought I was dying out of my head, but now he's avoiding me like I brought the fiends knocking on our doors.

It shouldn't bother me like this. *We're done. Our connection is broken, and good riddance. Now we need to worry about defending the Earth from a second invasion.*

Shockingly, that thought jolts my attention back to the present. "I'm going back," I say to Elle. "Come on. We might be Pyros, but we can't survive out here without food, water and shelter."

Technically, I can, since I'm Transcendent and virtually impossible to kill. But that won't help my argument.

"I know." She bites her lip. "I wish… you only just got back."

"Yeah, you'd think they'd have let us finish our party before attacking us," I say, in an attempt to lighten the mood. She gives a reluctant laugh. "Anyway. Let's go see Murray."

I have a list of questions for him the length of my arm, but no one will give him a moment's peace. Murray's the leader of the Pyros. But he's also Transcendent, like me. I found out during the fight with Jared, and I've yet to question him on his many secrets. Right now, he's surrounded by at least fifty people shouting questions. My heart sinks. *This is impossible. Surely he knows we don't have much time before sundown.*

"Leah?"

I turn at the sound of my name. Val stands with some of the other senior Pyros. I head over, Elle behind me.

"Hey," I say. "Are we going back to the base?"

Val shakes her head. "It's too risky. From what Cas told us from his last report, the whole mountain's unstable. Not even we can survive being buried alive."

"But…" *I* could survive it. But I'd never risk the others, and I promised Poppy and Tyler I wouldn't run off and do anything risky alone. Considering the circumstances, though, I have a feeling that promise is going to be tricky to keep.

"There's a town nearby," says Val. "Murray used to be friends with the leader, a few years ago. We've kept them safe from the fiends, so they owe us a favour. We can get supplies from there. They have some stockpiled," she adds, in response to my incredulous expression. I lived rough for two years following the fiends' invasion. The concept of sharing blew up in smoke along with half the planet. Most towns refused to let outsiders in, because they had enough trouble feeding their own populations. And they especially hated the red-cloaked strangers. I never could have imagined the Pyros would be my new family.

"If you're sure," I say, doubtfully. "Last time some of us knocked on the door of a town, we had guns shoved in our faces."

"This is different," says Val. "I've never been there myself, but if Murray knows them, there's a good chance we'll be able to get at least some supplies, if not shelter."

And if not? If they have guns, like the people at the town...

It seems like yesterday. The day Cas and Nolan found me cornered by a fiend in an abandoned house, after the energy blast killed my companions.

The last day I was in any way human.

The thought hits me like a blow to the chest. I suck in air, like I really have been punched. "I'll go, if you want me to," I say. "But... how close is the town to the divide?"

That's the other snag. The new fault line will doubtless have cut right through some surviving towns and villages. I don't know how many people there actually are left in what used to be the UK, let alone the rest of the world. The entire south side of the first divide could have been obliterated, for all I know. London was. So were the other major cities.

Val doesn't answer for a minute. I can't stop thinking about the first attacks now. Things were so confused back then, when we went from online updates on impending catastrophe to losing the entire world's power supply overnight. The end happened over a two-day period: destruction, death, the disintegration of the human race. And it started with the divide.

But the second divide didn't cause nearly as much damage. Which makes me suspicious. Though as half-invincible creatures which can energy-blast people to smithereens, they don't need a flashy entrance to be a threat.

Maybe they're already here. Hiding.

"Murray plans to go there himself," she finally says. "I can't talk him out of it. It makes sense, because they know him there, but we had to leave our radios behind. We have no way to contact anyone."

"He's the one everyone's turning to for answers." I suspect the latest bombshell, that Murray isn't fully human, is the only reason people aren't bombarding *me* right now. That, and the fact I nearly died less than twelve hours ago. A very good job my Transcendent body is good at recovering fast, otherwise I wouldn't have been able to run when our home collapsed.

"Then what? You and the senior Pyros... you can watch the group. Cas has turned into a one-man guard patrol on his own, right?"

"We're too close to the divide," she says. "Our best bet is to move away, but that'll take us into the hills. We're more exposed. And the town's the opposite way. Murray could walk it, but we need to decide if we're going to move first."

"And...?" Does she want my approval? I'm not exactly leadership material. I became Transcendent by total accident, when Cas healed me from certain death with his own blood. As an artificial Pyro, Cas has the resilience and deadly fighting skills of a Transcendent, but not all of our abilities. Like the energy blasts.

Wait. "You think the blasts are coming," I say. "Right? Because if the town's within a mile of the divide..."

It'll be wiped out. Last time the blasts radiated outwards, sending a ripple through the country, the world. Damn. I *need* to talk to Murray. If he knows about this...

"You talk to him," says Val, startling me. "I'll try to take over some of the questions. It's not a question of who's capable of leadership. It's a question of practicality and preparing for any eventuality, even if it means going against the obvious option. The first time it happened, I was far enough away to avoid the attacks, but I *saw* them."

I stare at her. I didn't know Val was outside during the first invasion. *Idiot.* She'd been with the army, I assumed.

"What happened?" I ask.

"I was with Murray after the Transcendent fell," she says. "He'd been injured, and couldn't fight. But he recovered fast. I guess it makes sense now."

So Murray never told her, either. He's killed her trust, and probably that of his other senior Pyros, too. If he leaves, anarchy might break out. Then again, that might happen anyway, judging by some of the vocal anger coming from some of the other Pyros.

Like we need to argue amongst ourselves now.

"I know," I say. "Well, you've known Murray for longer, but... even when he was being secretive, it was usually for good reason." I say this more for my own benefit than anything, because I need the reminder. I'm none too pleased about the lies either, but I understand. Sort of. Murray lied about Jared to stop the others panicking. Up until yesterday, only Cas and I had any idea that the tattoo marks on Jared's hand-picked favourites from the original Pyros were intended for blood control. The others are dead, apart from Val, Cas and Elle, and I've no idea why he picked those people in particular. Maybe as potential Transcendents.

There's so much I don't know. So much I could have found out, as his prisoner, if I'd at least pretended to cooperate instead of attacking him and pushing him into turning him*self* into one of the monsters. Maybe some people would still be alive.

Stop it. He's dead. You killed him. It won't undo what he did, but at least one enemy isn't coming back.

"There's a difference between secrecy and lying for no

good reason." Val shakes her head. "Garry says we should elect a new leader."

"Who?"

She shrugs. "You got a couple of nominations."

"Oh, no." I raise my palms. "I have no idea how to take care of a huge group of people out in the wilderness. Being powerful doesn't make a good leader." I hesitate. "Guess that's why they haven't kicked Murray out, isn't it?"

"He's never given any indication he might have *that* kind of power," says Val quietly. "But he was always the defender, keeping everyone safe, not fighting on the front lines. If he didn't use that power to defend us last time..." Doubt creeps into her voice.

"He wasn't *born* Transcendent," I say. "He made himself that way with fiend blood. Could it have happened after the attack?" I of all people know how hard it is to adapt when there's no information. Murray *told* me he gathered most of it after the last Transcendent died.

"He won't say." Val sighs. "Garry and some of the others are holding every word against him, which makes it difficult for the rest of us to get a word in edgeways. We shouldn't be fighting."

"I know that," I say. "I need to talk to him. Urgently, actually. It'd help to have a discussion without everyone wanting in on it. Especially when *I* have Fiordan blood, and I don't know for sure if it's stopped the connection..." I trail off, regretting telling her already.

"Have you spoken to Cas about it?"

"We were interrupted by the invasion," I say. "I haven't had any kind of visions since, but it's probably too early to tell."

"Oh." She frowns. "I would have thought... it's not an exact science, though, is it? This is why I wish Murray had confided in someone. Even Elle."

"He lied to her, too," I say. "But about what happened in the fiends' first invasion, I've only seen it in parts, in visions. I never got to ask Cas about the details. Did you know the Transcendent?"

"Not well," says Val, sweeping her ponytail over her shoulder, streaked with reddish dust from our escape. "I was at the back of the fighting when the invasion happened as I'd only just qualified as a Pyro. I had no idea she and Cas slipped away. I blacked out for part of it—I guess Jared activated the tattoo. When I woke up, there was chaos."

"And you knew Jared did it?"

She shakes her head. "You have to understand that he was one of our best fighters. He saved lives, not just Pyros but humans', too. None of us could have guessed he was working against us. When the fiends came, we were focused on our own survival. Nothing could have prepared us for an attack on that scale, because up until then, the Fiordans came through one, maybe two at a time."

I nod. Jared showed me a propaganda video when I was his captive, of the shapeshifting Fiordans appearing from nowhere. At least, that's what it looked like. But I didn't know how convincing his act was. *Bastard.* He'd better stay dead this time.

"So when they appeared with an army, there was nothing we could do. We lost all contact with overseas, even the rest of the country. We lost two thirds of our group, including our other base. The chaos… it was unparalleled. The most we could do was stop the invasion, but nobody knew exactly *when* it stopped. We regrouped and Murray told us Jared was dead, and so was the Transcendent. But at the same time, the fiends stopped crossing the divide. We'd had to move back, far back, because energy blasts were striking across the area near the divide and there were just too few of us. People were dying by the thousands…"

I can't breathe. Because I remember what I was doing at the time. I was at home, watching the carnage on TV, before the power outage. It took another twelve hours or so for the energy blasts to reach my home.

Time we could have been running.

I shake off the thought. This would have happened no matter what. Being Pyro is pure luck and barely kept me alive up until the Pyros found me. As for Transcendence...

"Was Murray fighting?" I ask. "There were other bases, but I guess like that lab, they got taken out."

"Murray... I have no idea," she says. "The Transcendent and Cas were on the front lines. Murray and Jared gave the orders. But Jared was supposed to have fallen into the divide, sometime in the chaos. I never questioned that was what happened until he came back, and..."

"Nolan said something odd," I say. "When we were in the fiends' world. He said Jared thought some of the Pyros survived. In the *fiends'* world."

Val blinks at me. "Nolan died, didn't he?"

"Yeah. At least I think so... it might have been one of the Fiordans, but he *acted* like Nolan, and... he's dead now, anyway. But he sounded convinced. I didn't even know there was another group."

"It's been a long time since any of us talked about them," says Val. "Our other founding members were amongst them, and they were lost on the other side of the divide. We couldn't get close for at least a week, and there was no trace left. Murray ordered us back to the mountain, and since then, we've lived in secret, only going out in small groups. Defending people where we can, of course. Trying to build up our numbers again. I can't believe so many..." She swallows, eyes glistening with tears. Guilt churns inside me. I didn't know any of the Pyros who died during the escape from our collapsing base, but I feel responsible all the same. You'd think we'd have had some warning.

You'd think I'd have learned by now that the fiends don't play fair.

"Could it be possible?" I ask. "I didn't think humans could survive over in the fiends' world. But Jared did. And he had spies flying in and out of the divide all the same. He said… he said only people with fiend blood could cross over. So…"

"He must have been lying about the others," says Val. "We can't worry about that now, anyway. We have to protect the survivors."

"I know," I say quietly. How many more had their lives torn from them today? What's the point in being all-powerful if we can't protect them? Small mercy that the energy blasts were relatively limited this time. For all we know, it *could* have been a prelude to something bigger. Not knowing *what* is the part that bothers me the most.

Val looks over at Murray, who's beckoning all of us to come closer. A chill runs down my back, for some reason.

"I hope he's thinking clearly," she says. "He's been through too much. Almost losing Elle…"

"Yeah. He owes *her* an explanation," I say. "It's a mess."

But Val and I walk over to join the crowd jostling around our leader. Murray has to call for quiet several times and three other senior Pyros, including Val, help calm the crowd down.

"We've come to a decision," says Murray. "I'm going to lead a small group to the nearest town and pick up supplies. There'll be time enough to debate over leadership when I return, but survival is our first priority. I'm going to ask you ten of you to gather groups to set up watch stations around our camp. Especially near the divide. There's no guarantee the Fiordans aren't planning another attack, and we've lost too many people due to being unprepared. I will answer as many questions as I can, but later, once we have basic necessities in place. We won't be taken unawares."

How can you know that? I want to ask.

Murray names ten Pyros. I'm one of them. I ask to patrol the area closest to the divide.

"I don't see why not," says Murray, to my surprise. *Good.* I can't be in three places at once, but at least I can watch the most likely place for the invasion.

"But that's the most dangerous," protests Poppy, with a glance at Tyler.

"Well, yes," I say. "I don't want the fiends sneaking up on any of us. You guys can be my backup, okay?"

Tyler gives me a faint smile. "Excellent."

They're a lot more optimistic than me. I arrange my group so I'll be closest to the danger zone, but I can't help hearing some of the whispers that Murray, our esteemed leader, is losing his mind. Just like Jared.

Maybe the fiends aren't the ones I should be worried about.

2

Murray departs for the town with his group. I'd hang back as long as possible to make sure certain senior Pyros, especially Garry, behave themselves, but I need to concentrate on the potential threat from the divide instead.

"All right," I say to Poppy and Tyler. "You stick behind me, shout if you see anything." We arrange ourselves across a range of low hills enclosing our camp, so we face the distant ugly line of the divide. I ask the others to trade positions every few minutes or so to make sure we cover the whole area. Maybe I'm not terrible at making decisions. But this isn't the same as deciding the fate of an entire group of people in the face of the second end of the world.

I quickly realise I hate keeping watch. I've learned to be vigilant from spending so long in the wilderness, but the idea of staying in one place when I'd rather be running, fighting, taking care of the threat, is more than I can stand right now. I didn't know how much the Pyros' way of thinking has affected me. Or maybe it's from being trapped in Jared's lair for so long. But I almost hope a fiend comes and attacks me just to quell the tension.

Minutes pass. Worry about Murray and his group makes me even more restless. I hope he knows what he's doing, and it'd be nice if he let the rest of us in on it, too.

I glance to my right to see Poppy and Tyler have moved close enough together that they can talk and still cover the same area of camp. Poppy waves me over. I keep one eye on the divide, but talking to another person might stop me going crazy over here.

"Nothing's around," says Tyler, fiddling with the end of a dreadlock, his eyes huge and exhausted. "Am I the only person thinking that's odd?"

"Definitely not," I say. "If there was a massive invasion, you'd think there'd be more signs. Like the energy blasts."

"I wish we could see what's happening on the other side," I say. "It makes no sense from our end, but if they have a plan, the Fiordans…"

Poppy shudders. Her dark skin is pattered with red dust fragments, and she looks as tired as Tyler. "Of course they have a plan. They're barbaric, bloodthirsty monsters. Murray said the reason they haven't struck back until now is because we wiped so many of them out the first time."

"He did?" I blink. So he really is telling everyone the truth now. But I have the sneaking suspicion it might be too little, too late.

"Yeah," says Tyler. "You knew, right? No… you weren't with us two years ago."

"I didn't know until recently, same as you," I say, guilt washing over me. "Jared told me more about the Fiordans than Murray did. Because he was trying to get me to join his cause."

"Creep," says Tyler. "That guy can't be dead enough, in my book. And he was like Murray, Transcendent?"

"Yeah, but he did it to himself. Something was going wrong in the end. He was going crazy. Even crazier than usual, that is."

"His own fault," says Poppy. "He injected himself with monster blood…" She trails off. My heart sinks like a stone at the glance that passes between them. *They know where my blood came from. Surely.* But I *look* human, and I guess it's easy to forget I'm closer to the monsters than any of us here, especially after their blood saved my life.

"I don't know what went wrong," I mutter, no longer feeling like talking. I want to move closer to the divide, but it's transparent from this side. From their side, too, actually. I've wondered more than once lately if the Fiordans ever had spies on our side. But we'd have guessed if they were amongst our own group, and the Pyros have always killed any fiends we've come across. No way anyone here's a traitor. Nobody in their right mind would side with the fiends.

So how could they know where our base was, to open the new divide right inside it? It can't be a coincidence. They must have known. Somehow, I think Jared had something to do with it.

"Sorry, Leah," says Poppy, startling me. "I know it's been hard for you."

I look away. "It's been hard for all of us. It doesn't matter now. All that matters is surviving… this." Whatever *this* is.

I let my gaze drift over to the divide again as I resume pacing my route. Cas, who ignored Murray's instructions, carries on walking alone across the back line of camp. Watching for fiends. Or for a sign. Hell, maybe even he's trying to spy on them. We're at a serious disadvantage here no matter which way you look at it. Jared might have been crazy, but he knew the fiends were coming. He might even have known about the attack.

Wait… there *is* a way. Jared's fiends, if any of them are still alive. We share blood, and some of them have *spoken* to me before. What if…?

There's no way I can sneak off alone. For one thing, I promised Poppy and Tyler I wouldn't throw myself in harm's way again. But it's hard for me to promise not to risk my life for the friends I've gained since meeting the Pyros, a comfort I never thought I'd have again. After losing my sister, I closed myself off from other people. Not hard, in a small group where we only spoke when necessary, surviving on the edge. I never expected I'd have reason to open myself up to friendship again. To trust. It's difficult not to be reckless when you're a Transcendent. But it's unfair on everyone to take a risk that might well be fatal not just for me, but for them, too.

For all I know, the Fiordans are waiting for us to make the next move and planning a counter-strike of their own. Their world is a dead zone. And yet if Nolan really *was* Nolan, the enemy was nowhere near that part of the divide.

Also, I can't help but remember all the fiends that broke into the base in the attack earlier… were Jared's. Engineered. I'm more convinced than ever that the Fiordans *aren't* responsible for the freakish mutations. Jared is. But why attack us now? And how *did* Nolan survive if he wasn't Transcendent? Cas killed him the second time.

I don't want to think about that right now. We have more than enough enemies already. It's painfully obvious that we're outnumbered by far, even if I don't know the extent of the fiends' army. Two hundred against countless thousands. Maybe more. The Pyros have been killing them for two years.

And there's only one thing we can do: find a way to close the divide for good. I always thought that was the job of the Transcendent. But maybe there *is* no way to close it. Maybe the damage the fiends did when they broke through the first time went too deep.

A sharp pain runs up my right arm, so sudden I gasp. Like pins and needles, times a hundred. It's an eerie reminder of the pain I felt through the connection with Cas. The tattoo.

Impossible. Firstly, Jared's dead. Secondly, the connection's gone, and I was never marked like the others. Jared did inject me with a drug for obedience, but it didn't work because Cas switched it out with blood. Mine.

My arm throbs. I push up my sleeve. Nothing unusual, except the veins in my wrist are maybe a bit darker than usual. I let my sleeve fall back and ignore the pain. I'm Transcendent, and any injuries will heal within minutes... *I think.*

I push the nagging worry down and concentrate on watching, waiting. It's enough to drive a person mad.

I'm so deep in a trance, it takes me a few seconds to register the appearance of a figure in the distance. But once I do, my hand immediately snaps to my weapon, my pulse races, and I step forward, approaching slowly. A human-shaped figure. But they're coming from the divide.

Human. Male. Not wearing a red coat. Dark clothes. Stumbling on the rocky ground.

I pull out my dagger all the same. I'll take no chances. Casting a glance to either side to make sure this isn't a set-up or trap, I walk forwards. I'm not about to let a stranger, enemy or not, get near the others.

The man spots me, angles his feet towards me.

I stop dead. *Impossible.*

His face is Jared's.

Three times, Jared's come back from apparent death. Three times, I've killed him. This time, it *can't* be him. I'm not hallucinating. I'm nowhere near the divide. Not close enough to start seeing things. And he's not just on this side, he's only metres in front of me.

This man's expression is fearful. Not like Jared's at all.

Wait. "Who are you?" I ask. There are two possibilities, and right now, a voice is telling me he's not one of the Fiordans. He wouldn't have confronted me so directly if he was. Right? But I can't count on anything.

Shoving back the memories of the torture I suffered at the hands of the real Jared, I raise my weapon. "Tell me, or I'll kill you."

The man stops. His expression, now I see up close, isn't familiar on Jared's face. Fear, for sure.

"Who the hell are you?" I demand, again.

"I… I don't have a name. You know that, Transcendent."

Transcendent.

"You're one of them." My voice drops, but a small amount of relief seeps through. I can deal with Jared's Transcendents. But whose side is he on?

"Three of us were buried in the ruins of the lab," says the man. "I've walked all day to find you."

"Why me?"

"You're the only one who can help us, Transcendent."

I almost laugh. This feels like a joke. One of Jared's experiments asking for my help? But they were never on Jared's side, and without his mark, they're free… but that doesn't mean I can trust them.

"Why do you look like Jared?" Stupidly, that's the first question I ask. But I can't look at his face without seeing the man who tortured me.

"Our shifting abilities are… limited," says the man. "After Jared last injected us, we stopped being able to shift back into our first bodies."

My stomach gives a sickening lurch. *Oh, God.* Maybe he's telling the truth. That level of sadism is like Jared, all right. Before, they were people Jared dragged in from nearby towns to use as his experiments. For some reason, possibly to freak me out, he transferred some of the Fiordans' shapeshifting abilities over to them, making them all look like Jared himself.

"So why do you need my help? Jared's dead."

No answer. His blank-eyed expression is nothing like Jared, always animated. And insane.

"How do I know you're not trying to distract my attention?" I ask, suddenly suspicious. "I'm not stupid. The Fiordans are planning something."

"They are," he says. "They're…"

"Leah!" A shout. Damn. Poppy and Tyler approach, weapons in hand at the sight of the Transcendent.

"Wait," I say quickly. "It's, uh, he's not really Jared. One of his Transcendents."

"So what!" Poppy brandishes her sword at him. "Get away from us, you monster. Val!"

Oh, crap. Val's within hearing distance outside the camp, talking to… Cas.

Of course, Cas is the first to march over, sword at the ready. Before I quite know what I'm doing, I move to stand between the Transcendent and the others. Not before glancing over my shoulder. Sure, he appears to be unarmed, but judging by Transcendent strength and whatever Jared injected him with, I'm not taking any chances.

"You're Fiordan," says Val, fury twisting her expression. "Get out of our world, you scum."

The Transcendent shakes his head slowly, hesitantly.

"Wait," I say. "It's one of Jared's Transcendents."

Val stares at me.

"They looked like Jared in the end," I say. "No idea why. It was after he went crazy, I think he wanted to mess with me so I didn't know which was the real Jared. Not that he wasn't crazy anyway…" I'm babbling. Mostly with relief. The Transcendents are no friends of the fiends, or Jared himself, come to that.

At least… they weren't. But with Jared dead, I can't tell where their loyalties now lie.

"How do you know *it* isn't lying to you?" Val draws her weapon, like Cas, and the two point the tips of their blades at the Transcendent.

"I don't," I say. "But he doesn't act like Jared, and the Fiordans would have kept up the act. He doesn't serve Jared now he's dead. He claims he knows something about the Fiordans' plans."

"That so?" Ignoring me completely, Cas marches past me and grabs the Transcendent by the wrist. Hard. I'm surprised he doesn't immediately skewer him, but instead he pushes up the Transcendent's sleeve to reveal Jared's mark. The blood tattoo. It's black, not red like it used to be.

"Answers first," I say quickly, with an imploring look at Val.

"We'll take him back to camp," she says. "He'll be our prisoner."

"He deserves worse," says Cas, glaring at him. I guess he, like me, can't see past Jared's face.

"If he has information we need—"

"Cas, bring him to camp," says Val, her expression hard. With a jolt, I realise that I've never seen her face to face with Jared. Not as herself, rather than his puppet. I forgot how angry she'd be with anyone who remotely looks like him, because he mind-controlled her and forced her to attack me.

Oh, shit. There's absolutely no way the rest of the group would accept them as allies even if they did have information. And if Murray let them in? They don't trust him anymore already.

This can only end badly, no matter what.

"Leah, you keep an eye out," says Val. "Just in case there are more out there."

"There are two," I say. "But Jared's dead. They don't have anyone giving them orders. They were buried in the ruins of the lab."

Damn. More than a few people are staring in our direction already. Cas grabs the Transcendent roughly by the arm and hauls him along. The Transcendent says nothing, just studies his feet and stumbles after.

Stumbles. Transcendents don't stumble.

Something's wrong.

My arm tingles, a shiver of pain running to my elbow. I watch the Transcendent as Cas leads him out of sight, until Poppy calls me back.

"I'll bet he was sent to distract us," she says. "The scum. We should have killed them all."

"They're unkillable," Tyler reminds her. "Damn creepy…" He trails off. My heart sinks further. I'm far from trusting the other Transcendents, but knowing how quickly the others judge, I'm one step away from becoming another enemy. Right now, only a handful of people really know what being Transcendent *means.* Or, being Jared's prisoner. And if I take the Transcendent's side in anything, I might lose their support. Not that Cas provided much in the way of *support.*

"Maybe they are," I say, "but we need information."

I'm not about to go anywhere, but I can't stop glancing over my shoulder every couple of minutes all the same. I'm not just worried Cas or one of the others might kill a potential ally. I'm more concerned with how the other Transcendents would react if they did. The very last thing we need is to bring the wrath of up to eleven more almost-invincible lab creations down on us.

Aren't you the same? The voice cuts in before I can stop it. The voice that carries the whispers of the few people who didn't join in the celebrations when I woke up after being injected with the cure.

Not human.

Unnatural.

Are we like Jared, now?

I try to shut the voices out, but they're relentless. Because where *is* the line? Have we already crossed it, in doing exactly what Jared did? How do I know there aren't people in camp who'd happily dissect our prisoner to gain a chance of winning the war? Murray himself let Jared lock people in cages, if those skeletons I found in the mountain cave are any kind of proof.

I'm not even sure I *know* Murray. And that might be the most frightening part.

Hours of watching later, I trade places with one of the other Pyros. I'd rather not move out of sight of the divide, but night's falling and judging by the noise from camp, Murray's back.

And I need to talk to him.

I walk through camp. No one notices me at first, because most people crowd around one area at the west edge of camp. I already know what I'll find there: Cas, watching over our prisoner. Val's there, too. And Murray—by the look of things, the crowd's waiting for him to wait a decision.

"Kill it," says Garry, who's hovering at Cas's side.

Cas shoots him a glare. "I would," he says, "but some people think we can get information out of it."

It. Like the Transcendent's not human.

"Hold on," I say, pushing through the crowd to Murray. "He's one of the Transcendents. He never served Jared willingly. I say we get information. Whatever he's willing to…" I trail off, my heart sinking. I wondered why the Transcendent didn't speak: he lies limp on the rocks. Knocked out, or dazed. Blood streaks one side of his face. "Who hit him?"

"Garry did," says Cas. "Though I was quite tempted myself."

"That's enough," I say. "Murray, you're in charge here. This Transcendent claimed to know what the Fiordans were planning. Of course, if *some* people hadn't decided to knock him out, he might have told us."

"Like I'd believe the enemy," says Garry, unimpressed.

Val cuts in, "They're too unpredictable. They served *him.*"

"Not by choice," I say. "They turned on him as soon as the spell wore off, tried to kill him."

"And how do we know they won't do the same to us?" Val counters. "I know you try to see good in people, Leah, but this is war."

"Exactly why we need information," I say.

Everyone turns to Murray, who runs a hand through his greying hair. "If he has information, it's in our interests not to hurt him and potentially antagonise the other Transcendents."

Thank you. "That's what I said. The Fiordans are out there somewhere, and I don't know about you, but I have no idea what they're planning. It's not like them to attack and run, not if they want to conquer Earth again."

I keep my eyes on Murray, wondering, not for the first time, if *he* knows more than he's letting on. Being Transcendent is a pretty big secret to keep, and considering how people reacted when he told them... what if he has other secrets, too?

"Perhaps not," says Murray. "We managed to get supplies, at any rate, so our first priority is getting our camp properly secured. Then I'll give everyone a more detailed explanation of our current options."

"The town let you in?" I ask, having completely forgotten the mission.

"Luckily, their leader remembers how we helped them in

the past. I only hope we can keep the fiends away from them."

"So that's the plan?" asks Garry, eyes narrowing. "We sit and watch? We're supposed to be soldiers."

"And we have a prisoner of war now," says Cas. "I'll get answers out of him."

"Cas," I say warningly. "Like Murray said. We don't want to provoke him *or* the others."

Val shakes her head. "They're not natural. They're not *human.* They have fiend blood, for God's sake."

Cas stiffens. Too late, Val seems to realise what she's said.

"I'll speak to him," I say quickly. "And we need to make sure no one's planning an ambush."

"Double the guard," Cas says harshly. "Especially near the divide. I think we should relocate the camp a few miles or so back."

"Wait," says Murray, before anyone else can speak. A fair few people are listening in. "It'll be nightfall in a couple of hours. We're all tired and hungry and stressed, and the last thing we want is to be out in the wilderness with the fiends roaming. This area's reasonably sheltered, and we have guards posted. That's all we can do."

And that's it. I'm torn between wanting to check for approaching enemies and waiting here for the Transcendent to wake up. He must have hit his head pretty hard, and I briefly wonder about the damage before remembering he can heal. *Idiot.*

So is he pretending to be unconscious?

Making sure no one's behind me, I sneak off while the others crowd around Murray's approximation of a campfire. The senior Pyros are in charge of setting up campfires. I'm starving, actually, but I'm not about to pass up an opportunity to question the prisoner. Who, I'm starting to think, has an agenda of his own. I crouch down beside him.

"Are you awake?"

No response. Frowning, I drop to my knees and lift his head. His eyes are closed, and his breathing is shallow. But aside from the dried blood on the side of his face, he doesn't appear seriously hurt. So why...?

"Talk to me," I say. "I'm not going to hurt you. Better you tell me what you know."

No response. Looking at Jared's sleeping face is creeping me out, so I place the Transcendent's head against the rocky ground again. Not exactly comfortable, but he doesn't move.

A shiver runs over my skin, prickling between my shoulder blades. What if Jared did something to the Transcendents? He's dead. The tattoo mark has no effect on him. But for all I know, he gave them an expiry date.

Damn. No way to tell. The Transcendent isn't awake, so I leave him and head back to camp again, managing to scrounge some food without being besieged by questions. The others are rotating guard patrols. I should be, too, but I want to hear what Murray has to say.

And I have some things of my own to say, before anyone makes a snap decision that puts us in danger. Okay, I'm thinking of Garry, mostly. And Cas, come to that. Hell, I don't even know what *Val's* planning anymore. I guess I was stupid to think having a prisoner who looks exactly like the man who wrecked all our lives would be overlooked.

But I can't help thinking of the Transcendent who turned on Jared. The one he tortured and locked in a glass case. The way he made them fight to the brink of death for his own amusement. If this one *is* innocent, it'd be, well, inhumane to torture and kill him.

I've seen humans do terrible things in the past two years, but I feel genuinely sick to imagine my friends tormenting another person. Before Jared turned him into a Transcendent, did he have a name? A life?

I'm driving myself crazy with my own thoughts. I look for Murray, and see he's taken up a central position near the campfire, others clustered around him. I head over that way.

Unsurprisingly, everyone's talking over one another and it takes several minutes of noise before Val says, "Enough! We need to come up with a plan, not sit around bickering. Murray has information. Don't you?"

The accusation in her tone is unmistakable.

"Yes, I do," says Murray. "Firstly, I gather you're aware that our mission was a success. It seems we have allies amongst the townspeople after all. But their defences aren't enough if the fiends mount a mass attack."

"And do you think that's likely?" asks Val. "We need to know. In fact, I think we all deserve to know the truth about what happened the first time. I've heard at least three versions of the same story in the past few days, and nothing adds up."

"Yeah, Jared being alive, for one thing," Garry cuts in. "And the Transcendent. You might as well start the whole story from scratch. And you better have a good reason for duping us."

"Quit it, Garry," says Val. "There's a time and a place for starting arguments, and this isn't it. Our survival's at stake, for God's sake."

"Thanks to them," says Garry, with a glare at Murray, then at me.

"Sure, I brought the fiends through the divide," I snap. "Shut up and listen to Murray, otherwise it'll be thanks to you if we die."

"Leah, that's enough," says Murray. "Garry, I appreciate your concerns, but she's right: our survival depends on putting our differences aside at least long enough to make a plan."

"A plan? They drove us out of our base," says Garry. "They

killed thirty of us, not counting the people who went after *her* and never came back."

Val steps in. "If you mean the people Jared controlled and killed, that wasn't Leah's fault. I was almost one of them."

"Enough!" says Murray again. "I'll tell you what I know, but bear in mind no one has an exact picture of what happened two years ago. I believed my brother to be dead, the same as all of you."

He waits for silence. Garry trades sullen looks with some of the other senior Pyros, but I guess he figures he'll get shouted down if he tries to object again. *Good.*

"Right," says Murray. "As far as we know, more than half the original Fiordans who started the war died in the first attack. They lost many of their own in the energy blasts, too. One group even turned on one another and slaughtered them. From my... *conversation* with my brother, as he taunted me before preparing to kill me..." Now, most of the Pyros appear cowed. Horrified, even. "He said there are three Fiordans with their sights set on Earth. Apparently, the part of their world that overlaps with the first divide is one of few inhabited areas on their world." He looks around at each of us. "The fiends are their soldiers, bred and branded for obedience. It was my brother who discovered they use blood control, but I never could have guessed he himself used that method on some of our own number. Not until he revealed his true colours during the first invasion, subdued me, and killed the Transcendent through the blood-bond. The Transcendent was supposed to close the divide. Jared lied and used her death to seal the breach. I'm assuming that's when he retreated to his underground lab. He'd already been using it before the war. He kidnapped and tortured a Fiordan to death to obtain their blood. He kept fiends, too, and enslaved them using a similar tattoo method to the one he used on some of the Pyros, though it was less effective."

Of course. The fiends were locked in cages. Maybe even his spies. I never found out how that worked. How he persuaded *them* to serve him.

The others are deathly silent, listening with rapt attention.

"He used them as spies, to keep tabs on the Fiordans' movements. That's why he always seemed to know what they were doing. He was one step ahead of us the whole time. He had two years to gain intelligence on the fiends. Luckily, he couldn't resist bragging to me when he thought he had me cornered. He didn't know I became Transcendent myself after the war."

I can almost hear everyone's sharp intake of breath.

"You were with *us* after the war," shouts Garry. And there are a few murmurs of agreement. "We thought you were dying."

"We thought you were *dead*," Val says quietly. Not loud enough for anyone to hear except me.

"I didn't know," I whisper.

"I knew we had to survive," says Murray, raising his voice again. "So I risked myself on a journey to the old lab, where I knew Jared had left traces of his experiments. I did the only thing I could and injected myself with the same concoction Jared was using on himself. I had nothing to lose, and I was willing to risk my life to protect the surviving Pyros in case it turned out Jared survived. It took me some time to understand that I'd altered myself irreversibly. I might not have used my abilities to their full extent, but I always intended to lead the army if the fiends were to attack again."

"Abilities?" Garry asks loudly. "You sure kept quiet when the rest of us were risking our necks. What about when we escaped the base?"

"I'm about to explain," says Murray. "I have healing capabilities, but they only work when I'm close to death. I think it's because I had a low dosage. I can't transfer the same effect to others, nor do I want to. Jared's despicable experiments in that area only cemented my decision. He intended to build an army of sorts, using Transcendents to transfer their blood to others. But the side effects invariably led to madness. I feared the same would happen to me if I used my abilities. Perhaps that makes me a coward, but Jared's callous decision to manufacture Transcendents cost dozens of lives."

I shoot a look at Cas. His face is chalk white, his expression murderous. I narrowly escaped the same madness. The same blood that almost killed me saved me in the end.

"So what, if it gave you superpowers?" says Garry. "Isn't that what we want? An edge over the enemy?"

My heart gives a sickening lurch. I can see why Murray didn't broadcast his being Transcendent.

He says nothing. Garry continues, "I don't think it's fair that you never gave us a say. You led us to believe that girl was our saviour, but clearly it wasn't true. If *you* can give yourself extra powers, why can't we?"

"Because you'd probably have been killed, moron," Ryan interrupts. "Didn't you hear? Most people died. And it's because of idiots like you that Murray didn't tell us."

"He didn't tell us because he's a coward," says Garry loudly. "He was scared of losing his power. Scared of his brother."

"Who isn't scared?" Val bursts out, and she walks to join Murray. "We're all scared of the fiends. The Fiordans. Life was hard enough without adding to our problems."

"Yeah, you'd defend him," says Garry.

"Times change," says Val. "Maybe he was wrong to keep the truth secret, but now it's out in the open. Now we know how the Fiordans control their armies. And we have *two* Transcendents now. That's two extra chances."

"Why not more, then?" Garry challenges. "Why not give us all a shot?"

"There was only enough for one person," says Murray. "Leah was dying."

And now everyone's staring at me. Including Cas. His eyes narrow. Great. Apparently he regrets saving my life again. Well, screw him.

"Before you start complaining that your life's worth more than mine," I say, directing most of this at Garry. "I'm planning to fight on the front lines in the next attack. Not hide away, which I'm assuming you did if you survived the last war."

Garry's expression is murderous. But Tyler and Poppy give me encouraging nods.

Cas, on the other hand, has turned away from me and is idly polishing his sword with the edge of his coat. I don't even know what to make of his behaviour. I wish I *didn't* care that he's pulled a Jekyll and Hyde on me again.

But seeing as everyone's listening, it's time to play my hand. I take a deep breath. "I think we should send in spies, too. Like Jared did."

Before anyone can shout an interruption, I say, "Think about it. Jared had the upper hand over us because he had spies in enemy territory. And some of us *can* pass through to the fiends' world unharmed. Cas and I did."

I can't help turning to him, even though it's a punch in the gut when he glares at me. I guess I never should have expected a show of support.

"When Cas and I—" His eyes narrow at the repeated phrase, as I planned—"went to the fiends' world, the army was miles away. Nolan said the fiends had abandoned their city, but that's miles from here, too, nowhere near this new divide." At least, I don't think so. I have no idea about the geography over there.

"A Fiordan," says Murray.

"Whoever he was, he acted like Nolan," I say. "I reckon the fiends did take him over there. He was carried off by the winged ones."

Poppy and Tyler exchange glances next to me. *The fiend I controlled saved their lives, too.*

"She's talking complete crap," says Garry. "How do any of us know she's even telling the truth? None of *us* were over there."

Oh, crap. I can't help looking for Cas's reaction, wondering if he'll actually stab Garry or something. But he doesn't move.

Anger floods me. "What reason would I have to lie to you? I was dying at the time. I killed Jared, too, if you didn't know that already."

"Again. No proof." Garry shakes his head. "It was Jared's fiends that attacked us. I reckon he's in league with them."

An explosion of questions. My heart sinks. I'd considered similar theories, of course, but I didn't plan on telling anyone without more evidence.

"Jared's *dead*," I say loudly. "I stabbed him and shattered his weapon. He died right on the edge of the divide. There's nothing left of him." I swallow hard, but more because of the ever-present memory of him torturing me, not what I did. I'm not sorry I killed him. "But that's not the point," I say, raising my voice again. "We have no idea what they're doing over there. I don't see the harm in me having a look. Some areas are hidden by hills. I can hide and spy from there. Even a quick search is better than doing nothing and being left in the dark."

"She has a point, you know," says Ryan to Val. "We need some kind of edge. Why not use the Transcendent powers?"

"And then what?" challenges Garry. "In case you've forgotten, the Fiordans are freaking smart. They can make themselves look like humans. What if they were like our Transcendents?" He glares at me, then Cas. I half-expect sparks to jump in the air between them. A fair few people turn to stare at Cas, having been unaware he was standing so close. Cas narrows his eyes and stalks off. It'd be funny, but it makes my heart hurt instead. No wonder he never told anyone. It's hard feeling sorry for someone who acts like an ass, but in all those visions, I never found out if he *tried* to make friends and was spurned for it.

I shove those thoughts into the *after the war* part of my brain. If such a place exists.

"The Fiordans aren't human," I say, though thinking of Jared, I'm having my doubts. "Not in the slightest. They might be able to mimic us, but it's easy to tell the difference. Though with *you*, I'm not sure."

A few laughs. Poppy and Tyler. A pang shoots through me. Here I am, offering to put myself in danger again. But what choice do I have? My arm throbs again, sharp and sudden. A rush of light-headedness shoots through my limbs. *Something's not right.*

Instinctively, I hide my left arm behind my back. My spine prickles like I'm being watched.

A crash from the far end of the group. I spin around, heart thudding. Cas has someone pinned to the ground, his sword at their throat.

The Transcendent.

"Wait!" I barely hear the shout over the noise of the crowd. Before I can question myself, I edge around the outskirts of the group to Cas, before he kills our prisoner.

"He was pretending to be unconscious," Cas says. "Listening in on us. Nice try."

The Transcendent shakes his head. "You don't understand…" he says.

"Understand what?"

"They hate you, Leah." He gasps. "They hate that you're alive. They'll take everything from you…" His nails rake over his face, drawing blood, and a chill washes over me. He looks like he's being tormented from the inside…

Like a vision.

Oh no. He was injected with… *my* blood? That can't be right. Unless it was Cas's. But my blood was tainted, before the new Fiordan blood saved my life. The visions were the first sign of the madness that almost killed me. And what he said…

"What do you see?" I ask quickly.

"Death," he whispers. "Slaughter and brutality. The Fiordans build their army to take down Earth, but they'll take you down in person. After destroying everyone… you care about."

He pitches forward onto the ground, coughs racking his body. Blood sprays the soil. "Death and madness," he croaks, and when he lifts his head, his eyes are almost red. "Death and terror… human terror…"

"Shut him up," says Garry loudly, shoving his way over.

"Gladly," says Cas.

"Wait!" Without thinking, I pull out my dagger and use it to block the edge of Cas's blade before he can stab the Transcendent in the heart. To my shock, I react quick enough to counter him, and fire flares along both our blades as they press against one another.

"You can't *kill* him," I say, hardly able to believe this is the same man I talked to this morning.

"He's dying," Cas says, voice sharp as his blade, though his eyes are on the ground, not on his target. "The visions and madness are taking over him. I'm doing him a favour."

Oh, God. Now I get it. But it's not enough to make me lower my weapon. We stare one another out, and there's unmistakable grief in his eyes. He doesn't want to watch anyone else suffer the visions.

Without warning, a tugging sensation erupts under my skin, familiar and sharp. I look up, my heart pounding. The last time I felt like this was when...

A familiar screeching shatters the night.

4

Cas is the first to react. Swearing, he withdraws his blade and moves in the direction of the noise. A familiar dread creeps over me as I see three dark, winged shapes flying towards us.

From the divide.

Oh, crap.

Lucky I already have my weapon. Without waiting for instructions, I run to the outskirts of camp, skirting around to find the quickest route to climb the rising cliff. My pulse races, fire already leaping down my arm to my fingertips and across the forearm-length knife that feels like an extension of my own arm. A tugging sensation under my skin pulls me towards my prey.

I sprint forward, wanting to put as much distance between me and the others as possible before I raise the now-aflame weapon as a challenge.

"Come and get me," I call up at the circling winged shapes.

And they come, in a swooping dive, clawed hands outstretched. So, definitely not the one I blood-controlled.

Without Jared, I'm guessing they've reverted to old habits, in which humans are prey.

They're about to learn not to screw with a Transcendent.

The claws swipe, and I jump, swiping the blade in an arc of fire. A screech tells me the other fiend's picked me as a target, too. Good. Though most of the others at camp are more than capable of killing these things, I'd rather not risk anyone getting injured when they don't have to.

The fiend bares its ugly teeth at me as my knife skims the tips of its claws. The second tries to dive at me from behind, but I spin and counter it. The air blazes around me, sending both fiends reeling back, bat-like wings flapping frantically.

"Too bad your master's dead," I say, and jump, once again swinging the blade in a full arc. This time, blood sprays out. I've cut off one fiend's claws, and it drops in the air, kicking out with its injured foot. I use its distraction to jump higher, underneath the other fiend, and stab the lower points of its wings. As it drops, I stab the flaming knife into its leg, causing it to lose its balance. Another swipe takes out a wing.

Now both my enemies are on the ground, as Cas runs up to join me. His blade flashes, blood sprays the ground, and one fiend crumples, cut in two.

One left. I face it, looking into deadened red-black eyes. "You're Jared's, right?" The words come out before I can stop them. "Too bad he's dead. I killed him."

The fiend hisses. I ready myself for the final blow—

And red light fills my vision as pain shoots up my left arm. The kind of sharp pain I associated with shifting into Cas's memories. A second later, the pain's gone, and so's the red light.

What was that?

Cas is already striding back to camp, leaving the fiends dead on the ground. I swallow, take one last look at the jagged line of the divide, and turn to follow.

It can't be happening again. The visions stopped. I'm cured. I'm not going mad.

So what the hell was that?

We run into more Pyros halfway to camp, and predictably, chaos erupts around us as everyone starts firing questions. Cas, clearly impatient with the noise, stalks away from the others, and I follow him.

"What?" he asks, without turning around. "I'm going to check there's no more of those bastards out there."

"Same," I say, scanning the sky above the divide. Nothing. Again, annoyance burns under my skin. Even the fight hasn't made me less restless, less determined to take action *now.*

"So you're not going to tell me how you knew the fiends were coming before you heard them?"

I blink. Oh, crap. "I felt them. Like something was pulling me towards them."

"I thought so."

Okay... "So you're not surprised?"

"I figured it was something like that."

"Fiordan blood," I say. "But you have it too. Some, I mean." This is awkward as hell, all the more because of the unspoken words—the blood once bound us, and means I know more about him than he ever wanted to tell me.

He turns away. "Apparently not enough to detect them. Are there any others about?"

I hesitate, then shake my head. "I first noticed it... the day I came to Jared's place. I knew the fiends were going to attack Nolan and me."

Cas's eyes narrow at the name. "A blood connection?"

"Why, you don't think the—" I swallow hard. "The visions? You don't think they're coming back?"

A faint head-shake. "I don't know. But if you can sense them, something in your blood still binds you to them.

Maybe the Fiordans, too. You didn't feel anything when we were in their world?"

"No…" In fact, not even when we fought Nolan. Or Jared. Both of them had Fiordan blood. But I didn't react to it. "Crap. Guess that means Nolan can't have been one of them."

"Not necessarily," says Cas. "You might only be able to detect regular fiends. I've no idea how it works."

"Great. I always wanted to be a TV aerial tuned into the monster channel." My head's throbbing too much to really feel like making light of the situation, but what choice do I have? It's absurd.

"Might come in handy," says Cas.

"Thanks," I say. "It'd have been nice if there was a handbook for this Transcendent thing back at the base. I can detect fiends. I can make crazy energy waves appear, but I can't stop an invasion." It happened too fast… but *could* I have stopped the Firodans opening the new divide?

"This is why we need spies," he mutters. "The Fiordans have had centuries to spy on us and learn to mimic us."

The prickling sensation on my spine is back again. "I figured," I say. "But if I can sense the fiends, does it mean they can sense *me?*"

He doesn't answer. Now I'm properly shivering. *No way. I can't be putting everyone in danger just by being here… can I?* No, fiends always aim for human targets. And Pyros. We're all just as vulnerable either way.

"Dammit," I say, and kick a discarded stone across the burned ground. Cas watches its progress, mouth slightly parted like he wants to say something.

But he shakes his head, and leaves without saying another word. I watch him walk along the perimeter of camp for before turning my back and returning to the others, my mind spinning.

I find Val in conversation with Murray.

"The fiends are dead," I tell Murray and Val. "But Cas is looking out in case any more appear." Most likely. I brace myself for the inevitable questions.

But Murray turns to Val instead. "We need to make sure everyone knows to watch the skies as well as ground level."

"They're too confident," says Val. "It's like they knew we were here. But none of you saw any fiends when you were on guard, right?"

I shake my head. "Not even on the other side. But I couldn't really see across the divide."

Apparently, no one gets my meaning—that the only way to know what's going on over the divide is to send someone to check. Like me. Instead, the camp breaks up into more debates. I can't help watching the sky, too weary to argue my point. And considering how angry some people are already, the last thing I want is to put the idea into certain senior Pyros' heads that my being here puts us at the centre of the fiends' attention. Logically, we stand out no matter what. Even if I left, the fiends would come back. Because that's what they do.

Even with the enemy gone, the prickling sense between my shoulder blades refuses to go away. I find it impossible to sleep that night. I'm mentally if not physically exhausted, but the ground is rock-hard, and my danger senses are in over-drive even with a tent over my head. It reminds me of expecting a phone call, back when we *had* phones, and jumping at the phantom sound of a dial tone.

Shut up, I tell my brain.

Eventually I fall asleep to half-formed dreams of armies marching and fire engulfing the world.

———

Three days pass, and we're no closer to a solution than before.

There's always something to do, of course. Patrolling. Hunting for food. Patching up injuries. I do my best to ignore the twinge of guilt that I don't dare risk using my own healing powers on anyone else. I can't help but wonder what might push me into that choice. *If one of the others was close to death...*

I shake the thought away, with difficulty. Maybe the heat's getting to me. Since the last attacks, the nights aren't cold like they used to be, and the days are long and thirsty. Even my healing powers can't protect me from sunburn.

Or the dreams.

Every night, I'm in the fiends' world, and everything's burning, and we're marching to war. I'm pretty sure even the visions when I was connected with Cas didn't show the future. It's never clear, always blurred, the colours distorted. But I always see fiends marching. Not humans. Just burned ground and red sky. Not too different from Earth now. So is this past or present? And could I be seeing what the fiends do?

The others are miserable, too. Tempers run high, arguments are a daily occurrence, and only fear that we'll attract the fiends stops me snapping, too. Garry in particular needs someone to talk him down. Whenever Murray's not around, he takes it upon himself to give everyone orders, and is constantly making unfriendly comments. About certain people in particular. Val. Cas. Me.

Doesn't take a genius to figure out why.

Finally, I manage to get Murray alone to argue, once again, about why I think I should be allowed to have a quick look over the divide.

"Come on," I say. "We've been stuck here for days. If the fiends had a counterattack at the ready, they'd have struck by now. All we're doing is giving them more chances to take us off guard."

"That may be," says Murray, "but the others look to you as an example. If you go running off, they have even more reason to doubt my leadership, even if I want to keep them safe."

"Yeah," I say. "But anything's better than waiting. It's pretty clear they're planning *something*."

I hesitate, on the verge of telling him about the dreams. But they don't make sense to me. Yet.

Cas hasn't spoken to me for days. I have no idea if he thinks he'll catch a disease from coming near me, or if he's still hung up on me getting an unwelcome peek into his history. Or maybe it's about our prisoner. The Transcendent hasn't given us any useful information, just mad ravings.

"Leah, this is difficult for you, but if people see you disregarding the rules, they'll take it as an invitation to do the same. We have enough arguments already."

I raise an eyebrow. Seriously? "Garry's friends don't go by the rules anyway." And they're more vocal by the day about Murray's supposed incompetence as a leader. I want him to confront them and shoot the rumours down, but he never does.

"There are too few of us to enforce them. I'd ask you to join the senior Pyros, but..."

"At this rate, Garry will have me kicked out," I say. "Seriously. Are we reverting back to the Stone Age? Pretty sure Jared said the fiends live in tribes. Maybe they're rubbing off on us and we'll be fighting one another over prey within a week."

Now I've done it. Murray's expression freezes. "Leah, I wouldn't say that in front of any of the others. Especially Elle."

"Sorry," I say. "But look at how some of them are behaving. You guys lived in peace when civilisation crashed and burned for everyone else."

"Because we're human," says Murray quietly. "Unfortunately, the word no longer has the same meaning for everyone."

"You're Transcendent," I say. "I'm not saying the most powerful person should necessarily be the leader, but it ought to make them think twice about challenging you, right?"

"Things aren't that simple." Murray continues to speak in a lowered voice, though most of the others are patrolling the camp at the moment. "I should never have mentioned the limited nature of my healing capabilities. If they see it as a weakness…"

A chill runs down my spine. "What, you want twenty-four-hour bodyguards?" Does he think *he'll* be attacked? Or kicked out? No way. He's held the Pyros together through one war already. But this is different. We both know it.

"I'm not quite that defenceless, Leah. I'm more concerned for the others' safety. They aren't thinking clearly, and that leads to errors in battle. This heat…"

"So it's not just me," I murmur. "The world's changing again. The last attacks…"

"I suspect they were a precursor, yes," he says. "As for the heat, it reminds me of when the sky turned red. Their world is seeping into ours."

"Then you should let me go," I say. "What if Jared's right and there are only a few Fiordans left? They wouldn't come without their armies of fiends. They'll be planning a massive breach."

It's not just the dreams that give me the certainty I'm right. It must take time to marshal thousands of warmongering monsters together into a proper army, even with blood control. Unless they're just waiting for the right moment to strike, when we're off-guard.

Murray nods to me. "Fine," he says. "Just a quick recon mission. If you see any signs of the army, or the Fiordans, get back over the divide *fast*. Don't fight unless you can win. We can't afford to lose you, Leah."

I half smile at him. "I know. Thanks."

"Go now, before it gets dark."

"What—now?" But he's right. It's midday. The others are nowhere in sight, and for all his posturing, I doubt Garry is anywhere near the divide. If I'm to slip away, now's the time.

"I'll tell them I sent you to look for fiends in the area," says Murray. "They know you can run fast. They shouldn't get too curious."

"Doubt Garry would care," I say. "Except—wait. The Transcendent. Who's going to watch him?"

"I am."

Damn. "I'll ask him if he knows anything before I leave," I say. "Just in case. Do you know what's happening to him?"

Murray shakes his head slowly. "I have theories, but…"

A sinking sensation in my chest. "You saw it happen before?"

"In the stronger Transcendent candidates."

I wince. Candidates. Created in a lab, or forcibly injured and healed.

"They all died?"

"Every one." He sighs. "Every time I think we're free of my brother's madness…"

I'm torn between feeling sorry for him and telling him to get a grip. He's supposed to be our leader. And now the idea of going off alone into enemy territory is even less appealing. But do I really have a choice?

"Right," I say. "I'll be back soon."

"Stay safe."

I'll come back. But first, the Transcendent. He's been moved into one of the tents, and one glance inside tells me he's in a bad way. His face is ghostly white, marked with scratch marks. At first I think he's been attacked. Then he rakes his fingernails over his face.

Okay...

"Hey," I say, warily. "Uh, can you speak?"

He stops scratching. I tense instinctively when he sits up, regarding me with eyes that I'd describe as bloodshot... *really* bloodshot. He doesn't look remotely like Jared anymore, not even when he was deteriorating from whatever he injected himself with. I swallow, now inexplicably scared.

"Transcendent," he says.

"What's happening to you?"

He coughs, blood spattering the ground. "Our fate."

I back up. *Not ours. But you can't save him.* Shake my head. "No." *Cas injected me with the cure. I'm safe.*

"We're... not..." He coughs again, back arching, hands spasming against the ground. Hands more like claws, now.

I flee. Cowardly as it is, right now, I'll take my chances in the fiends' world. I check to make sure there are no patrolling Pyros ahead, and jog to the outskirts of camp, climb the rise, and angle towards the divide. It's scary how this area looks more like the fiends' world than Earth, with not as much as a blade of grass poking through the ruined soil. Burned Spots. There'll be even more after the new divide opened.

A fresh pulse of rage washes the fear from the Transcendent's appearance away. I'm not going to be afraid, not even when I step into the monsters' world.

Of course, it's never as simple as I plan. I'm nearly at the divide when I spot a familiar figure. Too late to hope he doesn't see me, so I keep walking. It's eerily quiet outside the camp.

Cas turns to face me. "So you're going?"

I nod, warily. "You didn't think I'd stay here?"

"I guess not. But you shouldn't go alone."

I blink. Apparently, Jekyll Cas is back. Unless he has another motive for wanting to come with me.

"There's someone I might have asked, before he turned into a total asshole again," I say before I can stop myself.

Cas gives me an incredulous look.

"Oh, come on, you can't just talk to me one second then treat me like scum the next. That's not how it's supposed to work."

"Tell me how, then," says Cas. "I was planning to follow you anyway, to stop you doing anything stupid and getting yourself killed."

"That," I say, "is precisely what I meant."

"Precisely what?"

"Don't pull that one on me," I say, sharper than I meant to. "The constant patronising comments. Acting like I don't know what I'm getting into. Looking at me like I'm one of Jared's monsters."

Bad comparison. Guilt spears me as Cas's eyes turn sharp. "Forget it. I'm coming with you."

I blink. "That makes complete sense. Not."

"How many times have you run into dangerous situations now?"

"Like you've never done it."

"This is different."

Now I'm the one wearing an incredulous expression. "Different how? You think you're superior to me? Who's Transcendent?"

"Who nearly died?" he counters. "You of all people I thought would understand survival comes first. Unless you want to be a martyr, like—"

Like the first Transcendent. Oh. Cas fought alongside her,

EMMA L. ADAMS

not realising Jared had betrayed them and turned her into a ticking time bomb. Cas blamed himself for not being able to save her.

I don't want to get into that, so I say, "Yeah, fine. You can come. Just don't blame me if anarchy breaks out at camp."

Cas makes a disparaging noise. "As if my being there would make a blind bit of difference."

I don't answer, because all the responses that come to mind strike me as too insensitive. Sure, he might have made an effort to be nicer to people, but Val did, and Garry's lot are treating her like crap now. As for Murray...

I turn to the divide instead, scanning the jagged surface. As usual, the air above it shimmers like a heat haze, masking the world on the other side. It's thicker than before, like smoke.

I move closer. There must be a way across.

There it is. A semi-transparent bridge from here to there, from our world to the one invading it. Instinctively, I turn to Cas and nod before stepping into the divide.

5

I t's not like last time, when Cas and I fell through the
divide. This time, I'm balanced on what feels like a
solid surface. Before I can lose my nerve at the sheer
drop, I walk swiftly, trying not to think about how I battled
the Fiordan who looked like Jared on a similar bridge.

My feet touch down on burned ground identical to our
side. The sky's the same, too. Raging fire, like the world's
ending. *It's bleeding through into our world. The sky wasn't
supposed to look like that.*

No one's around.

I don't even get the prickling sense of being watched
from far away. No fiend shapes blot out the burning red sun.
No army waits on the horizon. No monsters in human skin
wait to ambush us.

No evidence the fiends have been here at all.

It's not right. Last time, I saw whole *armies*. But that was
miles from here, near the *other* divide. I have to start somewhere. Moving inland will take me deeper into fiend territory. West leads past our headquarters and towards the sea,

at least on our side. East leads the way we walked last time. I don't remember seeing a thing.

Except Nolan said…

Be quick, I think, remembering Murray. But I turn back to the left all the same. Less than a mile that way is the place where this world overlaps with our base. Where they broke through.

I draw in a breath, thinking hard. I left my red coat behind, figuring dark clothes would be less conspicuous. Like all Pyro uniform, it's fire-proof, immune even to energy blasts. Though every time I've seen the Fiordans, they've been impersonating Pyros, uniforms and all. Of course, the fiends might be nearby, too.

But I'm so close.

Screw it. This might be the last chance I have.

"What are you doing?" Cas demands as I start to walk.

"Checking out the place where they crossed over," I say over my shoulder.

"You can't."

Great. Back to asshat mode. That didn't last long. I ignore him and put on my best Transcendent speed, ignoring the heat of the sun, even harsher at noon here than on Earth.

I stop. Somewhere here, the fiends invaded my home. But there's no sign of anyone. Even the other side of the divide is blurred, hazy, like fire dancing over the gash in the earth. No mountain here.

I smack my palm into my face. *Idiot.* No mountain. The fiends *flew* through. The base is hundreds of feet up in the air.

"Finally caught on?" Cas asks from behind me.

I bristle. "All right, you don't have to take the piss out of me."

"You might have thought for a moment before charging off."

"You can talk," I mutter. "Great. So what's your plan? Go home? We don't *have* a home anymore. Thanks to them."

Cas says nothing. Turns his back on me, apparently watching the horizon. Where, I admit, I half-expected to see an army facing us. The fiends' absence is nothing if not creepy.

This way leads out into the ocean, in our world, anyway. Which means if there's going to be an invasion, it could be anywhere from the other direction. I curse under my breath. What a mess. As if I ever thought I could walk over here and run into the right information. And yet...

Right. Screw waiting around. I about-turn and back up from the divide, for one last shot at seeing if I can pinpoint the mountain on the other side. If we could somehow fly to the same height, I'd be able to get back inside and pick up supplies. Damn fiends. Damn Fiordans.

My hands clench. I march back a few metres, frustrated with myself. There's what, ten miles between here and the original divide? So... wait a minute. Unless the fiends are camped out somewhere between the two, they can't be around this area. I cast my memory back. The visions showed the fiends on the other side of the first divide. I think. The memory of the vision is hazy already, but from what I remember, they burst out of the earth on both sides. The angle means they *must* have been on this side. Somewhere between here and the other divide is where their army stood before they invaded Earth.

The Transcendent was meant to bridge the gap. To harness energy from both worlds. Can I do it from this side? It's completely mad, but logically... if there's really no one here...

I start to walk before I can debate the wisdom of what I'm doing. I'm risking my life. Hell, I'm risking Cas's, too. But from here, I can walk right up to the point where the invasion started.

From here, maybe I can figure out how to…

I stop dead. The ground ends abruptly at a cliff, plunging several feet down. I check for footholds, but it looks like I'm either going to have to jump or find a way around. Worse, another cliff waits opposite.

Cas's hand grabs my arm. "What the *hell* are you doing?"

"Exploring," I say, stupidly.

"You're doing *what?* Are you suicidal?"

"No." I snatch my arm out of his. "Don't tell me what to do."

That's when the edge of the cliff gives way. I tumble down several feet, barely catching my breath before I fall again, arms striking sharp rock, feet slipping every time I try to gain my footing. Gasping, I finally come to a stop in an undignified heap.

"I was going to warn you about that," says a conde-scending voice. Cas, of course, jumped down to land beside me.

My face heats up, and this time not with fire. Damn him. I scramble to my knees and glare. Even with my healing powers, my knees and elbows sting.

But Cas isn't looking at me. He's staring at the cliff face. Just staring at the rock.

And there's a cave opening.

I stare, too. *Fiends,* I think immediately. But the opening is barely wide enough to accommodate an average-sized human. Definitely not one of the monsters.

I turn and scan the area. Nothing. We might be the only people on this planet. Stupid thought. *People* couldn't survive here.

Just as the thought crosses my mind, there's a scrabbling sound. Footsteps.

A face appears in the mouth of the cave.

I freeze. The face is human. A man. Thirty or forty, maybe. Human-looking.

Not human. Never human. They can't survive here.

I go for my weapon. And he does the same, pulling out a knife the length of my arm. Like Cas's.

Like a Pyro's blade.

"You devils," he snarls. "Who did you take this time? Who was the girl?"

Rather than attacking, I'm struck into silence again. And Cas... hasn't even drawn *his* weapon.

Who the hell *is* this guy?

"Who are you?" I blurt. "You're—you're one of the Fiordans, aren't you?" Which means he's imitating someone. A Pyro. It wouldn't be the first time.

Who was the girl? The question makes no sense.

"Declan?" says Cas. Apparently recovering himself, he shakes his head and pulls out his weapon. "You Fiordans couldn't be content with just killing us, could you?"

"Hold it," I say. "Who's this guy?" I ask Cas.

"I'm Declan Lloyd," says the man. "Pyro leader and one hundred per cent human."

My heart misses a beat. "You're lying," I say. "Humans can't survive in this place."

"That's what we thought," says Declan, not lowering his weapon. "But we've adapted quite well. And I wouldn't take another step. You might think yourselves invincible, but we have ways of taking you to pieces that would make even you shudder to contemplate."

Impossible. It's impossible. For humans, for Pyros to have survived here... I wasn't prepared for this. But he looks and sounds sincere.

"We're not Fiordan," I say. "We're human, well, Pyro. We crossed the divide."

"Then you're not human," says Declan. "Or Pyro. They have better sense."

"Enough," says Cas, deadly-quiet. "Declan Lloyd died in the fiend invasion two years ago, along with two hundred other Pyros. The rest of us moved our base, and waged our own war on the invaders until they took our headquarters from us a few days ago. So as you can imagine, I'm a tad pissed off."

"You haven't changed a bit, if it even is you," says Declan.

"Neither have you, old man," says Cas. "Unfortunately, we both know the Fiordans are accomplished actors and have had centuries of practise imitating humans."

"That is true," says Declan. "But there are, to my knowledge, only three surviving Fiordans on this wasteland of a planet. Behind me are two hundred and five trained soldiers with the means to take you down. You're outgunned, Fiordan scum."

What? Maybe I should be worried about his soldiers, but it's the words *three surviving Fiordans* that ring through my head. Three. Jared told the truth?

"There's no need for posing," says Cas. "Two hundred and five? Really?"

Never mind the Fiordans. You have bigger problems, I tell myself. "You said two hundred died in the war," I say, slowly. "No… they didn't come through the divide?"

"We were stranded," says Declan. "Monsters every which way. Those of us with sense retreated underground. Luckily, the Fiordans had left an entire network of tunnels out of use. We adapted them, as best we could."

"And you've been here two years," says Cas. "Two years, without even trying to cross the divide and come back to…" He trails off, turning to face me. As though he can't help himself.

Only people with Fiordan blood can cross the divide.

No freaking way. They can't have survived this long.

"Without even trying? Many have died attempting it." Declan spits at our feet. "We waited until the Fiordans left, then claimed their underground paths. They rarely come here anymore. No humans on the other side. Until a few days ago…"

"They ripped open another divide," says Cas. "I'd have thought it'd be pretty damn noticeable."

"Energy blasts are old news," says Declan. "We just don't venture aboveground."

"So you won't have seen them," I say, half to myself. "They crossed over and attacked the base. We're stuck camping out in the wilderness, waiting to be attacked. Now it turns out there's not even a fiend army on the other side…"

"Was that what you expected?" Declan raised an eyebrow. "You're two years too late, girl. The army scattered, the Fiordans are too busy bickering and playing dress-up as unsuspecting humans. Last one I saw was weeks ago."

"The one imitating Jared?" I ask. "He crossed the bridge on the other divide. Well, he tried to."

He raises an eyebrow again. "You killed a Fiordan?"

"Yes," I say flatly, glaring at him. "Like I'll kill you, if you turn out to be one of them. The Fiordans are clever monsters. They wouldn't leave a whole bunch of tunnels empty." At least, I don't think they would. But then again, I don't know nearly enough about the Fiordans…

"The Fiordans are, as far as I know, under the impression that humans are incapable of making the crossing. This part of the country's abandoned."

"Really, now?" I say. "The Fiordans know about the Transcendents, right?"

Oh, crap. Definitely shouldn't have given that one away. Cas shoots me a murderous look and tightens his grip on his weapon.

Declan, however, only blinks at the word. "Last I checked, they didn't."

Impossible, I think, yet again. "Seriously? The one I fought was *waiting* for me."

"I thought Resa was the one," says Declan, nodding at Cas. Who freezes, hand still on the hilt of the blade.

A deadly quiet falls.

"She died," he says. Soft. Angry.

Oh. God. "She was the last Transcendent?" Dammit. Like I need to antagonise Cas now.

Declan raises an eyebrow and looks me up and down. "She doesn't look like much, but then again, neither did Resa, before."

"That's *enough*," shouts Cas. His hands are trembling. "If it turns out you're Fiordan, I'll rip you limb from limb. In fact, I might do it anyway. You don't have the right to know any of this, or to say her name."

"Well, damn," says Declan. "It really is you, Cas. And you are?"

I blink twice before I remember how to reply. "Leah," I say. "I'm Transcendent. I killed a Fiordan. Killed Jared, too."

Next thing I know, Declan's blade's pointing at my throat. I freeze, holding my breath as the sword edge nicks the skin of my neck. I might be able to heal, but I don't want my throat cut if I can avoid it.

"You killed Jared? Killed one of our own?"

"He wasn't one of our own," says Cas, through gritted teeth. "The bastard sold us out. He set us up to die, killed Resa and almost let the fiends overrun the world. He wanted their power. Reckon he wanted their army, too."

"That's the biggest load of bullshit I've ever heard," snaps Declan, still not moving his weapon. "Jared might have been a little extreme in his methods, but he also handed us our best weapon."

What does he mean by that?

Then I see he's looking at Cas.

"I'm not a fucking weapon." Now Cas's blade presses against Declan's throat.

We stand there, no one daring to make a move. I'm tempted to hit them both with fire and knock some sense into them, but I know that'd make things worse.

Cas glares at Declan. "I heard enough of that bullshit from Jared while he was torturing me in the name of research. Leah killed him, but damn if I don't wish I'd been the one to skewer the bastard."

Declan stares, chest rising and falling. "You're serious."

"Of course we are," I snap, jerking back out of range of the sword point. "We're on a hostile planet trying to figure out what our enemies are doing and when they're going to invade the Earth next. So we can stop them."

Declan moves the blade back, finally, giving me room to breathe. "You believe they…?"

"They did and they will," says Cas. "We killed Jared after his plans to create artificial Transcendents again created a bunch more monsters. And he must have drawn the Fiordans' attention. And…" He pauses. "You remember Nolan?"

Declan lowers his blade. "Blond kid, not very bright? Yeah."

I blink. This man really did live with the Pyros. That, or he's good at bluffing.

"He was one of Jared's, too. Jared marked us with tattoos. Blood-bonds. If we disobeyed him, he'd inflict unimaginable pain. We thought he died two years ago, but he appeared out of nowhere a few weeks back. Turned out he'd been hiding underground. Not unlike you." He eyes the tunnel entrance. "So he saw Leah and decided he wanted a pet Transcendent again. Nolan was terrified of the pain so he gave in and tortured Elle to force our hand."

Declan makes a choked noise. "No. You're lying. Not that little girl."

"She's fine," says Cas. "As fine as anyone can be. Jared captured and tortured Leah and me, killed almost everyone he marked, and kidnapped Elle. That made Murray snap and try to kill him. She got out okay, but his lab blew up, Leah and I were knocked over the divide, and we ran into Nolan again. He claimed Jared was looking for the other Pyros. You. I thought he was one of *them...*"

"I didn't see Nolan," says Declan. "But we rarely go above-ground. Especially with those unnatural screeching noises."

"Jared's fiends," says Cas. "That's another of his projects. He decided to engineer some of them. Oh, and his final act was to turn himself into a Transcendent. So was Nolan's, come to that, though he claims he had help on *this* side, from the Fiordans. Don't suppose you know anything about it?"

Declan shakes his head slowly. "You found out how to create a Transcendent?" There's no hidden meaning in his tone. He really doesn't know what Cas's blood can do.

Cas lowers his weapon. "You haven't earned my trust yet," he says. "I don't go throwing that information at anyone I see. Especially people who should be *dead.*"

They look at one another mutely, neither willing to give ground. As for me, I have no idea what to think. But this man doesn't act at all in a way I'd imagine the Fiordans to. They might be great actors, but the Fiordans can't have got close enough to the Pyros before the war to know what this Declan does.

What's wrong with me? Do I trust strangers so easily? I thought the past two years took that part of me away.

Still. I speak before the silence gets ridiculous. "So you're here, and you can't get back to Earth. But what if the fiends *are* attacking again? Invading? They took down our base and opened another divide. It suggests they're planning something big. And they had an army, but that was miles away from here."

"I can't deny it suggests they've rebuilt their technology," says Declan. "That's how they broke through the first time. But we took all their weapons from their abandoned base. Bombs," he adds, in response to Cas's raised eyebrows. "Think nuclear-style, but using their own technology. Like energy blasts."

That word makes anger burn in my veins. Cas and I look at one another. A thread of fear slides down my back. Murray was developing something similar. What he used to destroy Jared's lab. I know he got the idea from the enemy... but the Fiordans have enough of an edge over humanity already without adding *more* freaking explosions into the mix.

"*You* have their weapons?" asks Cas. "And the enemy definitely can't get at them?"

"They haven't found us in two years," says Declan. "Their fiends are too big and stupid to find the cave entrance."

I can't share his easy confidence. I've seen how intelligent the fiends can get. All the same, the idea of opposing them... using their own weapons against them like I did with the blood control... I can't deny it appeals.

Still, worry for the others twists inside me. "We have to get back," I say. "The rest of our group will be wondering where we are. But there's a hundred and fifty of us, or close enough. It's not enough for an army, but if you have the weapons to take down a bunch of fiends at once... and if there's only three Fiordans left..."

"You'll take him at his word?" Cas shakes his head. "There were dozens of Fiordans, and that's just the ones we tracked in the UK. Back when it existed anyway. They're near-invincible, they can't all have died in the war."

"There weren't dozens," says Declan. "Mostly it was the

same ones in different forms. I'd count ten, maybe less. Their armies were what did the damage. They were weak on their own."

It makes no sense, and yet it does. Nobody ever said the *Fiordans* were the ones who killed people. The fiends are everywhere, and their leaders live in the shadows. Fiordan blood control across an army? Definitely possible.

"Whatever," says Cas. "We'll tell Murray. Though I can't say he'll believe you. Or me, come to that. You should be *dead*, not living underground here of all places."

"Stranger things have happened," mutters Declan. "I never would have thought we'd find another Transcendent."

A pause.

"I wouldn't get too excited," says Cas, coldly. "And we might not be able to come back. But I'm interested in seeing your weapons."

The bombs. This whole scenario seems wrong, but how many more opportunities are we going to have to get potential information on how to beat the almost-unbeatable monsters?

"We'll see," says Declan. "I'll certainly be upping surface scouting after this. To think we missed another attack. Damned Fiordans. Maybe next time we'll be able to get out of this godforsaken place."

"Earth isn't much to look at, either," says Cas. "We'll see what Murray says."

My heart sinks. This could create even more problems. And who would believe humans survived here, even Pyros?

But I haven't survived this long by doubting the evidence of my senses. Declan's wary of us, but not a threat. Still, I watch my back as we leave.

6

C as doesn't speak as we hurry the mile or so to the divide. We've walked further than I thought, though I suppose I didn't pay too much attention at the time. Now, my head's spinning. More Pyros survived. We aren't alone. Even if we're on separate planets. And I was hoping to *close* the divide. If that's even possible.

One thing's for certain: we need a new plan.

Cas and I walk parallel to the divide, searching for a crossing-point. I keep one eye on the sky, too, wary of those winged fiends. To think they invaded us *right here*. There's nothing left now, no trace.

It's not right.

To keep from getting tangled in my own thoughts, I list what we *do* know. Two hundred and five other Pyros survived. They can't pass through the divide. Only people with Fiordan blood can. And fiends, I guess. Unless it's torn open again.

Supposedly, three Fiordans survived. It makes sense to think they're planning another invasion, and yet, there's no sign of an army. So what *are* they planning? And *where* are they? I ran into the first Fiordan on the bridge. He can't have been alone there.

He was imitating Jared. So presumably, he'd seen, or fought him.

Jared's place was right next to the old divide...

And his fiends were here...

I stop. We've reached the bridge. Last chance to look around. There doesn't seem to be anything to break up the monotony of lifeless, burned ground. No grass, no kind of plants. Even the air feels thicker than Earth, somehow, like it's full of invisible dust. No clouds in the red sky, which merges with the ground on the horizon. I think I see hills in the far distance, but it might be a mirage.

I assume the world wasn't always this way. The Fiordans ruined it themselves.

Just like they're trying to do to Earth.

"Come on," says Cas. "We need to get the hell off this rock."

"It's just..." I scan the red-tinged horizon, with barely a distinction between sky and land. "It feels like there ought to be *something* here. A clue. Like where the Fiordans even are."

He shrugs. "I've no clue. But I'm willing to bet they're somewhere along this damned line. Or the other one. Just a question of whether we want to risk running into an army."

I stare. "You mean, search them out?"

"They haven't attacked yet," he says. "And if we believe Declan..."

I can't believe it. Cas has always acted like we're doomed to lose this fight. For him to be considering the alternative... well, it's refreshing, to say the least. I already killed one of the Fiordans. Two, if Nolan was really...

Oh, shit. Nolan. We're miles from the original divide, where it overlapped with Jared's lab. Near where Nolan said he was held captive by... Fiordans?

Cas walks to the bridge. "We'll tell Murray. There's no way he won't let us come back after this."

It's not like Cas to wait for permission. But we left the others at a time when danger's at an all-time high. Not to mention the Transcendent captive back at camp. The image of his clawed hands and blood-red eyes flashes through my mind again, and I shudder slightly.

What happened to him?

Jared. I can't believe Declan didn't believe he was evil. How convincing was his mask? If he fooled even Cas…

Before we know it, we've reached the other side. Again, I scan for potential danger, above and below. Nothing. In fact, it doesn't look like anyone's patrolling near the divide. Then again, only Cas dared come this close.

My heart beats faster. I can't see how we're going to get out of this one without causing an argument. The last thing we need right now.

As we approach the top of the rise, two figures climb over the edge, talking loudly. Murray and Val, arguing. And they're dragging someone between them. A body.

The Transcendent.

"You're a fool," Val's saying. "You can't just go."

"I won't fight them," says Murray, sounding tired. He looks up, sweeping his greying hair out of his eyes, and sees us.

"What's going on?" Cas demands. "Where are you going?"

"Is he dead?" I ask, unable to take my eyes off the Transcendent's scratched, scarred face.

"Yes," says Val, harshly. "And this *idiot's* decided to leave the group."

I stare at Murray. "You can't be serious. You're the leader."

"Garry held a vote," he says. "Said I wasn't fit to run the Pyros anymore."

"They can't *kick you out*," I splutter. No way. I didn't think *that* would happen while we were gone. It's only been an hour. *They can't all have lost faith in him!*

"They can," says Murray, wearily. "It was a majority vote."

"Bullshit," I say. "This isn't like the government, it's survival."

"We're a democracy," he says. "I've always given everyone a say."

"But…" I splutter, totally incoherent. Murray might have lied, but he's Transcendent. Kicking him out goes against common sense, if nothing else.

"I did say you were being stupid," says Val. "If you leave, what's to keep them from kicking out anyone who disagrees with them? It's a slippery slope to the kind of savagery those scavengers practise. And there's your daughter to think of."

"Elle will be happier in the town. With humans."

"Murray, her friends are the Pyros," says Val, her tone gentler now. "I know you think you have to please everyone, but you've led the Pyros through Jared's betrayal, through everything."

"Yes, and there was never meant to be only one leader," says Murray. "There were three. I'm the one who never wanted to give the others the burden of responsibility for everyone's lives."

"You're an idiot," snarls Cas, marching up to Murray and grabbing him by the scruff of his neck. "Pathetic. You'd risk your daughter because you're scared of losing face?"

"She'll be *safe*."

"Amongst humans?" Cas laughs hollowly. "You've seen how they react to outsiders. They might tolerate you, but you'll never belong amongst them. What if they take on new leadership and decide you're a threat to their safety? People like us are going to face prejudice no matter what choice we make in this damned world."

Murray starts to speak, stops. He feebly tugs himself free from Cas.

"He's right," says Val. "If you leave, who'll be the next targets? Leah. Cas. Me. The people Jared took. If we're kicked out, it's the worse for all of us."

I clear my throat. "This is a bad time, but we found something over the divide. I need to talk to you about it."

Murray shifts, looks at me. "Danger?"

I shake my head. "I don't think so. It's complicated, and… you might not believe me at first."

"Oh, spit it out already," Cas snaps. "Or I will. Declan's alive."

Murray's face goes through planes of confusion, shock, and disbelief. He shakes his head fiercely. "The monsters…"

"He knew things," says Cas. "And he claims there are two hundred and five Pyros trapped in the fiends' world. They were stranded during the war, when the bridge closed. The Fiordans left a bunch of abandoned tunnels, and they're using them as a hideout."

Murray shakes his head again, apparently unable to speak.

"There's more," I say. "We didn't see a single fiend, or Fiordan. It doesn't look like the invasion's happening in that part of the world at all. There definitely wasn't an army. But when the base was attacked, it was just the winged fiends, wasn't it? Jared's ones. He'd have told them where our base was."

Murray looks at me. I can't read his expression. And it hits me like a sucker-punch. I don't want him to give up. If he gives up, a large part of the hope I've been clinging to despite everything—will be gone. Just like the old Leah, before she lost her sister.

I won't give up anyone else without a fight.

"Something's wrong over there," I say. "Here, too. I don't

see any other way we can find out. But the Pyros, Declan, they have Fiordan technology. They can *kill* them. They mentioned... bombs. Like energy blasts."

This time, Murray gasps. "Damned fool."

"You believe me?"

"I think it's preposterous." Murray shakes his head, again. "But you're no liar, Leah. If the Fiordans fooled you, you're not to blame."

"And do you think me easily fooled?" Cas challenges him. "I questioned him, asked questions only the real Declan would know the answer to. You know the Pyros crossed the divide."

"And *died*," says Val, white-faced. "You can't accept two hundred humans survived in that—place."

"Pyros," I say. "You know we're tougher than regular humans. And we can adapt."

"Evidently," says Murray. "I'd believe Jared would appropriate Fiordan technology and science, but Declan? He'd never touch it."

"Even if it meant striking back against the Fiordans?" Cas says. "You of all people know how much he hated them. At least as much as I did. And Jared..."

"I should have seen him for what he was." Murray's mouth twists. "I was blinded. He was my brother, and he wanted to save humanity."

"You never believed that," Cas says. "Not after what you saw him do."

He means creating the artificial Pyros. Like Cas. I feel like I'm interrupting a private moment. Cas runs a hand absently over the black tattoo on his hand. The mark Jared left on him.

"I can't say I'll believe Declan's alive until I see him with my own eyes," says Murray. "There's no question I trust the pair of you, but that place is poison."

"I know," I say. "But…" I glance back at the camp. "If they kicked you out, why not come with us to see proof?"

"Leah," Cas says, warningly.

"I get that it sounds insane," I say. "But you're the leader. And you knew Declan. You'd be able to tell if it's really him. Plus you can pass through the divide. Like us."

Murray shakes his head. "I'm not as advanced a Transcendent. I don't see how it would be possible."

"You have Fiordan blood," I say. "The tunnels are within five minutes' walk of the divide. No fiends were around, not even Jared's. The ones that invaded the base came in by air."

"So?" Cas says. "I'm not saying that guy didn't seem like Declan or a *really* good actor, but I thought you of all people wanted to keep your friends safe." He directs this at me.

Guilt rushes through me. Of course I do. And I never thought *Cas*, of all people, would be observant enough to pick up on that. Or care.

I turn to Murray. "If they kicked you out, odds are, we're next. Right?" Cas glares at me, but I meet his stare. "You know it's true. I'm doing more to keep the other safe by staying away."

Cas shrugs, his expression saying *your funeral.* I turn back to Murray rather than acknowledge the confused feelings I have towards Cas at the moment. I don't know whether he wants me out of harm's way, or if he thinks I'm *in* the way. Neither is particularly helpful.

Murray sighs. "I think splitting up is a terrible idea. But if the others are alive, it's my responsibility as a leader to at least…"

"Don't be stupid," says Val. "The fiends' world is suicide."

"Cas and I got back in one piece," I say. "Twice. I'm not saying it's not dangerous. But think about it. Potential allies are what we need right now. If anywhere has answers on what the Fiordans are planning, it's there. Declan said there were three Fiordans left after the last war. I killed one of them." Out of the corner of my eye, I can see Cas watching me, but I don't turn his way.

Murray blinks at me. "Even if it is him, he might have been mistaken."

"Nolan said the same," I say. "I think we should give this a try. If nothing else, they're stuck over there. Humans can't cross the divide, but… they were planning to attack from that side if the fiends start a war. I guess they aren't close enough to the other divide to have seen the army yet."

"Or he's not telling us something," says Cas. "But then, he thought *we* were the enemy."

"True," I say. "This whole thing's majorly confusing, but I reckon we should give him a chance. He didn't try to kill us, which is a step up from last time."

Except Nolan. If it really was him, we left him for dead. But thinking about that won't help us make a decision now. Cas's expression is more thoughtful than annoyed now. Maybe I've made my point.

"Okay," says Val. "Suppose we say he's telling the truth. You're risking life and limb over there when there are a hundred tired and angry Pyros right here. And your *daughter.*"

Murray grimaces. "She's in danger as long as she's with me. Transcendents draw the fiends' attention a million times more than any Pyro does. Besides, you and Leah can look after her while I—"

"Hold it," I say. "I'm not staying behind while you go over there alone."

"Nor am I," says Cas. "I don't entirely trust the guy. Besides, you think Garry and the other morons who kicked you out will leave Leah and me alone? We're beacons for the damned monsters, too. We don't have to be here." He looks at me, and my heart performs an inexplicable swoop. Now he's on my side. Whatever next? "What d'you reckon, death by fiend here or death over there?"

"If I'm going to die, it's not going to be because of the fiends," I say. "I'm going to kill the last of the Fiordans and kick every monster off our planet. And close the divide..." I trail off. I still don't know how to go about that last part.

"That almost sounded impressive," says Cas, and my heart performs another traitorous flip. *He's mocking you, for God's sake.* I glare at him.

"This isn't the time for jokes," Murray snaps, making me jump. "As for closing the divide, I'm not sure it's even possible."

"We're more likely to find out how to do it over there on the other side," I say. "They have labs. Fiordan technology."

I'm bluffing a bit. If I couldn't properly close the divide as the Transcendent and the last one *died* doing it—even if that was Jared's fault—maybe there isn't a way. Or maybe the idea of being responsible for the future of the whole *planet* is entirely too much for one seventeen-year-old girl. I can't afford to think about what might happen if I fail.

Nor can I think about how closing the divide would condemn the two-hundred-and-five Pyros on the other side.

How did things get so complicated?

As the thought crosses my mind, a screech rings out, drawing my attention back to the divide. I spin around, hands already on my weapon.

"Fiends." I scan the sky for the inevitable dark winged shape. They must be close. I run forward and left, my path taking me towards the divide.

Oh, crap. I skid to a halt at the cliff's edge. The noise came from the other side. One second there's nothing but shimmering air, the next, two giant winged bodies materialise above my head.

I jump back, swinging my knife in time to sever a fiend's claw. *Oh no, you don't.*

Fire flares from my hand, joining me to the blade, and we attack as one. First step: get the fiend out of the air. I duck underneath its flailing feet and swipe a couple of times. The fiend might move fast, but I'm quicker. Darting forward, I roll underneath its feet and tackle it from behind, stabbing the back of one wing. The fiend loses its height and drops to ground level as Cas rushes to join me.

But I'm standing too close to the edge. The fiend lashes out, and one stumble takes me into empty space, nothing but fiery light all around me. I tip backwards with nowhere to land. Damn. Which way is out? I run forward blindly—if it can be called running when there's no floor.

Next thing I know, my feet touch down on the edge of the fiends' world.

Three more fiends circle above.

Crap.

A fiend dives at me. I curse, raising my weapon to the sky and pushing the fiend back with a wave of fiery energy. It's easier here on the other side. The fire comes without conscious thought. I kick and dive and slash with my blade until I've brought two fiends down to fight on my level. One swipes a claw at me, which I dodge easily. As Transcendent, I have a speed advantage over even the engineered fiends.

And they're just as vulnerable to fire as the rest. Both cringe away from the flames leaping from my hands before I get within range. I don't even need to land a hit to send one fiend staggering into the other, growling in pain. A second hit knocks it down, and my dagger takes care of the rest.

Cas jumps out of nowhere to land on the edge, swinging his blade at another fiend. Blood sprays the dry red ground. As the third fiend hovers above, I send an arc of fire from my blade and knock it right out of the sky. The fiend drops with a thud that shakes the ground, and I dive at it, determined to finish it fast. One fire-edged punch to the jaw stuns it, and my blade finds its heart.

Murray lands beside Cas, twin swords in his hands, and the pair of them beat the other two fiends until they collapse into a heap of rubble. Dead.

"Five of them," I say, stopping to catch my breath before realising I don't need to. "They must have flown from somewhere else. We didn't see any last time."

"The bastards move fast," says Cas, kicking the rock-like remains of a fiend's head and reducing it to dust. "There's nowhere for them to hide here. Unless *they're* underground, too."

"We can't stay here," says Murray. "We have to go back."

"Wait," I say—and stop.

A person approaches, a black-clothed figure with a long dagger ready to fight. His hood falls back. It's Declan.

Murray follows my gaze. His jaw hangs slack, his hand falling to his side.

The two stare at one another for a moment before Cas snaps, "I'm not gonna do the introductions here. If you don't want us to get attacked again, get the hell on with it."

Typical Cas. Declan's eyes flicker towards him, then me. Then Murray. "So it's true," he says. "Did these two tell you everything?"

"As much as we knew," says Cas, seeing as Murray appears incapable of speech. "You're here, along with two hundred-odd other Pyros. Apparently you survived the war."

"Impossible," says Murray quietly. "You died. The last time I saw any of you was when you left for the war—"

"I thought you'd be happier to see me," says Declan.

"—before Jared turned on me," Murray finishes.

"So Jared really was the traitor."

"He's dead."

"I know," says Declan. "This girl claims to have killed him herself."

"It's true." I fold my arms defensively. "Jared's not our issue now. Looks like some of his fiends are roaming about."

"So that's what the noise was," says Declan. "I'd suggest you three come with me to the base."

"I don't trust you," says Murray. "The Fiordans are—"

"Masters of disguise and human imitation," says Declan. "I doubt they know every detail of how you brought three rivalling Pyro groups under your leadership with Jared at your side. How you roamed the country hunting for Pyros. I remember when you brought young Nolan in. And Cas himself, of course. I never did agree with Jared's methods, I admit."

"You know about that?" I ask, staring at him.

Murray interrupts. "You don't know what I found after— after the war," he says. "Jared had these labs set up everywhere around our bases. He kept humans in cages. Fiends, too. He lied about how many died in his attempts to make a Transcendent."

"That's enough," snaps Cas. "We're on enemy territory. For all we know they have eyes everywhere."

"*Not* in my base," says Declan. "Come inside and I'll tell you more about what happened two years ago. If you prove to not be what you seem, I've two hundred angry Pyros with weapons keen to take you out."

That's enough for me. "Come on, guys," I say. "Murray, I reckon he's telling the truth. If not, two of us are Transcendents. He's not."

Murray looks incredibly unhappy. But he nods. And we follow Declan, hoping we aren't walking into a trap.

7

We walk quickly. I keep one eye on the sky, but no more fiends appear. I want to know where they came from. If they were Jared's, I guess they're back to taking shots at Pyros again. They're stupid, but if there are more of them, they might attack Declan's group.

I tense automatically when we reach the opening to the tunnel. It reminds me too much of Jared's lair. I take a few deep breaths before following Murray. At least Cas looks almost as uncomfortable as I feel. His hand never leaves the hilt of his weapon.

Luckily, once we pass through the first part of the tunnel, overhead lights come on. A few metres in, we come to a door across a gap in the ground wide enough to jump. Flames leap up, like in the divide, and I instinctively step back.

"It's like our base defence," says Murray. "You managed to do that here?"

"It took a few attempts," says Declan, drawing his weapon. I tense, but he runs the blade across his own palm

3

and lets a few drops of blood fall into the flames. Immediately, they die down.

"Pyro blood?" I ask. Not for the first time, a bunch more questions about how this whole blood thing works rush through my head, but I don't yet know if we can trust Declan. Let alone how he'd react if he knew the three of us had the blood of our enemies running in our veins. Considering how the others reacted back at camp, it's probably best to keep that between us.

"It took a while to get it to work like the base," says Declan. "But yes. No one's tried to get in from outside, but it can't hurt to be careful."

"No one's... in two years? Never?"

"We were lucky," says Declan. "It was tough for the first few weeks, with the more impetuous younger Pyros racing off trying to find a way back. There are seven of us who assumed leadership, but we had some who took issues with authority. Especially during the first week, when we weren't sure we'd ever be able to survive here."

"But you did," I say slowly. "How?"

"This was set out as a base by the Fiordans," says Declan, unlatching several bolts on the doors. Once he's pushed them open, he beckons us to follow. Murray goes first, stepping over the gap where the fire sprang up from the ground. Cas follows. Then me. I don't look down.

"The Fiordans built this?" from Murray's tone, I know he doesn't believe it. "Besides, however did you feed two hundred people?"

"The Fiordans are more like us than we thought," says Declan. "This place is fitted with running water, sewage systems, light and heating. There's a cooler area where food's kept in storage. Nothing we were familiar with, mind, but fit for human consumption. I think most Fiordans live underground, probably because of the high temperatures and the risk of sunburn."

"Huh," says Cas. "The fiends can't have lived down here. This tunnel's far too small."

We have to walk single file. It's more reminiscent of Jared's place than I'd like to admit.

"The fiends... we've thankfully never run into one of their nesting places. Or whatever they call them." Declan leads us through yet more doors, into a proper hallway complete with strips of metal along the walls and ceiling that light the whole place up. Not exactly like fluorescent lights, but similar.

How can such depraved monsters build a civilised place?

Declan talks as we continue down the corridor, telling us about all the rooms they discovered down here. The technology. Books, even, though no one could read them. Machines that functioned like the kind of things we have on Earth.

It's wrong. All wrong. Sure, I knew the Fiordans must be intelligent. But it's wrong to imagine them as close to humans as our world is to theirs now.

No. There's a divide between us, like the divide between our world and theirs. We'll never be the same.

I fix that image in my head as I take in the views. Doors into rooms of machinery. Apparently it was gathering dust, until the Pyros here started fixing it up. A fair few of the Pyros here are scientists, who spend most of their time adapting fiend tech for human use. And building weapons. Yet they can't build a bridge back home.

Declan pauses outside another stretch of rooms. Behind one door, I can see Pyros sparring, training with weapons. There are so many of them here. Impossible as it seems.

"Right. I think we'd best start with one of the labs, if that's all right. I mentioned you to our lead scientist, who naturally thought I was addled from the heat, but here goes..."

He opens the door on our right.

"Holy shit," says the man inside. He's younger than I expected. Thirty, maybe, with fair hair and sideburns. "It's really Murray." He takes a step back, frowning. "And if it isn't, I've enough ammo in this room to turn you into wallpaper paste."

I almost laugh at the incredulous expression on Murray's face.

"It's me," says Murray, recovering. "And you know Cas, of course. This is Leah. Leah... this is Ray."

Ray's eyes flicker towards me. "Pyro?"

"Transcendent," says Declan. "All of them are, apparently. I'd say we have some catching up to do."

Ray doesn't take his eyes off me as Declan closes the door behind us. While there are seats, Cas remains near the door, as uncomfortable as I've ever seen him. Murray himself takes a seat, leaving a reasonable amount of distance between himself and the other two. The rest of the room is taken up by tables covered in what resembles an engineer's workshop more than one of Jared's labs.

It takes five awkward minutes to fill Ray in on the situation on Earth, not to mention Jared's betrayal.

"Knew there was something not quite right about the guy," says Ray. "He was too interested in the Fiordans. Though I can't really talk now, seeing as the crap they left down here saved all our lives."

I can't wrap my head around that. So I listen instead.

As they talk, I realise... they have a history. The Pyros' history. One I wasn't a part of back then. These people were friends with the current Pyros. Mourned by them. I fidget uncomfortably as Murray tells Declan the names of all the Pyros who've died over the past two years. Declan does the same.

There are a lot of names.

A lump rises in my throat. How could the others kick Murray out as leader? He cared about all of us. It should be obvious to anyone.

"It's all very well talking about the past, but if we keep at it, we'll never get anywhere," Cas interrupts. He's grown more and more impatient by the second, hovering near the door with one hand on his weapon like he expects fiends to drop from the ceiling and attack us. Considering that's exactly what happened in Jared's place, I suppose I can't blame him.

Declan turns to Cas. "You, young man, haven't changed a bit."

"So you said." Cas narrows his eyes at Declan. "I don't trust you. Or you," he says to Ray. "What's all this crap for, then?" He indicates the unidentifiable mess of wires and metal and rock all over the tables.

"For one thing, I started out researching how the Fiordans ran their society. This was built to withstand outside attacks, so I'm guessing it's some kind of war base. I think parts of it might have been like bomb shelters."

"Just for the Fiordans?" I ask, frowning. "If the fiends can't fit underground, it must have been, right? But you said there were only three of them. This place looks awfully big for such a small group."

"Yes," says Declan. "Believe me, we've argued about that one for months. My theory's that there used to be a lot more of them, and they died out fast. Maybe it's what prompted them to attack Earth. They used to appear in small groups. Of course it's possible they just abandoned this part of their planet, but I'm led to believe most of it's like this. Wasteland."

"Seems too convenient you'd just walk into a safe place," says Cas.

"We didn't," says Declan. "We lost dozens of people. Our forces had scattered, and there were fiends everywhere. No

Fiordans, though, and we wore the fiends down eventually. Once the fighting died down, we'd scattered, and we were running around trying to find anywhere to shelter. A few people saw a city, a couple of days' walk from here, and a small group went there to have a look. They never came out. It's the Fiordans' place, for sure."

"Nolan mentioned a city," I say. "In fact, I think I saw it, though we were on the other side of the divide at the time. In the distance. Which means, yeah, a few miles from here. Damn."

So's their army, a voice in the back of my mind reminds me. From what Nolan said, it sounded like they abandoned the city to gather their army. The one I saw on the horizon. From here, in their world, it feels closer. I shiver, clenching my hands on the edge of the seat.

"That place is bad news," says Declan. "I wouldn't try to walk it, not with those fiends around."

"Wait, there are fiends?" asks Ray. "When did they come back?"

"Today," says Murray. "They attacked us on the other side of the divide. Before we came here. Do they not come here usually?"

"Not since the war," says Declan. "The first few weeks were rough, like I said. Those of us with sense stayed underground. But they stopped coming. Hasn't been one of those things rampaging around in over a year. And we're more than a match for them. It's the Fiordans we were afraid of, but no one's seen any of them, either."

Part of me still thinks what he's saying is impossible. Either way, I have a feeling we're about to destroy their carefully-constructed peace.

"The one I fought was near the other divide," I say. "But that's... I don't know how many miles away from here. At least a days' walk. On Earth, anyway."

"Sounds about right," says Declan. "None of us has walked that way since before, but we have a vague map of the area."

"There's not much in the way of landmarks," says Ray. "Obviously."

"You never said what you were doing with that lot," says Cas, reaching to pick up a piece of metal from the desk. Ray slaps his hand away, which makes me stare. I never thought Cas would let someone get away with that, but he shrugs.

"Firstly, figuring out what the Fiordans were doing," says Ray. "I think they must have taken all the useful stuff with them. We found vehicles without working engines, for instance, but we don't have reason to explore the surface anyway. Our focus is on weapons. We also tried to build a bridge across the divide, but that fell through. Literally."

"But we had success with weapons and explosives," says Declan. "We've made new hand-to-hand weapons that are resistant to Pyro fire, and explosives. But we've only tested them in controlled conditions. Obviously, we don't want to cause any damage or draw attention to ourselves."

"Though that's how we found out this place is damage-proof," Ray adds. "Accidents happen."

I don't know whether to laugh or not. Shockingly, Cas is unamused. "You're lucky you lasted this long."

"Perhaps," says Ray. "It's something to do. But mostly, I want to know how they opened the divide. And I want to know if it's possible to create a way back."

Murray looks back at Cas and me. I can't tell what he's thinking. Is it wise to share what we *do* know? Confiding that we have Fiordan blood wasn't on my plan. But then again, he's a scientist.

He also hates the Fiordans, but that's a given.

Damn. There's no way he'd want to inject everyone with Fiordan blood so they could safely get home. It might kill them, not to mention there's not much to return to.

I fidget. "Hope Val's got everything under control back there. We kind of left things… hanging," I add, as Ray looks at me.

"That's one way of putting it," Cas mutters.

"What happened?" Declan frowns at Murray. "Not like you to be quiet. I'd have expected you to start poking around that technology by now."

"Yes, well," says Murray. "That's what got us into this mess in the first place, isn't it? There was a dispute amongst the group. They've voted me unfit to lead, for keeping secrets from them."

"They *what?*" Declan and Ray exchange glances. "Who's in charge?"

"Val," I say. "But there were people starting arguments. It's because of Jared. Murray didn't tell them, and…"

"I can guess," says Ray. "For God's sake, Murray. You really caved in that easily? I thought you people were still at war."

Murray studies the ground rather than looking at him. "We've lost enough people already. Morale's at an all-time-low, and after I lied about my brother, I no longer deserve their trust."

"At least you know your buddies survived," says Ray. "That's got to count for something."

"I'm glad," says Murray, slightly hoarse. "Glad you made it. I wish there was more I could do to help you. I couldn't save our base."

"Because the Fiordans opened a divide right through the middle of it!" I snap, suddenly angry with Murray for giving in. I'm equally angry that we're here instead of there, on a hostile world instead of with our friends. But if we're to save them, maybe the answer's here.

"Bet you have your hands full with this one," says Ray.

"I'm surprised she's not making a bid for leadership. But you strike me as the independent type, Leah."

"Maybe I am," I say. "There's too many damn problems and the last thing we need is our group to be tearing itself apart. But I thought the fiends were right on the doorstep. Apparently not."

"The winged ones move fast," says Cas. "It'd make sense if they're planning to attack from the sky."

"Unless..." I trail off, my throat closing up. The world has two divides now. Logically, I'd expect there to be more people on the other side. Our base was almost in Scotland, and though the fiends already attacked the major cities, we passed a fair few towns when I was part of Randy's group of survivors. Maybe the fiends are attacking them first. Even Pyros can't pass through the divide to stop them.

"They definitely have a plan," says Ray. "Sounds like they wanted to drive you out of the base. But it doesn't add up, you're right. I'll bet it shocked you to find us on the other side, huh?"

"Of course it did," Cas says irritably. "We expected an army. Now we find a bunch more people we have to save."

"Cas!" I say, shocked, but Ray laughs.

"Some things never change." He brushes his hair back, picking up a red metallic-type device. "So. Want to meet the others?"

"I don't think that's a good idea," says Declan. "They'll get swamped with questions."

"And we need to check on the camp," I say. I feel bad for these guys, of course, but I belong with the other Pyros. On Earth.

Of course, it isn't that simple. Declan scouts ahead and returns to tell us there are winged fiends circling overhead.

"We drew their attention," he said. "We were field-testing explosives."

"They attacked us earlier," says Cas. "Our group was the target."

"Damn," says Ray. "You're in a tricky situation, I'll give you that."

To go home and risk being spotted, or risk the others getting attacked again? There doesn't appear to be an easy way out. We stay in the lab, making periodic checks on the surface. The fiends are circling, but don't appear to be heading in one particular direction. Frustration wears me down and I end up sharpening my weapon, sitting inside the hallway. Cas stands opposite, leaning on the wall, not speaking. Ray finds the whole arrangement amusing for some reason, and brings us food so he can stare at us.

"Not much of a conversationalist, is he?"

I shrug. "Neither am I. You get used to being quiet in the wilderness."

"You lived outside?"

I end up answering his questions as we eat the odd, dried food they found in storage here. It tastes bland, but edible. Ray asks about my life on the road with Randy and the others. How we avoided the fiends. I tell him about everything except Lissa, and how she died. I can't talk about my sister with strangers. With anyone, really. The wound is fresh, spiked with guilt about how if I'd known I was a Pyro, I could have saved her.

But I didn't have my healing abilities at the time. I hadn't met Cas or Nolan yet. I tell Ray that part. How they found me in an abandoned house, cornered by fiends, determined to fight to my last breath.

Then I hesitate. I know better than to go shouting my mouth off about Cas's ability, but maybe Ray knows about it. Declan does, if he knows Cas was meant to be the Transcendent.

But Ray asks first, "So when did you find out you were the Transcendent?"

I hesitate. "After I'd been with the Pyros a few weeks. I sort of eavesdropped on Murray."

Ray laughs. "I figured you'd be a challenge. How'd you two get so tight, anyway?" This time, he turns to Cas, directing the question at him, too. Cas himself hasn't said a word through my story.

I'm fed up keeping secrets. "We were both Jared's prisoners. That's a long story."

"We have time."

"No, we don't," Cas snaps. "Those damn monsters aren't gonna leave us alone, are they? Want me to go scare them off?"

"You'll draw attention to this place," I point out, though if they're circling around, they must have some idea we're here. Maybe it's because we made a racket when we came through the divide while fighting those fiends. Or maybe they're looking for their fellow monsters. I haven't a clue. But it strikes me as a bad sign.

"I think we're going to draw attention to ourselves whether we like it or not," says Ray. "And I've no intention of sitting around underground while they attack Earth again. Whatever we can do from here, we will."

"You can mount a stealth attack," I say. "They won't be expecting it. But it depends *where* they're planning to attack."

"Exactly," says Ray. "I think you might be a leader-in-the-making after all, Leah."

How should I respond to that? Staying here feels too much like abandoning everyone on Earth. But going outside with the fiends roaming around might draw their attention to the base. Sure, these Pyros have survived two years here relatively unharmed... but it's certain something big is happening outside. Somewhere on this world. How long before it reaches Earth?

Despite Cas's complaints, it's clear we'll have to spend the night. The fiends remain outside, and though Declan has guards on standby in case we have to push them out of the base, I know they're Jared's engineered monsters. This place might be fortified, but they can still do some damage. And, more to the point, bring the Fiordans right here. Less than a mile from the part of the divide next to the Pyro camp on Earth.

Have we doomed them all?

———

I'm standing in front of a crowd. Not humans. Fiends. Too many to count. Hundreds, thousands. Most are regular fiends, over-muscled russet-red-skinned monstrosities with swinging fists and long tusks. A smaller group—though there are at least a hundred—of winged fiends waits in front.

On either side of me is a... person. Whoever I am, I'm looking at the crowd, so I can't see my companions' faces.

But I can see the people tied up in front of me. Four of them, lying on the ground, hands and feet bound together.

And all of them have Jared's face.

"Where is the Transcendent?" says a male voice. The person on my left. It's not a familiar voice, nor can I place the accent.

"I don't know," one of the Jareds says, spitting out blood. "Please... let us go. We were victims, too."

The man steps forward, but his back's to me so I can't see his face. He's wearing dark red, the same colour as the burned ground, and remarkably similar in style to Pyro uniform. He holds a long dagger, too, also just like ours. I glimpse a hand, pale but marked with black on both sides as he turns the knife over and moves towards the tied-up Jareds.

"Victims? You wear the face of the human who pillaged our world. He made a mockery of us, and stole our technology. I confess I would be content to watch him destroy the human race, but he was far too dangerous to keep alive. As are you." A knife gleams, pressed to the man's throat. "But you have information we need. The Transcendent."

"I don't know."

The blade flashes, blood spurts, and the man's head falls to his chest.

"Next." The Fiordan walks to the second Transcendent. "Tell me where the Transcendent is. She escaped your master's clutches, did she not?"

"Yes. She escaped. She's pure-blooded, she's strong."

Some part of me wonders what the hell they're talking about. Pure-blooded? They must be talking about me. But why would the Fiordans ask where to find a Transcendent when he has four, no, three, right in front of him?

"And you didn't track her?"

"We were buried in the lab when it collapsed," says the Transcendent. "We escaped, but there was no trace. The new divide you opened... she may be on the other side."

"You'll never know that," says the Fiordan dismissively. Again, blood spatters the ground.

"Set," says a female voice on my right. The other Fiordan. They have names? "Have you considered there might be more than one of them?"

"Many times," says Set, without turning around. "But humans are weak, and the transformation breaks them. When it doesn't, it results in pathetic creatures like these." He indicates the Transcendents. "Some are unaccounted for, but unfortunately, that one was right. Our new divide has cut the humans off from one another, but has also made it more difficult for us to track individuals. The blood should win..."

"And that's how we'll know the Transcendent," says the woman.

"His or her blood doesn't react, it cannot be traced. They are, for all intents and purposes, one of us."

"Don't you say that," snaps Set. "They will never be one of us. And we have to kill them before they find out their potential. Humans are nothing if not imaginative. Evidently." He kicks one of the other Transcendents. "You're all worthless, aren't you?"

The Transcendent gasps with pain. "Please... we don't know. Jared never told us a thing. He wanted us to fight for him, but he's dead. We will happily fight for you."

Set laughs harshly. "We have an army. We have no use for you snivelling savages." He turns to... me. Whoever I am. "Do you want to finish this one off, Dek?"

"With pleasure."

And there's a knife in my hand. It looks like a Pyro's sword, rust-red. Blood and ashes, blazing red then white.

I strike. The Transcendent falls.

8

I wake, gasping. That felt too real to be a dream. But I thought the visions stopped…

Not again. It can't be happening again.

I can't be dying again.

I take a few deep breaths. *It was just a dream. You're not dying.* At least, I don't feel like I did when the visions took me over last time. Maybe it's an aftereffect.

Or something new.

Does it have to do with my blood belonging to them? Murray injected me with a higher dosage of Fiordan blood to save my life. Has that *tied me to them* in some way, like Cas and I are—were—connected?

Rather than freaking out about the vividness of seeing through the Fiordan's eyes, I examine what I know. The vision took place in the same way as the others did. My dreams were never this distinct and memorable, before or after the world ended. Not even at the time I'd awakened as a Pyro. Only after Cas saved me.

And it's been over a week since the Fiordan blood brought me back from the brink of death. I've never been interrupted by a vision, unless you count those odd shooting pains in my left arm.

The Fiordan I saw in the vision had a tattoo on his left hand.

Oh, shit.

Rather than panicking, I try to make sense of what I overheard. The Fiordans are looking for me, but they can't know about our camp. Or even where the mountain base was. That's... odd, if nothing else. If they knew I was with the Pyros, they'd have sent more than a couple of fiends. Which suggests the ones that attacked us were acting of their own devices. But if I'm to believe the dream, or vision, the Fiordans have Jared's fiends on their side now, too. Unless they engineered those wings themselves. Considering the technology they left here, it's perfectly possible.

Except it means a real Transcendent, whatever that is, is one in a million. The others apparently don't count. *We have to kill them before they find out their potential.* For what?

I rub my forehead, trying to remember what else they said. And forget the line that's burned into the front of my mind: *they are, for all intents and purposes, one of us.*

"I'm not one of them," I whisper aloud. Like it helps. Oh, God. What if it's true? I don't have the visions anymore. They might have been killing me, but they were proof I was close enough to human that the monster blood was poison. "Quit it." I hit myself in the forehead with my palm. I'd be *dead* without the Fiordan blood, for God's sake.

I need to get a grip.

Wherever the Fiordans are, it's a place big enough to hold an army. Definitely nowhere near here. But which side of the divide? The fact that there are *two* divides now doesn't make it any easier to picture.

Maybe someone here has a map of this place.

I pull my clothes on, picking up my weapon. I never did

have a good memory for geography, and I don't even *know* what the Earth looks like now. But the Fiordans clearly went near the old divide where it crossed with Jared's lab. That's where they captured the Transcendents. But they've apparently not been... east? West? Whichever direction leads to our base. Maybe because it's close to the sea. No humans to attack.

My head's spinning. I need air.

I leave my room and immediately get lost. I can't remember where Cas went, nor Murray. I wander the corridors until I almost run smack into Ray.

"Oh, it's you," he says. "Murray and that grumpy ass Cas are with Declan in the lab."

Of course they are. "Okay," I say. "Uh. Thanks for letting us stay."

"Just as long as you don't touch anything in the lab, you're welcome."

I find the right door once Ray points it out to me. Inside, Cas stands near the door and doesn't look at me as I walk inside. Murray converses with Declan. Sounds like they're filling each other in on the past two years.

Is this really the time to be playing catch-up?

"Are those fiends outside?" I ask, interrupting. "Because the others back at the camp will be wondering where we are."

"I know," says Murray. "We're waiting to hear if the coast's clear. But you know I'm not welcome back there. I was leader of these people, too, and they're trapped here."

Oh. Now I get it. Typical Murray, thinking he has to be responsible for everyone here as well as the Pyros back on Earth. Maybe I'm being unfair, but aren't the people who've looked up to him for the past two years a priority? Except... the people here looked up to him, too.

Damn.

I think it over. We *could* stay here, because we can move back and forth between here and Earth... but they can't.

"People can't pass through the divide unless..." They're injected with Fiordan blood. I'm *not* taking on the job of persuading two hundred people to do that. We don't even *have* any Fiordan blood left, not even at the base.

They used the last of it on me. And Jared's place is buried underground now.

"There must be a way," says Murray. "Plainly, some kind of explosive was used to open the divide before. Both times the fiends attacked Earth. I don't think even the Fiordans have that ability."

"What if it was a bunch of them at the same time?" I ask, though I really don't have a clue. "We don't know everything about them, even here."

"We know some things," says Ray, walking in and shutting the door behind him. "I've studied their way of life, as best I could here. The fiends, too. They're completely subservient. If you ask me, the way to stop the war is to eliminate their leaders."

"If we knew where they were," Cas breaks in impatiently. "And some of them must have died in the last war. The Transcendent didn't do it, so how?"

He has a point. Only Transcendents can generate energy blasts, which is how I killed the Fiordan on the bridge. And Jared. But there was only *one* Transcendent there two years ago.

"Maybe they killed each other?" Murray suggests. "From what you're telling me, it sounds like they don't get along with one another. Too many overpowered beings in one place."

Oh. Maybe blood control doesn't work on other Fiordans.

Is that why it didn't work on *me?* Jared hinted the reason he didn't mark me was because I'd be resistant to it...

For all intents and purposes, one of us...

"That's a pretty big assumption to make," says Ray. "If they can control a whole army of those brutes, why would they turn on one another?"

A pause, where I try to look at Murray out of the corner of my eye. And Cas. Should we really be trusting strangers with this? And yet, Declan and Ray are experts on the fiends and their world. They can't know about the blood connection with no actual fiends or Fiordans around to study, like Jared did.

I take a deep breath. "I think Murray should explain that one," I say. "If you want to." I know Cas and I don't have the same implicit trust with these people. Me, because I didn't know them before. Cas, because he doesn't trust anyone.

"Explain what?" asks Ray.

"I've been through this crap enough times," Cas mutters. "I'm going outside."

Murray shifts. "I don't think that's a good idea."

"The coast's clear," says Ray. "That's what I was going to say before you distracted me with all that talk about the monsters having rivalries."

"Right," I say, relieved for the distraction. "I want to take a look outside. You mentioned a city, right?"

Declan frowns at me. "Not that I'm about to start lecturing a Transcendent, but the last time anyone went near that place, they never came back."

"That was two years ago, though, right?" Unless Nolan wasn't lying, and the Fiordans really did hold him captive there. But I have no idea if he was telling the truth. And even if it is booby-trapped, there's not much that can bring down a Transcendent. How else are we to know what's out there? Murray can explain to the others what we *do* know, but there's gaping holes in our knowledge. If answers are anywhere, it's a place the Fiordans lived recently.

"Yes…" He looks at Murray. "I don't suppose I'll be able to stop her once she gets going, right?"

"Nothing stops Leah when she wants something," he says, with a flicker of a smile. I blink, pretty sure he's referring to how I went after Cas to save him from Jared. I can't help looking at Cas, but he doesn't meet my eyes. *Stop it. Like that should bother you now.*

"I know the dangers," I say. "I won't bring any monsters here. If I see anything, I'll hide."

Unless it heads for the divide and attacks Earth.

"Transcendents move fast," says Murray. "She'd be back within the day. This is the real reason you wanted to come here, isn't it, Leah?"

I blink again, not sure why I'm surprised he noticed. Murray really does pay attention to everyone he cares about. I'm part of that. The group. Even the Pyros here. A mixture of relief and pride seeps through me. Right now, I don't feel any less or more than human.

I say goodbye to the others once Declan's unlatched the door and got me through security, back into the tunnel leading to the surface. It comes as no surprise to me when Cas follows silently behind.

I turn to him once we're out in open air. "You want to come with me, then?"

"I want to see the city," says Cas, shielding his eyes from the sun. "There's no point us being here if we don't try to know our enemy."

Hmm. If I admit it, I want proof that they're *not* like us. We walk for a while, our Pyro speed clearing ground in no time. Every inch of this planet looks the same: burned, red, lifeless. Dead. I hope I've remembered the direction right, but we've time to cover ground. I keep one eye on the sky, but no fiends appear. It's like they vanished into empty air. According to Ray, they headed the opposite way to the divide. Not to attack Earth. But I'm suspicious.

I turn to Cas as we walk across yet another a stretch of flat, burned ground. "So. A city. What do you think?"

"The Fiordans used to be an advanced culture," he says, with a shrug. "You can't deny it, considering Jared stole their ideas. Not to mention what Declan's doing."

"Guess not."

"Besides," he says. "This is an opportunity we've been searching for for months. Years, even. A way into the fiends' world, to find out some of their secrets for ourselves."

I blink. "Doesn't seem to me most people liked that idea."

"Before all this shit happened," says Cas. "When we were recruiting new Pyros, we spent half our time raiding old labs. It's risky, because so many of them were close to the divide. That's why Murray was fixated on them, though."

"So you don't think it was the Fiordans' combined powers that opened the divide?"

"Maybe," he says. "It definitely has to do with the Fiordans. The energy blasts are like contained explosives." Cas shrugs. "I have no idea about the technical crap, but it makes logical sense for it to involve Fiordan blood in some way. Only people with their blood can pass through the breach. It'd explain why they were dead set on killing us off."

"Blood. Like…"

An image flashes through my head. The blood-defence at the entry to the base.

No way.

"You don't think they set it up this way on purpose?" I whisper. "So they can get at Earth, but we can't strike back?"

"It wouldn't surprise me," says Cas. "I've been thinking about it for a while. Why does blood make such a difference? I reckon the key's finding where and how it opened in the first place. You temporarily closed the breach before."

I nod. Yeah. I did. And if there's anything that might make me feel better about what I overheard in that dream, it's the thought that being Transcendent means I'm the one who can stop them invading Earth again. For good.

But am I a sacrifice? Like the last Transcendent?

No. She was betrayed. I won't let the same happen to me. I repeat the thought in my head, and it actually does keep the worries at bay. For now.

I keep my eyes on the horizon as we approach what looks like a collection of hills but eventually becomes distinct enough to make out the low shapes of buildings. The city's in a valley between hills, and we'll have to climb down a sloping path. I scan the air for threats, and Cas does likewise. Nothing.

Did they really abandon this place?

"Should we?"

"We're already here," says Cas, and leads the way downhill.

The buildings are made out of the same red rock as everything here, and are shorter, squatter than buildings in —I inwardly shudder as I catch myself thinking, *human* cities. These buildings housed monsters. The fiends *lived* here.

The city's dead, it's pretty obvious. Many of the buildings' windows are cracked, and some walls have collapsed. Heaps of red stone lie in the wide streets, but there's no kind of boundary around the outside of the city to protect them from danger. Though I suppose they *are* the danger.

Cas's already found a path into the maze of buildings, leaping down from a small cliff into one of the deserted streets. I draw one of my daggers, just in case, and follow.

It's eerily silent. I breathe in the scent of burning, like everywhere in the fiends' world. Not strong, like near an energy blast, but enough to make the hairs rise on the back of my neck. I clench my fist around the dagger and peer through every window we pass.

Fiends' rooms are sparsely furnished, containing, if anything at all, nothing more than a handful of crudely-cut stone seats. Sometimes cupboards and beds, and other oddly-shaped furnishings. Once again, I have to remind myself that this is the place the enemy called home.

The streets are wide, forming a crisscross pattern, but there don't seem to be any kinds of vehicles around.

"I don't understand how this place survived," I say, in a whisper. "It's primitive. Surely it should have been wiped out along with the fiends."

We try to keep moving forwards without deviating too much—the city's bigger than it seemed from a distance, and getting lost is the last thing we want to do. We find a main street, or what looks like one, given that it's wider than the others, and contains the ruins of what appear to be shop carts or vendor stands. A shiver goes down my spine, and the image of a similarly-ruined town on Earth flashes through my head.

In the centre is a platform, and even though the ropes hanging above it have mostly rotted away, there's no doubt as to its purpose. Several whipping posts lie at the other side of the square, stained with old blood. Made of stone, like everything else. I wouldn't expect anything less from monsters like the fiends.

And yet...

The fiends as I know them are brainless killing machines, who wouldn't even be capable of building this basic city. They get into brawls with each other, attack at the slightest provocation, and would be impossible to keep in any kind of order. But for this place to exist, *someone* had to have been in charge. The Fiordans, of course.

On the other side of the city square, things change

dramatically. The buildings become taller, and Cas strides ahead to one of them and pokes his blade through the collapsed door. The two halves of the stone door fall away, leaving a gaping opening.

I stare. Metal strips line the walls in the dusty hallway, clashing sharply with the world of red stone outside. Cas holds his knife steady as he prowls through the hallway, which has several openings off the sides, though the rooms lead into one another with no doors in between. But there's glass in the windows, and strange metal devices in some of the rooms. In one, there's a single, roughly-cut mirror—nothing else.

"Figures," he mutters. "I'll bet only the Fiordans had access to their technology. That, or they had the fiends under blood control all the time."

"Why would they need those whipping-posts, then?"

Stupid question. Cas turns to me, his expression dark. "Because they enjoy torture."

We leave the house and walk to the end of the road, where we come to an area of parked vehicles. Not cars, but humped metal shells, each with one single door at the back, far taller and wider than a human vehicle. Some have odd contraptions strapped to the sides and roofs—and my heart does a sickening drop when I realise they're weapons.

They're military vehicles.

The largest building of all is at the end of the car park—not tall, but as wide as four regular houses put together. Covered in metal all over, gleaming in the red light from the sun above. I approach warily, but the door's open. Abandoned, like the rest.

Cas's already entered by the time I finish gaping at it. I follow on his heels, peering into the gloom. He comes out of a room on the left, shrugging.

The interior of the building could have been copied from

Jared's underground headquarters. Tunnel-like corridors lead into endless rooms—all around the same size, all empty. So many of them.

"It's a prison," says Cas. "At least—part of it is."

A prickling sensation crawls up my spine. We're being watched, I'm almost certain of it.

"Do you think there's—something alive in here?" I look in the cells to the left and right, but all are deserted.

Cas shakes his head. "I didn't hear anything."

"Nor me." But the prickling sense persists all the same. We walk deeper into the building. Soon, the cells come to an end, though several other corridors branch off. We reach a series of spacious, metal-walled rooms. There's nothing left inside but blocky furniture. I suppose it'd be too much to hope that the fiends left something behind we could actually use.

"Labs," Cas mutters.

"How do you know?"

"I just do." He prods the wall with his blade. "Dried blood. Also, the ceiling's lower, and look at the doors. Can you imagine a fiend walking under that?"

He has a point. The opening to the room is wider and taller than a human house's by far, but not wide enough to accommodate a full-grown fiend, unless it was knocked to the ground and dragged.

I suppress a shudder at the sudden, vivid memory of being trapped in the cage with that fiend.

So they had labs, same as Jared. What were they doing in here? Questions nag at me, like a puzzle with a key piece missing.

Cas slices through the wall, cutting a deep trench in the metal from floor to ceiling. He steps a couple of metres to the side and does the same, the blade slicing metal like butter. He kicks at the wall with a *clang* that echoes on the metal walls around us. I press my hands to my ears.

"Are you mental?"

He kicks the wall again and a whole piece of metal falls away, leaving a gaping opening.

Leave it to Cas to find the hidden room. Metal lines the walls, but unlike the other rooms, it has furniture. Metal chairs, grouped around a stone slab to serve as a table. Crudely carved stone shelves lined with… books.

"What in the world?"

Cas walks to the nearest shelf, picking up one of the books. It looks surprisingly new, the pages faintly yellowed but not damaged. In this alien world, this is the most alien thing yet. Books mean civilisation, intelligence, records of the past.

"A record room?" I suggest, thinking of all Murray's files, back at the base.

"Thought so," he says. "They were gathering intelligence —on *us.*"

My heart misses a beat.

He holds out the book. I take it carefully, even though there's no reason for me to treat it with respect.

The double-page spread is covered with sketches of humans. Not fiends, not even the Fiordan leaders—humans. Surrounded by rough, harsh writing, odd symbols and criss-crossing lines. Handwritten.

A strange haze washes over my vision, and a pain pierces my temple. I blink, trying to bring the page back into focus.

A word leaps out at me: TRANSCENDENT.

I blink again. The word is written at the top of the page, in large block letters—no, symbols.

I can read it. I can read the fiends' script.

Transcendent.

A chill breaks out across my skin at the familiarity. I step back, and again. "Can you read that?" I whisper.

Cas looks at me with an exact mirror of my own emotions, so intense it knocks the breath out my lungs.

"They were making Transcendents," he says. "It wasn't our idea. It was theirs all along."

I turn back to the page. I wish I couldn't read this. Because if it's true...

Other images. This one's clearly a fiend. Not a winged one, but a regular one. Again, the words rearrange themselves before my eyes into something familiar.

And horrifying.

"The fiends *are* Fiordans," I croak. "A handful of them doctored their own and turned them into slaves so they could have all the power for themselves. They're related."

"I figured," Cas says, his tone flat. "I *knew* there couldn't be so few of them. This city's built for Fiordans, not fiends. At least, it was originally. They must have...turned the others into fiends and dominated them with blood control."

"Who wrote this?" Why would they leave a record?

Cas turns to the book's cover, flipping to the introduction. My eyes take in the text even as my brain struggles to unscramble the meanings. It's like reading English, but with the letters rearranged in such a way that it takes a few seconds to read each word.

And I don't like what I'm reading. "This is written by the first Fiordan to gain Transcendent power," I say. "A... scientist, I'd guess." And I can guess what happened. He experimented on himself, recorded the findings, and someone else got hold of the information. A handful of Transcendent Fiordans dominated everyone else in their world. It seems impossible, and yet I've seen what blood control can do...

Cas turns the page. The text blurs, but the same words

keep cropping up: *fiend. Fiordan. Slave. Energy. Energy-slaves. Superior.*

Transcendent.

"The Fiordans are Transcendent," I whisper. I can't speak louder. My breath comes too fast.

"This looks like… some kind of measurements."

"Levels of Transcendence," Cas says, eyes narrowing. "Measured in… energy. Not blood?"

I can't even begin to understand that. My head spins. "I don't know what that means. But Transcendents and Fiordans… we share blood. It should have been obvious."

He shakes his head. "It *was* obvious. Jared tortured Fiordans and fiends, he could have got the information from any of them. He took their blood, tried to make a human who was equal. But clearly he didn't read about this energy crap."

I can't stop myself looking at the page again. At the text I shouldn't be able to read.

Pyros have created a weapon called "transcendent". Supposed to be… I have to pause before whichever part of me understands the text fills in the gaps… *like Fiordans. The Pyros were weak. Now they are dangerous. They have stolen blood from us, from their enemies, and intend to use it to win.*

But the Pyros are made of weaker substance than we Fiordans. Bodies can be enhanced, made strong. Their minds, however, are fragile. Pain will break them. And if not, they become the being they hate the most.

9

Cas leans over the page, right next to me, his elbow brushing mine. Another shiver runs through me, but this time, it's not because of what I read.

I tilt my head to look at him. His eyes narrow as he reads, and I see a crack in the mask—raw emotion gleaming through. Pain's etched on every line of his face, like a man standing at the gallows, faced with his own doom. It's an alien expression as far as *Cas* is concerned, and yet I know it's genuine.

His eyes meet mine, and the mask is back.

"That's interesting, isn't it?" he says, shutting the book with a snap and taking it from my hands.

"They studied us," I say. I don't even know what to make of what I read. "They knew—knew everything about the Pyros. Even the Transcendents." I'm babbling, avoiding the real issue—the fact that we're both products of the Pyros' attempts to get around humans' natural weakness to the fiends.

And that last paragraph...

But the Pyros are made of weaker substance than we Fiordans.

Bodies can be enhanced, made strong. Their minds, however, are fragile. Pain will break them. And if not, they become the beings they hate the most.

Pain. It's what Jared used against us. Cas and I both understand what it means to be powerless enough that you'd say, do anything to make it end.

The beings they hate the most. The Fiordans. Like what I saw in my dream. I'm… just like them.

I want to tell Cas. Yet my throat's dry, my heart's pounding. We could be on opposite sides of a gulf. Human. Not human.

I'm the monster the Pyros face.

He raises an eyebrow ironically. "Yeah, it was pretty obvious they were studying us, seeing as they've always had the upper hand. They watched us like people watching ants stumbling around in the sun, and one of them always held a magnifying glass."

Now *he's* changing the subject.

The room feels too small, too enclosed, and too much like the cage Jared locked me in. Trapped by blood. The blood that makes me one of them.

"I used to wonder about it, you know, when I was a kid," says Cas. "Why Jared made me. He wanted to create a shifter like the Fiordans. Spies to blend in with the enemy. The best he could do was those fiends. Most of his experiments died in the lab. They were too frail."

I've no clue what to say to that. I just listen. He's holding the book in one hand, head slightly bent. Voice quiet, yet the metal walls catch every word, like a secret.

"The same happened when he tried to mirror their other abilities. He did have some success with weapons, evidently. The Fiordans are the same as us—they're bound to their weapons with blood."

"Blood," I say. "That's the key to everything, right? It's

what gives them—and us—their power." But the book said something about energy, too. I don't understand that, but maybe it's linked to whatever power the Fiordans have in their blood, too.

Cas's expression darkens. "Don't you get it?" he says, in a low, tortured voice. "Their blood is our blood. Normal humans aren't built to stand it, but he made it so we have no choice. Jared got the idea of using the tattoos from their blood-bonds. They used them to control their armies. And the population, too, if this place is any indication. Think about it, who'd be able to keep a city of those fiends in line?"

"I never pictured them living in cities anyway," I say. "They're savages. I'm surprised they didn't wipe *them*selves out."

Cas shoves the book back onto the shelf. "Now we know," he says. "I don't think the fiends were always killers."

My heart drops. "You what?"

"The fiends are driven mad by pain. That's what the Fiordans use to control them. Through their blood. Guess I get how they managed that." He glances back at the book's spine, the text that looks both foreign and familiar. "Question is, how do we rank on the monster scale?"

Something knots inside me. "If we're going by blood, I'm more like the fiends than you are." I clench my teeth together before all my fears come pouring out, right in front of someone who's already proven he doesn't give a crap about me.

The hurt in his eyes knocks the breath from me. "You really think so?"

Great. I can't think clearly with him looking at me so intently. "I don't know, you tell me."

"Leah…" He speaks through clenched teeth.

"Well, do you think I'm a Fiordan or not?" I cross my arms. "I'd like to know."

"What kind of question—of course not."

"Then you're not one either."

Cas's jaw tenses and he looks away.

"What's the problem?" When he doesn't answer, I press on. "Are you so used to thinking of yourself as a monster you can't accept the facts?"

"*What* facts?"

"That we *all* have Fiordan blood," I said. "All Pyros do. We share their blood. It's what gives us our powers in the first place."

Cas finally looks at me. "Are you finished?"

"No." If he's going to start an argument over the slightest thing, then we need to solve this before the war breaks out. "Not until you stop acting like what Jared did to you makes you an outcast, or whatever the hell your issue is. Because it seems to me you brought it on yourself."

Cas's hand clenches. "You *what?*"

"What I said." It's time we talked this out. This isn't ideal timing, but maybe there's no such thing. "You think of all humans as collateral damage. You can barely stand to be within a metre of another person, human, Pyro or whatever. But not me." My face heats up, and not because of the fire. Because he's literally a metre away from me and staring at me like I've started speaking the Fiordans' language. "And you know what? I find that insulting. You want to hang out with the other monster, is that your game?"

Cas's mouth is hanging open. "What? Why would you think that?"

"Hello? You've never spoken to anyone else the whole time I've known you, except Murray. And Declan and Ray, I guess. I've definitely never seen you have a proper conversation with anyone about anything other than the war."

"Because it's *right out there.*" He gestures out at the world in general. "Never, for a second of my life, have I been allowed to forget it." He's breathing heavily, and I know he means every word.

And I can't let the pity that strikes my heart stop me from making my point. "Cas, you're an annoying asshat, but I like you." His eyes go wide. "Believe it or not. I'm just *bored* with your Jekyll and Hyde act. *Why* did you save my life?"

"What kind of question is that?" His eyes narrow again.

"Am I supposed to know the answer? Did you save me because I'm Transcendent, and because you knew the world would be doomed if you didn't?"

"What? No. Of course not."

"Or because you didn't want to be the only part-Fiordan part-human monster on the planet? You wanted someone else to make you feel less of a monster?"

"That is *bullshit*, Leah. I never thought of you as a monster."

"You thought of *yourself* as one," I point out. "And that makes me worse by default."

"Bullshit." His jaw's set. "You just said you liked me. I think you're proving the opposite."

"No, I'm trying to get an answer. To be honest, I'm not sure why I'm wasting my time." Maybe I am, but the nagging feeling that's been following me around since I survived the last blackout persists. That connection I felt with him... I put it down to the visions.

So why hasn't it gone away?

"I don't even know what you're asking. I saved your life because—" He stops.

"Why?"

"I don't know, okay?" he shoots at me. "I forgot how damned aggravating you can be. I don't have to answer your questions."

"No, you don't," I fire back. "That's the thing, Cas, you have a choice. Jared doesn't control your life anymore. So you can choose to be your own person and actually own up to the decent things you've done, or you can carry on acting like you're the only person in the world who's suffered. In case you've forgotten, everyone I knew from the world before is dead." My breath catches, and I swallow. "I saw my parents die. My sister died in my arms. My friends for the past two years were blown to pieces in front of me." I pause for breath. "But you know what? I can still remember the good times. I have friends. The war isn't my whole life. And if we win this, it never will be again."

That intent look is back in his eyes, but he doesn't say anything.

I go on. "What about you, then? What're you planning to do when the war's over? When all the fiends are dead?"

A long pause. It's like trying to draw water from a rock. But I'm not giving up.

"What do you want me to say?" he finally asks. Not really like a question. More of an afterthought.

"Don't try to push it onto me."

"Well, it seems to me you'll find something wrong no matter what I say."

I raise an eyebrow. "What?"

"You can't deny it." He looks away again. "I don't know what the right answer is, okay?"

"The right answer?"

A tugging sensation under my skin, like an itch. Like we're being watched. I step back, instantly tense.

Cas notices. "You felt something?"

"Yeah."

That wary expression is back again.

"See? You *do* think I'm like them."

"You're claiming you can read my thoughts?" He backs towards the door. "That's *not* what I was thinking. I don't think we're alone here."

Me neither. I look everywhere as we leave the building, but I can't see anything hiding behind the vehicles. The sooner we get out of here, the better. We never should have stayed so long. And I'm more confused about Cas than ever.

As we find our way to the main road leading north, a shrieking noise reaches my ears.

"Fiends," I say. Sounds like Jared's winged ones—the ones I can sense. We look warily around, into the abandoned buildings. No signs of life... I can't tell how close that noise was. The air crackles with tension, mingling with the burning smell.

Another shriek, and something falls out of the sky. I jump back, daggers held high, braced for a fight.

A gigantic body crashes into the city, sprawling, motionless, over a nearby rooftop. It's one of the winged fiends, head dangling upside-down right in our path, tipped back and crisscrossed with scars.

We have no choice but to walk around it. Cas takes the lead, holding out his sword like he expects it to attack. I go next, edging past its ugly, tusked head. I can't help looking at the blood dripping over the edges of the building, at its slitted eyes.

Cas hisses, "It's alive."

I half-gape at him, then the fiend moves. Its head rises painfully, and its eyes open a fraction and focus on me. "Tran—scen—dent. He is here. He's looking—for you." The fiend's words trail away, and its eyes close, its head drooping.

My heart hammers. He? Who's he? The Fiordans? Do they know I'm here?

I hate how open this city is, especially as *something* knocked that fiend out of the sky. It could only have been another fiend. Which means there's one around here somewhere.

We pass more empty buildings, most stone, some metal-plated, and a few vehicles. I catch myself trying to picture what life might have been like in a place like this, and mentally shake myself. What does it matter how the monsters lived? They did a pretty thorough job of destroying *our* way of life, sending cities toppling into the divide, energy blasts wiping out a thousand people at a time.

And yet... what if it's true, that they were at the mercy of their leaders? That they were victims of twisted experiments, which broke their minds?

The city ends against a cliff face which climbs a hundred feet into the air.

"What d'you think?" I ask. "Should we climb up, or walk back the other way?"

The fiend came from the opposite direction, but hanging from the cliff, we'd be easy pickings for winged fiends. We'll have to move fast.

"We climb," says Cas.

Cas doesn't waste any time, swinging up the vertical cliff face. I reach for the nearest hand-holds and start climbing. There's virtually nowhere to rest on the way up and we sometimes have to leap up three feet at a time to find the next hand-hold. I fall into a smooth routine—reach, pull, jump. Eyes on the sky above, and the edge of the cliff peeking out above our heads. The exertion pushes the worries to the back of my mind, though I go tense whenever I think I hear a sound that might be wingbeats. I do my best to imagine the weight falling from my shoulders as I climb. The weight of knowing what I do now.

At last, Cas disappears above, onto the cliff. I put on a spurt of speed and catch him up, a rush of relief sweeping me as I clear the cliff top.

The relief swiftly disappears. Someone's standing not ten feet away. A human-shaped figure with wings.

Nolan.

10

C as reacts first, drawing his weapon. "You Fiordan scum."

"I told you I wasn't one of them," says Nolan, stumbling forward, knife in hand. He's bleeding, red rivulets streaming from both arms. Did *he* knock that fiend out of the sky? "If you'd listened to me, I wouldn't be stuck here."

Oh, crap. We killed him—or Cas thought he did. But if it's really him, what have we done?

Cas glares at him. "What the hell is your game? Why did you abandon the city?"

"I'm not Fiordan," says Nolan. "I was telling the truth. They made me Transcendent, gave me their blood to heal myself, but I'm not one of them."

"You… what?" I have no idea what to say. My first instinct should be to attack, but I can't forget Cas and I left him bleeding over by the other divide when I killed Jared. Obviously, he flew here, but that doesn't explain why he's alive.

"I thought you were one of them," I say.

"He is," says Cas, sharply. "Don't let him trick you. He's the Fiordans' minion."

"I'd be dead if I wasn't Transcendent," says Nolan.

"Fiordans can heal themselves as well as Transcendents," I retaliate. "Prove you're Nolan."

"I saved your life!" he says. "When Cas and I found you in that abandoned house. The fiend was about to kill you. I saved you."

I raise my eyebrows as he blurts out everything, from when I first went to join the Pyros. The trip to the abandoned lab. The fight with Jared, when he attacked Elle. And the last time I saw him, when I let him out of jail to help me find Jared's place and save Cas.

Either the Fiordans did a good job torturing every detail out of him, or he's for real. But why would the Fiordans torture him if there are only three of them left in charge of an army?

"Enough," snaps Cas. "If it's really you, you're lying scum all the same."

"I didn't lie to you," he says. "I was sorry for what I did. Leah will tell you."

"Don't you dare," I say, all sympathy fleeing as I remember he betrayed me. He attacked Elle. "I'm not about to start grovelling to you now. You as good as admitted you're working with the enemy. Now tell me why you abandoned the city. Where's this army?"

"You know?" said Nolan, eyes wide. "You can't have seen it up close. They'd have taken you to pieces. I barely got away from them."

"The Fiordans," says Cas. "If you want to talk so much, tell us where the Fiordans are. How many are there? How big is their army?"

"I... don't know." Nolan shuffles back, both eyes on Cas's weapon. "There are three Fiordans. They wear human skin, most of the time, but they can fly. They're bringing the army together. Over there." He points at the horizon. I can't see anything but unbroken red ground.

"And you?" Cas demands. "Are you part of their army? Or a trap for us?"

Nolan blanches. "I didn't want to work for them. I pretended I did so they'd keep me alive. They were torturing the others."

Transcendents. My dream was real.

"Others?" asks Cas.

"Jared's," says Nolan. "They were angry, some of his fiends. But they're all under the Fiordans now."

"So the Fiordans attacked the base?" I ask.

"Attacked the base?" Nolan shakes his head slowly. "No. Why? The others are all right, aren't they?"

"Don't tell him a thing, Leah," says Cas harshly. "He's playing you for information. The others are where you'll never reach them, so don't even try."

"You can't take down an army," says Nolan. "They're going to claim Earth, there's not a thing any of us can do about it. They caught me, they were going to kill me. The divide almost did. Humans aren't meant to cross, but the fiends carried me. I didn't exactly have a choice in the matter."

"Are we supposed to feel sorry for you?" Cas's eyes narrow. "The Fiordans will only have kept you alive if they thought you were worth something. Let alone made you Transcendent."

A pause. Nolan's mouth twists into an almost-smile. "You're right."

Then he attacks. Cas's sword flashes out, but one wing-beat and Nolan's in the air, out of reach. Cas swears, swiping with his blade, but Nolan draws his own weapon and dives at me, pure rage in his expression.

I don't even get chance to be frightened. I jump out of

range, readying my weapon. Adrenaline floods me. I turn to face my opponent. *Enemy. Not Nolan. He's not on your side now.*

"You did this, Leah. You ruined my life."

He grabs at me with a clawed hand. I swipe my dagger but miss, my hand unsteady. *No. I can't be uncertain.* He wants to kill me. I swipe again, pretending I'm attacking one of those winged fiends. Not Nolan. I knew he was a traitor and a coward. But I never thought even he would side with the *Fiordans.*

"Is that how it's gonna be?" I say. "You spent years training to fight against the Fiordans. Now you're best friends for life?"

"That's not how it is," Nolan howls, striking out. His claw grazes my scalp. He's freaking *fast,* quicker than the other flying beasts. Transcendent. "You could have saved me. I was trapped here with those monsters."

We trade blows, but he keeps flying high, out of reach even from Cas's blade.

"No, you weren't," I say. "If they made you Transcendent, you could escape any time you want."

"What?"

Oh, shit. I shouldn't have said that. No, the Fiordans must know they can walk through the divide and humans can't. They're the ones who set it up like that. Right? But I guess they didn't tell Nolan that.

I take another stab at Nolan to avoid having to think of a reply. He dodges, wings carrying him upwards, and returns to hover opposite me. "I couldn't escape," he says. "They marked me, but it doesn't work for some reason."

Blood bonding. He already has their blood—he's Transcendent.

Crap. We're in trouble. As if that wasn't obvious.

Nolan hovers out of reach. "I didn't want to hurt you. But you're the Transcendent. They'll torture me if I let you go."

"I couldn't give a shit," says Cas, jumping to swipe at Nolan. "If you're supposed to be invincible, why are you still a bloody coward?"

Nolan flinches away and Cas's blade forces him to move to the side. Then I step in on the opposite side, dagger pointed up at him. Between us, Cas and I manage to get him more or less pinned, unable to move closer to the ground without one of us stabbing him. He looks plaintively at me. "We can talk," he says.

"Not interested, unless you can tell us your Fiordan masters' plans," I say. "They wanted you to kill me because I'm Transcendent, right? Why bother? I can't protect every single person on this planet." My voice cracks on the last word. I can't even protect my friends. But Nolan knows I'm right.

"Because you're the only one who can kill them."

That's not the right answer—any Transcendent could. It's because I can close the divide. But I can't give anything away, in case word gets back to the Fiordans.

"Seems to me they should have sent someone to kill me themselves," I say.

"They sent me," says Nolan. But he doesn't try to attack me again. He glances over his shoulder, his expression changing to alarm. "There are more of them coming."

"Pity for you." Cas jumps, higher than I've seen him move, and knocks Nolan right out of the air. The two of them slam down into the dirt, Cas pinning him down and raising his weapon—

Nolan screams as he's skewered through the middle. He writhes, choking, "You can't kill me!"

"There are other ways to make your life hell," says Cas, softly, apparently unperturbed by the blood splattering his coat.

"What do you want from me?" He gasps and writhes, but

appears to realise it'll only hurt more if he moves. Tears streak his face, blood spreading across the front of his coat.

"You're the one who attacked us," I say, pushing back the rising nausea. "You're working for the enemy. You attacked the base."

Nolan winces, lines of pain creasing his face. "I didn't have a choice."

Anger burns away my disgust and a sensation too much like pity. "So you did tell them where to find us."

"You got out, didn't you?"

"What?"

"I did that," he says quickly, eyes flickering to the blood pooling around his chest where Cas's blade digs in. "I told them I'd only need to take a small group to wipe you all out. I said the Transcendent wasn't there. I don't think they believed me, but they let me go."

"A likely story." Cas twists the blade, and Nolan screams. I wince despite myself, feeling sick.

"So you told the fiends where to find us," I say, looking at Nolan's face rather than the wound.

"No. I've given them the wrong information," Nolan chokes. "They've tortured me repeatedly, but they can't kill me. They say I'll die myself soon enough. There wasn't enough blood to make me a full Fiordan. Like you."

I freeze, almost flinch, like he's punched me in the chest.

No. It isn't true. A hollow sensation fills me. I'm not...

"So you can't kill them?" I ask, slowly. "Just a—pure Transcendent?" I can't say *Fiordan*. But it explains why Jared's Transcendents never tried to fight back in the vision.

Nolan nods.

"So they know I'm here, in their world?"

Nolan shakes his head. "I didn't expect to find you on this side. I was heading for the base."

"The base is gone, thanks to you," I say, angry when my

voice shakes. *It can't be true. I'm Pyro, if not human.* "I'm here to find out how to kill my enemies. *Your* enemies. Or they used to be, before you turned traitor for the last time."

And my hands are on Cas's blade where it skewers him. He twists his head to look at me, surprise flickering across his expression before it hardens again. "I might let her finish you off," says Cas. "It's a mercy."

"I told you, I can't die," Nolan groans.

Cas gives him a critical look and then stamps on Nolan's hand. The bones shatter with a horrible noise, and Nolan lets out a high-pitched scream.

"Right," says Cas. "There are three Fiordans, and an army. If the Fiordans were to die, what would happen to the fiends?"

"They'd be free," says Nolan, face screwed up in pain. "But they're mad beasts. They'd attack anything that moves."

"We've dealt with that for long enough," Cas mutters. "Does that include Jared's fiends?"

"He's dead," chokes Nolan. "They belong to the Fiordans now. And all his pet Transcendents are dead."

Considering what I saw in that vision, I'm not surprised.

A familiar screech echoes overhead. *Oh, hell.* Sure enough, two winged fiends appear, fast approaching. I curse, glad my weapon hand's free, because Cas's is pinning Nolan to the ground.

But they move too fast to avoid both at once, diving at us in unison. I run to them, my knife already flaming. My first swipe misses and talons graze my forehead. I duck, cursing as blood drips into my eyes.

An awful noise comes from Nolan as Cas wrenches the blade free and strikes, sending one of the fiends plummeting to the ground. I wipe blood from my forehead and stab wildly at my opponent. This time, my dagger sinks into its leg.

The fiend screeches, wings beating, and I stab its leg again, bringing it to the ground. Cas has already made quick work of the other one, which lies on its back, unmoving.

Time for me to finish this one off. The fiend lets out a whine, which I ignore, once again slashing its leg.

Something's not right. The first wound's closing, healing itself.

My heart sinks like a stone. *No. They can't have given the power to the fiends, too.*

The fiend stops, hovering in the air, eyes blank and red and staring.

Staring directly into my eyes in a shockingly familiar way. And it hits me: my own blood was on my weapon hand when I stabbed it. The cut on my forehead's healed already, but...

"Hold on," I say to Cas, who's standing on Nolan's coat, presumably to stop him from getting away. "I think I accidentally transferred my own blood over. Like before."

"So?" Cas is unimpressed. "Kill it."

I don't. "You'll obey me now," I say to the fiend. "Fly over there."

I point, and it obeys, wings beating in time with my instructions. Oddly, I feel like laughing.

Nolan half-sits up, mouth falling open. "How are you doing that?"

Oh, crap. I forgot Nolan could see.

"See?" I say to Cas. "Reckon I can convert all their army?"

In fact... now I think about it, flying on one of these things would give us a way to get right up close to the fiends. To the Fiordans.

"No, you can't," says Cas. Still unimpressed. "Don't try it. The Fiordans would kill you before you got to all of them."

"How about we sneak up on them?" I ask. "Air transport. We can ride these fiends and get right over the fiend camp and…" *Drop a bomb*. Wasn't that what Declan and Ray were developing underground?

My pulse races. This is it. I can't think of a better way to wipe those bastards out in one go. What else is there to do?

"Don't do anything stupid," says Cas. "Get that fiend down here and kill it."

Seriously? He won't even consider it? "No," I say. "It won't hurt us as long as it's under my control. We can fly back…"

"I'm not *flying* on it," says Cas.

Despite everything, I burst out laughing at his expression. Really, I'd have suggested hitching a ride on the fiends earlier if I'd known it'd get this much of a reaction from him. I gasp for breath, doubled over.

Cas, on the other hand, gives me a blistering glare. "Are you done?"

"No," I say, trying to get myself under control. "Nolan, you're going to tell us *exactly* where your Fiordan masters are hiding."

I'm aware he's grasped at least part of my plan. But right now, I can't bring myself to care. For the first time in what seems like forever, the prospect of victory doesn't feel hopelessly out of reach.

I'm not letting this go now. Not if it gives us a fighting chance of ending this battle before it reaches Earth.

Nolan gasps. I glance at him, and see the wound's healing already. Damn. How do we get rid of him if he can't be killed? I should have seen this one coming. He looks pathetic, but if we let him go, he'll fly right back to the Fiordans and ruin any chance we have of making a plan.

Cas marches over and grabs him by the scruff of his neck, apparently no longer considering the winged fiend a threat.

"Tell us," he says. "I'm going to make your life a misery either way."

Nolan swallows, trying to pull away from Cas. "This

whole world looks the same, but they're at camp. That way." He points to our right. I squint, but I can't see anything. "The army's divided into winged fiends and regular ones. They're going to attack from the air first, scouting to find the base camp. The new divide was dangerous to cross for a while, but they'll find your friends. Count on it. They want to kill you, and they'll stop at nothing. Even if you avoid them, they'll kill everyone you know."

"Screw that," I say, but my heart's beating faster. I can't protect everyone. But can I take down three of them at once?

"I have some theories about killing the bastards," says Cas. "I think I'll practise on you."

He reaches and grabs Nolan's weapon from his limp hand. Nolan gasps.

"Hang on," I say. "We can't—"

"We can't leave him alive," says Cas, harshly. "Right."

A screech rings out. Two more winged fiends, I think —*Wait, since when could I tell how many there are, before I even see them?*

Sure enough, two batlike shapes appear on the horizon, getting closer fast. Before they're on us, inspiration strikes and I slice open my own palm, letting the blood drip onto my blade. Then I motion to Cas to stand back.

Cas himself has other ideas. He stabs Nolan's hand as he tries to grab his weapon back. Nolan falls back, whimpering in pain.

The winged fiends approach in a swift dive. I jump and slash at my first target, slicing across its leg.

"Stop!" I yell.

And it does. The second, however, dives. I duck its claws and stab it in the back of the leg with the bloodied blade.

"You'll both obey me," I say, as they land beside me.

"That's very dramatic," says Cas. "I was hoping you'd do the sensible thing and tell them to kill one another."

"Uh." I guess that'd be logical. In fact… "If I set them against the Fiordans, they'd know we were here."

"Pretty sure they'll know soon anyway," says Cas. "You're gonna have to make a choice, Leah. They're after you, and they'll kill the others to get at you even if you're not back at camp."

My heart sinks. He's right.

I turn to him, my brief triumph forgotten. "You think I don't know that? I'll draw their attention."

Nolan coughs, reminding me of his presence. By the looks of things, the wound in his chest is almost healed.

"Here?" says Cas, one eyebrow raised.

"I have a plan," I say. "First, we need to get rid of this guy." I point at Nolan, and he pales.

"You can't—"

"Shut it, you," snaps Cas. "You've outlived your usefulness, but we're not going to let you go telling tales on us to your masters."

"They're not my—"

"Pick him up," I say to one of the fiends.

Nolan twists to stare at me, but the fiend obeys instantly, scooping Nolan up in its claws.

"Take him somewhere far away from here. Nowhere near the Fiordans or any other fiends."

Nolan makes a strangled noise. "No! I can't stay in this place."

"It's fitting," I say. "You're lucky."

"Yeah, you are," says Cas. "So, what's this plan of yours?"

He might be asking for my opinion, but his derisive tone makes me bristle. Sure, I might be improvising a little, but I actually do have an idea.

The fiend holding Nolan takes off in one wingbeat. Nolan lets out a hoarse scream, but it's too late. In seconds, he's in the air, flailing and howling.

I turn my back on him. "Right. We get the fiends to carry us back to Murray and Declan. I need to talk to them."

"We do *what?*" Cas's eyes narrow.

"Don't start," I snap. "Those things move crazy-fast. We can cover more ground. I've flown with one before."

"I am *not flying.*"

This time, I'm more annoyed than amused. "Fine. I'll leave you here and fly back. Grab some of Ray's bombs, then fly to the fiends' camp and mount a stealth attack. We can cripple their army without them even seeing us until it's too late. The bombs are energy blasts, they might even be able to kill them."

Cas gapes at me.

"Admit it. It's all we've got, and as an added bonus, it'll keep the Fiordans well away from our group. They'll know they have enemies on this world."

"They know that already," he says. "They'll know we're coming, for sure. This is suicide."

"No, it isn't," I counter. "No more than walking right into their camp and challenging them. We don't have much time."

Cas swears loudly, running his hands over his weapon like he wants to stab the winged fiends through the throat.

And I get an idea. "One of them can carry both of us at once," I say. "I'll get the other to make sure Val and the others are safe. Can you speak?" I ask both of them.

A pause, then: "Tran... scendent."

That figures. "Is that all you can say?"

"No."

I almost laugh, more at the expression on Cas's face than anything.

"Right. That's our plan. Cas, you can come with me or you can walk back and miss out on the action. Your choice."

Cas's eyes narrow. Sighing, I walk to the first fiend. "Pick me up and follow my directions," I say. To the second,

"You're to follow us, then follow my directions when I'm on the ground."

And they obey. My heart jumps when the fiend's claws close around me, but I've done this before.

"All right," Cas snaps, moving alongside me.

"Him, too," I say to the fiend. "Don't drop us."

Cas makes an angry hissing noise, but secures his weapon before letting the fiend pick him up in one clawed hand. I bite back a laugh at his expression when we take off.

11

I 'm right about covering more ground. The flight is short, if uncomfortable. Once we reach camp. I order the fiends to touch down, then I give one of them directions to our group. I tell it to fly high, out of reach, and try not to be seen. So the others don't panic.

Cas doesn't speak a word. He's acting like I have the plague and it's catching. Again. What happened to the man who looked so devastated down in the Fiordans' house when he read that we're becoming the monsters we despise?

Maybe that's the problem. Even if we win this war, in all likelihood, Cas and I will be the only survivors. He's been through that once before already. Sure, mutual traumatic experiences can make two people form a bond pretty quickly, but I've no idea what Cas and I have, now, with the blood-connection gone. But he might have had a point. I don't know what answers I expected from him, but maybe pushing him like that was unfair.

I take a deep breath and approach the cave entrance.

Declan's there on duty. "You're alive," he says. "That was quicker than I expected."

"Uh, about that," I say.

"Leah, watch out!" Declan jumps up, blade in hand, and swipes at the fiend. The wings flap, carrying it out of reach.

"Wait!" I say hurriedly. "It's on our side." That came out wrong. "I'm blood-controlling it. I can control them with my blood. They obey me."

Declan's expression suggests I've declared allegiance to the Fiordans. *Oh, crap.*

"It's true," says Cas. "Her blood's similar enough to the Fiordans' to let her do the blood-control thing."

An unexpected rush of gratitude almost knocks me over. *Similar*, he said. Not the same as the enemy. I'd stare at him to check he's actually Cas, except now Declan gapes at both of us.

"Leah, if you don't kill that thing, I will."

"Didn't Murray tell you about the blood control?" I ask, desperately. "He told you what being Transcendent—what it means, right? Their blood is mine. That's why they want to kill me, because I'm the only person who can kill them. I can even turn their monsters against them. I came back because I think I know the way to the fiends' camp, and I need your help."

Declan stares some more. I shouldn't be surprised, and yet I'm impatient. "Is Murray around? He knows I can control them. I've saved people's lives that way before." It's true. One of Jared's fiends went on the rampage in the lab after I used the blood control, giving us the chance to escape, and got Tyler and Poppy out when I couldn't help them.

Declan sighs. "The others aren't going to like this. They know about you by now, Leah. I've had to work hard to convince them we've really found another Transcendent. But the Fiordans, well, they're the enemy. No way around it."

"I have their blood," I say. "So does Murray. And Cas, too. If it helps us beat them, surely it can't hurt. I have a plan."

Declan glances over his shoulder. "I'll give you the benefit of the doubt for now, but I'm keeping an eye on that *thing.*"

"I will," says Cas. "You know I'll kill it if it moves. Let Leah explain the plan to you and Ray."

Damn. *Who are you and what did you do with Cas?* I want to ask. Instead, I nod. "What he said. The quicker I explain, the quicker I can get the plan underway before the Fiordans figure it out. They're bound to, eventually. They sent Nolan to kill me."

I fill him in as we go through the tunnel, past the defences at the entrance, to the lab. Murray and Ray are talking inside, but stop as soon as we walk in.

I'm expecting resistance, but they let me explain my plan in silence. I brace myself for the backlash.

Ray speaks first. "That's a plan worthy of you, Murray."

"It's too risky," Murray says.

"What about the *blood-controlling fiends* part?" Declan asks. "It's downright suicidal. I'll bet that's one of the reasons the Fiordans want the Transcendent dead. You could build your own army."

Of humans. A sickening jolt goes through me. I shake my head violently. "No. That's what Jared did, and look where it got him. I don't want an army, I just want to kill the Fiordans. They're not invincible. And it wouldn't hurt to know how to close the divide, too."

"We have a theory about that," says Murray. "Declan's map marks the areas the main attacks happened from *this* side. I had a map like that back at the base, but I can remember the essentials. If we work out where each divide originally opened, I think that's the key to closing the breach."

"But there are two of them," I point out. "It'd be a lot easier if I killed the Fiordans, but—with the breach closed, you'd all be stuck here."

A pause. Declan shakes his head. "We've already resigned ourselves to never going back to Earth. If it keeps those bastards out, I'm willing to take the risk."

"But…"

"Look at the map," says Murray, pointing to a large sheet of paper spread out on the table. Two lines are scored across it, with a few markers in between. "You were there." He points to a marker. "The city. Did Nolan say where the army was?"

I frown. "I'm not good at telling directions, but he pointed that way…" I trace one of the lines on the map. "Is that the first divide?"

"Yes," says Declan.

It's closer to the city than I thought. I forgot how much ground I can cover as a Transcendent. And even more with a winged fiend on my team.

"If we go by the map, they must be here," says Declan, pointing at a spot somewhere to the right of where the city's marked on the map. Next to the first divide. "So logically, it's the place to attack them. Except we can't move fast enough to intercept them without them seeing us."

"That's why I need to sneak up on them," I say. "If I fly in, I can ambush them. Not to mention I'll be able to get at the divide. Where do you think it opened the first time?"

"From this side? It's difficult to tell." Declan sighs. "It might not work from this side. You might only be able to close it from Earth."

Damn. More complications. And yet…

"So they'll be invading Earth from there?" asks Ray, pointing at the map. "Looks that way. There were a bunch of towns over that side before."

"Not necessarily," I say. "They're looking for the Transcendent, but I don't think they know about our new camp yet. Unless their winged fiends found it." I clench my fists. I want to keep the other Pyros back on Earth safe, but right now, it seems like the best way to do that is to stay away from them. "I sent another fiend to check on them to make sure they're all right. It's following my commands. It won't hurt them."

The others' sceptical expressions suggest otherwise.

"Look," I say. "I know this is crazy, but the invasion's coming to Earth and they'll do anything to find me. The best thing we can do is get the jump on them in a way they don't expect. They definitely wouldn't expect us to dive-bomb their camp. At the very least, we can scatter their army, even if the bombs don't kill the Fiordans outright."

"She has a point," says Ray. "I don't like it, but those two walked right into the Fiordans' city and came out unscathed. If anyone can pull this off… we have plenty of bombs waiting to be tested."

"We need the best you've got," I say. "If it doesn't work, I want to close the first divide, because there are only humans on that side. Not Pyros."

"Yes," says Declan. "I know you're the Transcendent, but you can't fight here and on Earth at the same time. The other Pyros… they're ready to fight, aren't they?" He looks at Murray, who nods.

"As they'll ever be." Murray sighs. "I did tell some of the older members to take Elle and the people who can't fight to the nearest town, if need be. The others will fight to the death to defend Earth."

My heart sinks. Fight to the death. Everyone's lives depend on me pulling this off.

I draw in a breath. "All right," I say. "How do those bombs work?"

Ray explains. It makes my head spin, and I wish I could practise before using one on the Fiordans, but it can't be helped. I do my best to remember the instructions, and cram as many destructive devices into my pockets as possible.

"I think I should go with you," says Murray.

"No." I shake my head. "I don't think I'll be able to keep Cas away, but there's a good chance they'll be heading this way if the Fiordans survive. They'll be majorly pissed off."

"Got it," says Declan. "I've two hundred Pyros here spoiling for a fight. We won't make it easy for them."

"The winged ones will get here first," I say. "I wish I could blood-control all of them, but it's not possible if we don't have much time."

And we don't. The pressure's like a ticking clock. We're lucky to have escaped this long. A sharp pain in my left hand is a reminder. I'm connected to the Fiordans somehow. If it isn't killing me, I have a feeling the only way to stop them getting at Earth again will end in my death.

But I can't afford to let those doubts distract me. I'll save Earth. I have to. I have to close the divide. No matter what the cost.

Maybe Cas suspects. He doesn't look me in the eyes when I walk outside again. The second fiend has come back, and he and Cas are having what appears to be a glaring contest.

"Are the others safe?" I ask the fiend.

Its head dips. I assume that means *yes*.

"Are there any fiends over there?"

"No."

"Holy shit," says Ray from behind me. "She's talking to it. And do I hear you're planning to hitch a ride, too, Cas?"

"I'm not happy about it," Cas mutters. "Where are these bombs?"

Ray repeats the instructions. Declan hovers behind, with Murray. Both of them wear grim expressions. My heart plummets. If this plan doesn't work, I've effectively doomed the others. And Earth.

My plan relies on the fiend camp looking exactly like it did in my dream, or vision.

"We'll prepare," says Murray. "I can speak to the others over the other side, too."

I turn to him. "But they kicked you out."

"And I shouldn't have let them." His face is pale, but his expression is firm. "I let them undermine my authority at a time when we need to be united. I left Val to deal with the fallout." He shakes his head. "I've been a coward, I admit it. But I'll tell them to be prepared."

He means in case this doesn't work, and the invasion reaches Earth.

I nod, words clogging my throat.

Cas studies my face while I shove the bombs into the pockets of my coat.

"You're not planning to throw *yourself* into the camp, are you?" he asks.

I blink at him. "Of course not. Why would you think that?"

He shrugs. "Just hard to figure out what you're thinking."

"I could say the same for you." I don't want to argue with him now.

"If this doesn't work, we're dead," he says. "You do realise that, right?"

"Yes," I say. "But that doesn't give me license to be an asshat to people. That's the point I was trying to make. If anything, it's an excuse *not* to treat people like crap."

Cas's gaze drops. "You and I had very different lives. I don't know how to think the way you do."

"Well, you can start by not calling people collateral damage."

"When did I say that?"

"You don't remember when we were on our way to Jared's the first time?"

"You think *that's* the part I remember?" He shakes his head. "I've said some shitty things to you, yeah, and I'm sorry for that."

"You apologised for treating me like crap before," I say. "Then you went back on your word."

A pause. "The world's ending," he says. "We're at war. The fiends caught us off guard when they attacked the base. All I could think about was trying to stop anyone else getting killed. Including you. You're not invincible, Leah."

I hear another name. *Resa*.

"I'm not her."

He looks away, jaw clenched. "I know you aren't. But you have the same habit of coming up with these whacked out plans and expecting everyone else to follow through."

What? "You don't have to come."

"You think I'm staying behind?" His eyes are angry blue chips. "You think I'm about to let you go running off again? This goes against everything Murray taught us in training. He taught me to give the orders. He trusted me." He glances back over his shoulder, and I see the extent of the responsibility he accepted. He was my age at the first invasion. He watched countless Pyros die. I saw his memories, but that was just an outsider's view. It didn't show how he coped afterwards, but I can guess.

Because it's not so different to the way I coped the two years after the invasion. I barely spoke a word to anyone. I kept my head down and followed Randy's orders to stay alive. I never thought I'd experience any kind of friendship.

I never thought I'd be leading an attack against the invaders.

"Cas," I say, "just trust me on this, okay? And just... imagine what it'd look like if we win. *When* we win. Earth will be safe. The fiends will be gone."

"Winning the war won't kill them all," he says. "Besides, they'll keep trying to come back."

"Isn't that why the Pyros exist? We'd need something to do with our awesome fire-power after the war." I half smile at him, though I don't get one in return.

"After the war," he repeats. "There's never been an 'after'. Not as far as I'm concerned."

"*If* there is, then," I say, "just think about it. Have you ever considered you don't see yourself as human because you've never let yourself act like it?"

"What?" Disbelief colours his tone.

"Human. As in, having goals in life other than being a great Pyro soldier. Talking to other humans and actually considering their opinions. Maybe having actual human feelings." Great, I'm blushing now. But I've been inside his head. I know he has emotions buried in there somewhere.

I know he cared about Resa.

I'm not jealous. All I feel is the need to make him understand what I'm trying to say.

And what I'm not saying. But there's no time to examine my own jumble of disconnected emotions. Not when we have a war to win.

"*If* there's an 'after'," he says, "I'll remind you how downright suicidal your plan was." He moves towards the fiends.

I've no idea how to take that, so I join him by the fiends. "And I'll remind you how you hitched a ride on one of Jared's ugly minions."

The fiend bristles. I wonder if it can understand me. Oops.

Cas tenses at the mention of Jared's name. "If there's an 'after', I'm making sure Murray gets reinstated as leader so he can stop anyone who might get stupid ideas about following Jared's lead."

"See? You can imagine. It's not so hard." I climb onto the

fiend. It's more sensible to ride on their backs so we can position ourselves in such a way that if anyone looked up from below, they wouldn't be able to see us. Not that it would help if the Fiordans saw two of their fiends flying out of line, but there's little we can do about it.

"I can imagine," he says, climbing onto his own fiend, "how much I want to be back on the ground."

I turn around and give him an amused grin. "I'll never let you forget this. I bet no Pyro's ever won a battle this way before."

"Don't get ahead of yourself." He checks the bombs concealed in his own coat, and I check mine again, giving the fiends a set of instructions. If there are other fiends in the air, they're to blend in until we can slip away. If there's no way to avoid the Fiordans, we're to approach from behind and fly directly overhead, as high up as possible.

There's no practise run. If this goes wrong, we're as good as dead. And so's everyone else.

Go time, I think, as the fiends take flight in unison. Cas already has a bomb in his hand. He's unusually quiet. Maybe even he knows we're in way over our head.

I can't afford to imagine anything other than victory.

And then we're flying over burned ground. Though we're aiming for the fiends' camp, maybe I'll be able to see where the first divide opened from here. In fact… if it's far enough from the Fiordans, maybe I can close it before they notice us. If not, at least we'll draw attention to ourselves rather than the others.

My heart thuds frantically. My arm throbs, though I've no idea why. I check on Cas occasionally. He clings to the fiend's back, his face set.

In what feels like hours yet no time at all, the jagged shape of the divide cuts across the ground below. There's no sign of the army, but from my memory of the map, it's some miles along the same line. I order the fiend to fly higher, much higher. On the left is the coastline. Near there is the place I first spoke to a fiend. Some miles to the east is Jared's first lab, which was destroyed. Further along is the buried ruins of Jared's other lab, underground.

And on the distant horizon, I can see the army. Even from here, it's a blur of red shapes, an entire stretch of ground given over to the monsters. We're too far away to be spotted. Too high. My breath whistles in my ears. I'm sure if I was still human, I'd have passed out from lack of oxygen by now.

But I'm not human. I'm Transcendent, even here, clinging to the back of a monster.

I let go with both hands and try to find the fire. Even here, it rises to the surface, flooding me to the fingertips. But I can't get a handle on the energy the way I did when I closed that gate.

Cas flies directly below me. He's shouting something, but I can't make out the words.

Okay. It looks like the original plan will have to do. The fire's warmed my numbed hands, but the fiend doesn't like it. It makes a hissing noise, rocking beneath me. Oh, crap. I'd better keep the fire away from it. I know I can't die from a fall, but plunging fifty feet into the fiends' camp because I've killed my ride would be a humiliating way to end a stealth attack.

I direct both fiends to fly towards the fiends' army.

This is it. Once again, the time that passes might be an hour, but is probably less than five minutes. Not enough time to mentally steel myself. My hands are numb, clumsy, but I ready the first bomb.

Cas swears softly behind me. Even the vision can't have prepared me for the sight of thousands upon thousands of monsters, all in lines. My throat closes up. *So many...* From above, it looks unreal, like a painting of a war about to break.

Except there's only one army, and every soldier is facing the same way. Towards Earth.

Just like my dreams.

The fiends remember my instructions. I can't see individuals from here, but the Fiordans are much smaller than the monsters they command. Maybe they're hiding amongst the army. I'm not about to drop within sight. We have the advantage as long as we're out of reach.

Kill them.

I fly close enough to Cas for him to see my face and understand what I'm about to do.

The bomb leaves my hand in a burst of fire. Cas's does likewise. We move on, soaring over the army. We've thrown a half-dozen projectiles before the first one hits the ground.

The explosion rends the air in two. "Higher!" I scream at the fiend, hoping both of them have the sense to get out of the way. The ground below disappears in red smoke which swiftly rises to surround us. I'm forced to cling on with both hands as the impact of the explosion rocks the fiend beneath me.

It's not over. Grabbing another bomb and hanging on tight with my other hand, I direct the fiend over to the part of the army that hasn't disappeared in smoke. The roaring sound in my ears is like a tidal wave, the starbursts of red as the bombs hit the ground—it feels like I'm watching through someone else's eyes.

The last bomb comes too soon. By now, the ground's almost completely obscured. My ears ring. The pain suggests I've deafened myself several times over and my healing power's barely keeping up. But it's enough. The fiend remembers my instructions, and apparently Cas's does too, because it follows us. Cas is half-hidden behind smoke and I can't see his expression.

The last bomb falls. I don't even hear the impact amongst

the blur of red smoke. I can't tell how many have died.

"To the divide!" I scream, or I think I do. I can't hear my own voice.

But my words must get through somehow, because the fiend flies us still higher, out of reach of the noise. Is this what the Fiordans felt like when they tore open a door into our world, when their explosions obliterated our cities? I refuse to feel sorry for the mass of writhing bodies below. *They did the same to us. They'd kill us in seconds.*

The divide appears through the smoke—the explosion reached even here—and the fiend picks up speed, apparently eager to get away. As the ringing in my ears dies down a little, we're over the divide, and falling—diving—

I gasp for breath. The fiend pulls out of the dive sharply, on the same level as Cas's.

"What the *hell?*" he yells at me. "You could have killed us both."

"Thought you wanted to live dangerously," I say, but nausea rises in my throat. How many of them did we kill?

We had to. They'd have killed us.

We skim near ground level, passing over the places where the divide tore through towns and villages. And Jared's place. I don't even recognise it at first. The ground's totally flattened.

"What are you looking for?" Cas snarls. "Just use your energy thing and get it over with."

Right. I do my best to ignore the aches and pains all over my body as it objects to the abuse.

But I let go of the fiend with both hands and call the fire again.

Warmth floods me. I didn't realise how *cold* I was, but we flew so high, my skin's turned to ice-cold rock. I gasp as heat rushes to my fingertips, as I try to reach the energy.

Nothing.

Damn.

"Touch down," I say.

The fiend seems to understand. Seconds later, we land on burned ground. Not anywhere I recognise. Cas lands beside me and instantly jumps down.

"How many do you reckon we killed?"

"I haven't a clue," he snaps. "Get bloody on with it already. We're giving them too many chances to strike back."

"All right, all right." They'll be held back for a while at least. But I need to figure out my Transcendent abilities.

Ignoring Cas's presence, I walk closer to the divide, trying to remember what it felt like when I faced off against that Fiordan on the bridge.

Stay out of our world. Up close, this divide appears smaller than I remember. The other one's right near our group. The quicker I close both of them, the better.

I reach for the fire, for that flood of energy I felt last time. Jared could use it without thinking. But I was too scared of hurting the others to practise. And now I don't know what I'm doing. *Stop it. It's like the Pyro power—all instinct.*

I push on the energy, push at the divide. *I'm Transcendent. I was meant to do this.*

Energy flows to every inch of my body. I'm barely aware of my own feet, now standing over the edge. And yet… nothing's happening.

It's not right.

"Leah!" Cas shouts, and I turn.

He stands, sword outstretched, holding the fiend back. The monster growls, baring its teeth.

"Stop that!" I shout at the fiend.

A claw lunges at me. I draw on the Transcendent power without even thinking and send it flying back a few feet. The fiend staggers, but launches itself forward at me again

"Stop!" I yell.

Crap. This is bad. I didn't realise the effects of my blood-control would wear off. I didn't think it was possible.

But if we kill them, we've no way back.

Cursing, I draw my dagger and slice open my palm again. With two swift strikes, Cas drives his opponent to the brink of the divide, blade to its neck. He's already cut open both its clawed feet. I do the same, but this time, it has no effect.

"Shit," I whisper.

We've no choice but to kill them.

As I lunge in for the killing blow, a blast of energy sends me off my feet. My back slams into the ground, knocking the breath from my lungs. I sit up, groaning, the fiend advancing on me.

The fiend can't have done that.

Cas has stabbed his opponent through the neck. The fiend lies on its back, its lifeblood spilling onto the burned ground.

I ready myself to attack again. Screw caution. I send my own blast of energy at the fiend, and it goes flying in a whirl-wind of fire. For a second, I'm caught up in the flow of battle. A kick to the shoulder knocks it down, and a final burst of fire.

The fiend disintegrates in a mass of rock-like particles. I step back, the fire dying down and hopelessness settling in. How the hell are we meant to get back to the others now?

A winged shape flies out of the divide, touching down beside the body of its fallen brothers. And a human-shaped figure steps down from its back.

Murray.

I freeze, weapon still in my hand.

Impossible. Murray's back at the base. This is one of the Fiordans.

Oh, God. They're not dead.

We brought them to us.

12

"Transcendent," he says. "I knew you wouldn't be able to resist seeking us out."

He planned this? The thought flashes through my mind as the air around us ripples. I barely have the time to raise my dagger before I'm thrown back several feet in a whirl of energy. My feet dig into the ground, but I still feel off-balance. Shaken. *It didn't work. We failed.*

Murray reaches up to his face, which is stretched in an unnatural grin, and pulls. The skin peels away like paper, revealing red skin like the fiends'. The Murray-shaped skin falls away, revealing the short, savage figure of a real fiend, a Fiordan.

He looks almost identical to the one I killed last time. The Fiordan bares razor teeth in a wide smile.

Heat rushes through me to my fingertips, my dagger igniting. I snarl and lunge forward, and fire erupts around us.

I strike once, twice, three times. The third strike catches him in the arm, leaving a crimson trail. I've done this before. I'm faster than they are. Stronger.

That's why they're afraid of me.

The fire surrounds us in a halo, reducing the world to a small space where the two of us struggle against each other. The Fiordan dodges my dagger and leaps at me with clawed red hands outstretched. I jump up, whirling around in a manoeuvre Val taught me in one of her lessons, a lifetime ago. Strike low, where the monster doesn't expect it. The dagger severs two claws from his left hand, and he hisses at me.

Power thrums beneath my skin, the kind of power that would reduce the Fiordan to ashes—power that could even bring down the army.

The dagger penetrates the Fiordan through the neck, point first.

He staggers, dropping to its knees, making a horrible choking sound. Blood streams from his neck.

He looks up at me. Grinning. Then jumps back, my dagger coming free. The blood flow is slowing. Healing.

Oh, hell.

"You should know better, Transcendent. Our blood runs in your veins, after all. You might call us... siblings."

"I'm not like you," I say, heart beating fast. I reach for the fire, for the energy blast I used to kill the other one, but the Fiordan splays a hand and sends me staggering back again. I should have practised using the power. I don't know enough, and I'm at a desperate disadvantage.

And where the hell are the other two Fiordans? They might be attacking the others. I should have guessed they'd think of the same idea, flying on the winged fiends' backs. Avoiding the bombs.

I have to kill it. Fast.

But the Fiordan lunges, wielding a dagger that could be identical to mine. Fire leaps into life along the blade, forcing me back.

"You humans stole the fire from us," hisses the Fiordan.

"Our blood runs in all Pyro veins. You stole our life, and we deserve to take your world as compensation."

"Like hell."

The Fiordan throws the dagger at me. I'm not prepared for the move and have to throw myself flat, skidding across the ground. The dagger misses, but so does my attempt to grab the Fiordan by the legs and pull him down. *I thought he couldn't let go of the weapon!*

But the Fiordan darts forward and the dagger's suddenly in his hand again. The blade almost takes my fingers off. I've never fought an opponent like it. All my training was focused on fiends, and possibly humans. This short, monstrous creature with a deadly blade and a healing power is far outside my comfort zone.

"Is that the best you have, Transcendent?"

The sword blazes, creating a wall of pure fire. Two can play at that game. I concentrate on my own power, letting it flow into the weapon in my hands, and leap at the creature again. If I can strike hard and fast, maybe I can get a hit in. Slow it down.

The enemy's blazing sword deflects every one of my hits, barely appearing to move at all.

Does the Fiordan intend to tire me out? I don't have time for this. My world is dying, there's an army waiting to invade, and only I can stop it.

"I was told you're a legendary fighter. Or was that the other one?"

He's trying to put me off. Ignoring the rasping voice, I dig my heels into the ground and launch myself into the air. I sail right over the Fiordan's head and land behind him, daggers slashing back. A spray of blood tells me I hit my mark—but the wounds will heal within a few seconds.

The Fiordan's sword presses to my neck, and it's too late to dodge.

"Goodbye, Transcendent."

The sword cuts through the air—

And misses, because another sword's in the way, cutting off its path. Cas stands in front of me, blazing fury, towering over the Fiordan.

It's fast, too fast to watch, even. The air crackles with flames from both weapons, and I back away, out of Cas's path. Already, the bruises from the broken rock are healing, the blisters fading to nothing.

But though I might be Transcendent, even I can't get an opening in this fight. Cas and the Fiordan are locked in a deadly dance, two warriors fighting for victory. A fight that can only end in one of their deaths. I've never seen as thoroughly as I do now that this is what Cas was born to, that he's nothing without the fight. Because it was why he was created, and why he lives. He said something like that to me once, and yet this is the first time I've really seen what that means.

And he's winning. He's driving the Fiordan back towards the edge of the cliff.

The opponent seems to realise this, and leaps over Cas's head, slashing at him from behind. Cas easily deflects the blow, and retaliates with one of his own.

Pushes the fiend's weapon aside, and stabs him in the heart.

I know he hit the heart, because of the precision of the strike. Nothing Cas does is by accident.

The Fiordan topples over backwards, gasping, lifeblood flowing from his chest. Yet he tries to stand, raises the weapon feebly. Cas paces over to his dying enemy, eyes hard and cold. He raises his blade. What's he doing?

The blade sings through the air, and the Fiordan's clawed hands are severed. Cas bends down and lifts the enemy's sword from his limp hand. The awful thing is, the Fiordan's moving, limbs twitching, but the light around the sword is going out.

Cas lunges, piercing the monster through the neck with his own sword.

"That should do it," he says, into the silence.

I walk over to join him. The Fiordan's back arches, blood sputtering from his ruined neck.

"Your world is ours, Transcendent! My blood lives on. He'll die. Just like the rest of you. Our blood..." The Fiordan falters, his head dropping.

Dead.

I move forward. "Why'd you need to stab it like that, too?"

"Figured they couldn't be immortal," he says. "I noticed Nolan didn't heal when I cut him with his own weapon, so..." He indicates the Fiordan's two wounds—the one on its chest looks like it's sealed, but its neck remains open, a gaping red slash.

"Damn," I say.

Cas flashes me a sideways look. "I can't let the Transcendent have all the fun. It's only fair."

I half-laugh, more in relief than anything. The Fiordan's dead. *One down, two to go.* "They should have died when the bomb went off," I say, and I don't feel like laughing anymore. "You don't think they saw it coming, do you?"

Cas doesn't answer. I step closer to the edge of the divide. This is probably a bad idea, but even with whatever hellish chaos is happening on the other side, I can't see a thing from here.

My skin prickles. Why couldn't I close the divide?

Come on. Fire. It comes without conscious thought now, flaring across my outstretched arms as I *push* against the curtain of red rippling in front of me. Pain flashes up my left arm, sharp and burning, but I ignore it. *Close the gate...*

A hand closes around my throat. I choke, the fire

quenching as though doused with water. A haze cloaks my vision, but not enough that I can't see the person attacking me.

Cas.

"Wait!" I try to speak, but the word can't get past my lips, because my throat's being crushed. Pain takes over and I can't even scream. No. Cas wouldn't hurt me…

But he is. The cold, dark eyes that stare into mine, as he crushes the life out of me, are no longer those of my ally.

A gurgling laugh comes from the Fiordan. "I told you, our blood lives on. Jared stole our power and used it for his own benefit. Our blood is superior."

My vision dances. Pain shoots up my left wrist. The tattoos. They've taken control of the tattoos. Just like Jared did.

But it doesn't work on me. And that's why they want me dead.

Fighting the haze, I kick out, with both feet. One connects with something, and the chokehold loosens. Another kick. Cas snarls, raising his blade, and I desperately hold my dagger in front of my face to block his strike. He casually knocks it aside, and presses the sharp point of his own weapon to my neck.

The haze recedes, my healing powers kicking in, bones fitting back together. But my mind's a maelstrom of confusion.

"Oh, Transcendent, you shouldn't have killed him," says another voice, as Cas stares blankly at me, knife pressed to my healing throat.

Another Fiordan stands beside the first, having stepped through the divide. Small, skinless, ugly. Teeth bared in a snarl. This one's female, I remember from the vision.

"Cas," I whisper, feeling blood trickle from where the blade cuts my neck.

"The boy belongs to us now," says the Fiordan.

"No," I croak, struggling to break his grip. "It's not true."

"You know I speak the truth, Transcendent," the Fiordan whispers. "You know it in your heart. Your Cas is no more. His blood is mine. His will is mine, and you will watch as he destroys everything you hold dear, Transcendent."

I reach for my Transcendent power and pull hard, breaking free from his grip. Cas and I face each other. There's no recognition in his expression.

"I know you're in there," I say. "Cas, fight it. You're too damn stubborn for this. Fight it, stop letting them control you!"

"It's hopeless," the Fiordan hisses. "I will take everything you have, Transcendent."

Cas's knife comes down, and the world explodes in white-hot agony.

Don't black out. Don't give in. I push back against the pain, shove it to a dark, screaming corner of my mind, and narrowly dodge another strike. Somehow I raise my dagger in a counterattack, our blades connecting.

But the pain's fading, and the fire's coming back. I let it flow to the weapon in my hand, whirl around, and throw a blast of energy at the Fiordan. Cas staggers back, but he's not caught the brunt of the blast.

The Fiordan also staggers, but doesn't fall. Damn. I can't access the extent of my power with Cas fighting me.

"Cas!" I shout. "Don't you do anything you'll regret."

No response.

"My blood will be your end, Transcendent." The Fiordan's mouth twists in an insane smile beneath gleaming eyes.

Cas turns on me, blade flashing fire. Eyes blank.

Too late to block him.

Too late to run.

A vision bursts across my eyes. I'm in the air, hovering over a battlefield, red ground soaked in blood.

No. No, I'm not. *Focus, Leah. Not now.*

It's not a battlefield. It's chaos, it's slaughter. The remaining fiends on the ground are running, covering ground, flying.

Flying in the direction of the divide. Towards Earth.

No!

I blink fiercely, willing my sight to come back. The dust clears enough to reveal I'm a few metres from the cliff leading down into the ravine. No sign of Cas or the Fiordan. The smoky air makes it hard to see the divide beyond.

But the army's coming this way. We didn't kill them all—we just made them raging mad.

This is my last chance to act.

I reach past the pain and horror, to the fire.

Get out of our world.

The pain and anger feed the fire, as I push against the divide, against the army on the other side. My blood is more than Fiordan. I'm human. I'm superior.

"And I won't let you take Earth!" I scream.

Then… I feel it. The gates holding the divide open, like gears under the surface, under the rippling fire-like curtain. I push them back.

The resistance gives. My vision flickers between this divide and the other, between the two gulfs, and the power's draining from me even as I pull it from the line in the earth. I feel it more than I see it, like the click of bolts closing, the thud as two sides of a gulf slam into one another, becoming one again.

I fall to my knees, and the world fades away.

I'm flying on the back of a winged fiend. Below, chaos reigns, monsters swarming against one another. Opposite, another figure rides another fiend. No, two of them. One, small and goblin-like. The other is Cas. They're flying towards the other divide, which appears twice as big as before, covering more ground. Like the divide I destroyed… in the waking world…

"That way!" yells the Fiordan beside Cas. "The girl's friends are that way!"

Oh, God. He told them where camp was.

The shock sends me slamming back into my own body, curled on the ground beside where the divide used to be.

There's nothing there anymore.

I didn't imagine it. The divide has gone. The plague that's split our world for the past two years has gone. Yet there's barely an echo of energy. Compared to what I saw in the vision… *The other divide.*

I reach for the energy again, but I can't feel anything. The surge of adrenaline is gone, and even with my Transcendent powers in overdrive, I'm tired, so tired.

A horrible ache rises from somewhere deep inside me, clogging my throat, making my eyes burn, turning my limbs to water.

Cas is with the enemy now. I've lost him for good.

I curl up, my head pressed to my knees. Not a vision, not the torture of Jared or the fiend—just the incurable pain of pure, helpless misery.

I've lost him.

You never had him.

And that, more than anything, is what hurts. That *after* world… can't exist anymore.

Tears burn my eyes, the regret leaving a metallic taste in my mouth. I can't get the image of the way he looked at me in the fiends' city out of my head. Like someone desperately looking out for a connection. A moan of pain escapes through my clenched teeth.

Get up. Leah, you have to get up.

I push to my feet, ignoring the pain in my limbs. I'll heal. I can walk. Move fast. I have to.

From here, I can see nothing but empty ground, a gigantic Burned Spot where the divide used to be. Several miles north of here is the second divide. If I run, I can reach it in less than a day.

But that won't be fast enough to stop the winged fiends reaching the base and attacking my friends.

And Cas...

No. I won't think about him now. Once again, I push the pain down into a small, dark, screaming part of me, put one foot in front of the other, and run.

13

I f not for the urgency, I'd stop to stare at the chaos the divide closing has left in its wake. The whole Earth must have shaken, yet I barely felt it. Because I was the earthquake. I was the energy blast.

I am the Transcendent.

And the only reason the Fiordans aren't attacking me is because they want to hurt me first. To take my friends away from me, one by one. Probably, they want to have Cas torture me to the brink of death. Or maybe they want to watch me kill him. They're easily as bad as Jared. But Jared never really understood how the Fiordans work. I'm not even sure I do.

They have an army. I have to warn the others.

I run so fast, I might as well be flying. My feet skim dead, burned ground. The divide's left a permanent mark.

But within an hour, the shapes of towns and houses start to appear. I pass by patches of grass, yellowed in the heat, but clinging onto life. Even a stretch of woodland that might be the same one the winged fiends nearly killed me in. Where Cas saved me. Everything looks different now.

Stop. Stop thinking. Run.

And I do. A continual tremor follows underneath my feet, whether from the divide closing or from an oncoming army, I've no idea. I pick up the pace, like I can outrun the memories of all the nights I spent outside, under the cold moon. Sleeping by the roadside, running from Jared's lab, leaving Cas, leaving him…

There was nothing you could do. Jared marked him before you even knew him.

I stop, clutching a stitch in my chest, and let a few tears fall. It doesn't help.

Run, Leah.

A sharp sting in my left arm follows me, but no visions come. I have no idea what's happening on the other side, back in the fiends' world. I run like if I move fast enough, time will slow down for me. The Earth will stop. The army will wait.

The army doesn't wait. I skid to a halt at the top of a small hill, a hundred metres from the second divide, at the sight of countless winged fiends like a flock of bats soaring through the sky.

The first wave of the attack is already here. I can't even count them, but they surely outnumber the hundred and fifty or so Pyros hiding amongst the hills.

I glance around desperately. No towns nearby, but I leap down the hill and sprint towards the divide all the same. If I can get on the other side, I can draw their attention…

Maybe I really do have wings. It takes seconds for me to reach the edge, and I jump without thinking, the air carrying me along. I scream as fire folds around me, though it doesn't burn.

"Come and fight me!" I yell at the winged fiends, raising my blade to the sky and sending fire arcing overhead.

And they do. The army turns around as one, seeing me

hovering over the divide, between one world and the next. Either side of me, the air shimmers. *Can I close the door from here?* I can't see the Fiordans.

But Murray, Declan and the others are back in the fiends' world, and Cas...

I shouldn't have hesitated. A blast of energy hits me between the shoulder blades, sending me flying, out of the divide and onto rock-hard ground. Earth, I think immediately, as a dozen winged fiends fly right at me. Too late to dodge.

Definitely too late to turn them against their masters.

But I can fight them. My dagger remains glued to my hand, even as I slam down on my back. I push to my feet and send a wave of energy right at them, knocking more than one of them out of the sky. Some recognise they're outclassed and fly away, back over the divide and into the Fiordans' world. Some try to slash at me only to be driven back by a wave of fire. I'm controlling the fire at last, the fire from the divide itself.

But I'm too late. And there are too many of them. The fire's power dies down to a trickle even as I push desperately at the divide, like I did the first time. *Come on.* It's like something's muting the fire inside me, or whatever connected me to the energy inside the divide. A resistance. Have the Fiordans put up some kind of defence?

Come on!

It isn't working. The divide grows brighter, if anything, and I know with a sinking certainty that the energy I pushed away from the other divide somehow ended up here. I'm not strong enough.

The thought hits me like a sucker-punch. *I'm not strong enough to close it.*

A dozen fiends descend on me, wings beating, teeth bared. Dragging my attention back to the present, I jump and slash and send a fiery wave that knocks three of them out of the sky, but I'm outnumbered. Individually, I could take them down, but all I can do is call the fire and push them back until sweat runs down my face, until pain rocks me on my feet—pain from all over my body, like whatever makes me Transcendent has been pushed to the brink—

Like I'm going to burn out.

I let the fire drop. No way am I going to let these bastards kill me before I have my revenge on the Fiordans. And there's no way I'll let them get at the others.

I leap and stab one low-flying fiend in the wing, sending it crashing into another. My dagger finds its throat and cuts deep. The fiend's corpse drops at my feet and I jump over it, the momentum carrying me directly beneath the five remaining fiends stupid enough to stay even when I drove them back with fire.

The second fiend falls before I have the chance to attack, a dagger buried in its neck. I blink, totally confused. Two red-cloaked figures pop up from behind the opposite hill.

"You didn't think we'd let you have all the fun, did you?" shouts Poppy. She and Tyler leap forward and join in the fight. The sudden arrival of the others sends the fiends into a confused frenzy. All three dive for Poppy at the same time, like they think she's the weak link. She proves otherwise before stabbing one of them in the throat, and Tyler leaps on another's back, fire lighting his red uniform. I shout a warning at the last one, and it turns on me, sharp eyes glaring.

Dagger in hand, I jump the last two feet and crash into the fiend. Fire ignites my fist as I pound its face as hard as I can—the image of Cas's face flashes before me—a wordless scream of rage escapes and my hand keeps punching even when the fiend's head is reduced to nothing more than rock fragments.

Tyler and Poppy stare at me like I've just walked out of my grave.

Swallowing hard, tears burning my eyes, I back away from the fiend. My whole body is trembling as I scan the sky, checking for more enemies. The sky attack must have been ahead, because they'll have been able to escape the bombs.

Like the Fiordans did. And they could be anywhere.

"Earth to Leah?" says Tyler. "Not gonna thank us for saving your neck?"

"I—sorry, guys. Thank you." I sink to the ground, tremors racking my body. "How did you know I was here?"

"Girl, you lit up the sky like a beacon," says Poppy. "You don't think we'd let you get away with sneaking off again, did you?" She runs over and hugs me, as does Tyler.

And the tears break free. "Oh God… guys, I thought you were dead. I saw the army. I couldn't—"

Between gasps, I tell them the gist of what happened. I have to warn them there's an army on the way, led by two enraged Fiordans who'll stop at nothing to make me suffer.

And that Cas is our enemy.

Poppy's eyes grow round, but she doesn't interrupt. "Murray and the others are alive?"

"I don't know," I say, honestly. "Those fiends just flew right over their hiding place. It wouldn't surprise me if the Fiordans knew about it by now." I have to take practical steps. Cas isn't around to lead the army. Which means I have to do it.

I stand, still shaking. "I'm going to have a look over the divide. It won't take a second."

Poppy and Tyler follow with noises of protest, but the divide's almost translucent now, the fiends' world appearing clearer than Earth on the other side. No sign of any fiends, on land or sky. I walk alongside it, heading to the point where I crossed over the last time.

"They're not there," says Poppy. "We came right up to the edge when we realised you'd gone. Val's gone, too. I think Garry must have driven her out."

My heart drops. No. She had Jared's mark. And she wasn't Transcendent, either, so passing through the divide would be fatal for her.

"Or she's like Cas," I say, refusing to voice the inevitable. If I lose anyone else, I might break into shards.

"No," says Tyler. "Val's strong. We'll beat down those Fiordan scum. I reckon they're hiding like cowards."

I shake my head. "They had a plan. They saw us coming all along, that's why they used the winged fiends."

"You couldn't have known," says Tyler. "Sounds like you beat the shit out of half their army."

"All I did was make them mad," I say, in a choked whisper. "They'll do anything to hurt me now."

"You have to come back to camp, Leah," says Poppy.

Yes. I need to warn everyone. "All right," I say. "But Murray's over there. I need to tell him what—what happened."

"There's no need," says Tyler, pointing at another group of Pyros heading back in the direction of camp. "He's there."

I blink. It really is Murray, talking urgently to a couple of older Pyros I vaguely recognise.

My heart sinks.

"Murray," I say, walking over to him quickly.

"Leah. Thank goodness you're alive."

"Things are bad," I say, and give him a rundown of events. Like the more times I say it, the more real it will become. Cas belongs to the enemy now. The invasion's coming.

"Don't panic," Murray says—apparently, the emotions warring inside me showed on my face. "We're soldiers. We were meant to fight the fiends, on the front lines. I've already asked for Elle and anyone who can't fight to be taken to the town. And Declan and the others are more than ready to fight."

"I need to go after them alone," I say. "The Fiordans had Cas try to kill me. They'll set him against all of us if they can." Maybe they're just trying to break me, but it's working. I can't watch my friends kill one another. And... oh, God. Elle and Val have the marks, too.

"Leah, all we can do is fight. Declan and the others are setting traps on the ground over the other side to slow the army down. It won't slow down the winged ones, of course, but it'll give us the chance to prepare. We need to regroup."

I nod mutely. Wishing I'd thought of a more sensible plan. Killing that Fiordan feels more like a defeat than a victory, even though the Fiordans had the means to use Jared's tattoos against us whenever they felt like it. They've been playing us all along.

Unsurprisingly, everyone looks at me like I came back from the dead. Not for the first time. I ignore the stares and follow Murray to the centre of camp.

"Hold it," says Garry, coming over with some of the other senior Pyros. "I thought we made it clear neither of you are welcome here anymore."

"You didn't say anything like that to me," I point out. "Besides, we were just attacked. The war's literally on our doorstep, and there's an army of fiends marching this way right now. If you want to stand there and make stupid threats, that's your issue, but I reckon everyone else here is going to want to listen to what we have to say."

I talk right over the interruptions. We don't have time to argue, and I'm far past caring.

"Right," says Murray, as silence falls. "I can't pretend I've been a perfect leader. But whether we like it or not, the war we've trained to fight in is coming here, to us, right now. Those of you who want to fight, stay here. If you don't, you're welcome to go with Ryan. He's going to take some of you to the nearest town. Obviously, you're all prepared to fight fiends, but this time, the Fiordans are with them, and they're likely to appear first. As I told you, they're shape-shifters, as cruel and manipulative as Jared ever was. They're likely to attempt to deceive you by imitating people you know. Like Jared. Like me. And…"

Go on, I think, bleakly. *Just tell them. Tell everyone Cas is our enemy now.*

Murray draws in a breath. "I'm sorry I couldn't prepare you for this. But it's likely the Fiordans will be here by the end of the night. Leah and I recently learned that two hundred other Pyros survived the war two years ago. They've been hiding underground in a ruined part of the Fiordans' world all along, and from there, they intend to make their final stand. We're not alone in this fight."

Whispers break out. More than a few people think Murray's losing his marbles. I suppose I can't blame them. With the number of bombshells we've dropped lately, they have good reason never to trust another word he says. But he didn't mention Cas. Why?

"Is that where Cas is?" asks Elle, looking on, wide-eyed. "With the others?"

I can't tell her the truth, so I nod. Murray doesn't answer. He walks amongst the group, offering reassurances, answering other queries. Garry and his friends stand in a huddle. Probably scheming to make a break for it. I'm not bothered about them now.

Perhaps I'm imagining it, but the ground faintly trembles under my feet. Like the rumble of a distant quake, or a fast-approaching storm. Above, the sky boils with red clouds. Like the world's coming to an end, again. But no more fiends appear.

"You can't leave me behind," says a quiet voice. Elle. "I thought you were *dead*, Leah."

"I'm sorry." Damn. I blink tears out of my eyes. "I had to do something to stop them, but I ended up making things worse. But I'll tell you what happened."

No one's queuing to ask *me* questions. I'm not sure whether it's because they implicitly trust Murray as their former leader, or because they *really* don't trust me. Whether because I'm Transcendent or because I've repeatedly gone behind everyone's back, it hardly matters now.

And whether they trust me or not, I'm going to do everything in my power to keep them safe. But first, I owe Elle the truth.

I tell her everything, about the other Pyros hiding underground. About my fight with the Fiordan. Trying to close the divide. Victory, at the worst price.

"He's not dead," says Elle, finally. "Not to you. I reckon that's why my dad didn't tell the others. He thinks you can save Cas."

"I can't," I say. "There's no way around Jared's spell. Apart from maybe giving him *my* blood, and he'd never forgive me for that. Besides, how do I know it won't make things worse? Only a full-blooded Transcendent is completely resistant to them. I don't know why it worked for me and not for the others."

The others. There are no more Transcendents, apart from Murray and me. And only I can close the divide. But for some reason, I can't grasp the raging energy I felt when I closed the last one. It's stronger. *God. I wish I'd figured it out before.* Before. When Cas and I were—friends? Maybe. I swallow hard, push those feelings into the *after-the-war* part of my mind, which is shrinking by the second.

"I'm going to keep watch," I say to Elle. "You go with Murray. You'll be safe, I promise."

Who am I kidding? She has Jared's mark. If the Fiordans get any hint we're friends, they'll turn her against me. Like Cas. Like Val. Who knows where she is now? I hesitate, torn, but I can't hold back. I need to reach the others.

I walk to stop myself thinking, becoming aware I'm being followed when Poppy and Tyler catch up with me at the top of the rise. The divide cuts through the land ahead, a shimmering curtain of fire above it. On the other side is a sky as red as the one above our heads, the land as dead and cracked as the ground under our feet.

Even though there's no one on the other side, I imagine the Fiordan swooping in on its winged fiend and obliterating everything. There's nowhere to run. They'll find me anyway, take everything from me again. I've already lost my friends, my home, my world—and now, Cas. I'd thought I was strong, but not anymore. Maybe Jared broke me, or maybe I broke myself when I over-stretched my powers closing the gateway last time. Or maybe I've been breaking all along, like a tiny crack in a window growing until it shatters. The final straw was failing to close the divide and stop the invasion. Shutting the first divide only made things worse. Some Transcendent I am.

I never even saved Cas.

"Tell me about him," Poppy says. "Please. I hate this, I hate the silence. Talk to me, Leah. It'll help. Please."

"I—" My voice cuts off in a sob. "What do you want me to say?"

"Anything. What did Cas mean to you?"

Like it's a funeral or memorial or something. She believes he's gone. That, or she's genuinely wondering what I could possibly have seen in him. Did I really hope Cas and I could ever have anything? I don't know. I thought I'd have time enough to think about it later. After.

Just thinking that makes a jagged shard of pain rise in my

chest. I push it down, squeezing my eyes shut. "I honestly have no idea. He saved my life—you know that already. We wanted nothing to do with each other. But then we were stuck together when Jared threatened everyone, and I saw that—that Jared tortured him." I have to get out the words, because they're like pieces of glass cutting me apart on the inside. "We never got along, but I cared about the idiot. He doesn't know how to relate to people, but he was alone after the last Transcendent fell, and I think he wanted to stop the same thing happening to me."

I look up at Poppy, who's said nothing throughout all of this. She moves and hugs me, hard, shaking as much as me.

"I'm so sorry," she says. "I was stupid, selfish. I thought you two ran away together, that..."

The shards dig in again. Ran away. Like two people who could be together without repercussions. The thought never even crossed my mind, but I wish she'd never voiced it all the same.

"That would never happen. It's never been like that, anyway. He didn't even want to be friends." I bite down on more bitter, angry words before I can say them. It isn't true. He did want to be friends. He just didn't know how to say it. And I was too stubborn to give him the chance to. I shake my head. "He couldn't think about after the war. I was stupid enough to, and now... if this wasn't happening. I might have had..."

Had what? Happiness? A brief spark, perhaps, before it was snuffed out. But in this world, those tiny sparks, those brief, bright moments, are all the more valuable. Regret is worse.

"You couldn't have known, Leah," Poppy says, and Tyler nods agreement.

"I knew we didn't have much time," I say. "Even at Jared's

place. He risked his life to help me. I could never pay him back. And… and I can't kill him, I just can't."

"He'd—Leah, I know you don't want to hear this, but he'd want you to. I didn't know him that well, but he'd want that. He'd want you to live, want you to defend the world even if it meant killing him."

She's right. He was a Pyro, through and through, in a way I can never be. If our positions were reversed, he'd kill me without a moment's hesitation. I've always known it. He was prepared to watch me die before, when the visions consumed me. But he didn't try to put me out of my misery. Because he thought I could be saved? I shake the thought away. What might have been doesn't matter, because in this world, it isn't possible. Cas is a Pyro. He lives to defend the Earth, lives to fight. And I'm the same. Jared might have tried to break me, but the fire lives inside me, and will as long as I do.

"Leah, you're stronger than me, you're stronger than anyone."

"Yeah, you are," adds Tyler. "You know that."

"No." I shake my head. "I might be Transcendent, but I'm not immortal."

"No one's immortal," says Poppy, swallowing. "That's why you're human. I think you can stop him. And Val."

Oh, God. Val. How could I forget the enemy has her, too?

I refuse to let that, or the thought of Cas, put me off. We're the only people left to defend our world.

"It's not about how strong you are," I say. "In fact, that reminds me. Cas killed one of the Fiordans even though he's not Transcendent, by stabbing it with its own weapon."

I turn to Poppy and Tyler. "If I don't make it—"

"Don't talk like that."

"Well, if I'm not around, then," I say. "They like to trick us and split us up. It wouldn't surprise me if they used some kind of distraction to get me away from you guys, then attacked. If you get their weapons away from them and stab them with their own blades, I think any of you could kill one of them." I draw in a breath, speaking with every ounce of confidence I possess. "There are two of them, but a hundred and fifty of us. Not to mention over two hundred over the divide."

"Exactly!" Poppy's eyes gleam. "I reckon they're scared of you, Leah."

I want to argue, but don't, because—what if it's true? They're scared of someone using their own power against them. It's been obvious from the start. We *do* outnumber them, even if they have thousands of fiends on their side.

I do my best to smile at the others. "We'll mow them down, before they can hurt anyone else."

"Absolutely," says Tyler. "We'll win, or die trying."

Die trying. They've accepted our fate. I've never been alone in this war, not since I found the Pyros, even standing on the brink of the divide. Maybe being Transcendent means I'll outlive everyone. But as long as my heart's beating, I'll fight alongside them to rid our world of the fiends.

I raise my eyes to the sky, to the unmistakable shape of something big flying on the other side of the barrier.

"This is it," I murmur. "Guys, run back and warn the others."

There's no protest. Their retreating footsteps echo in tandem with my pounding heart and the heaving Earth under my feet.

Blade in hand, I prepare to face my enemy.

14

―――――

I hear the fiend's cry before it properly crosses the barrier. My weapon's at the ready, blazing bright. A warning. The fiend drops immediately, diving at me with wide red eyes.

I stop. It's the fiend I blood-controlled. The one who took Nolan.

"Are you an enemy?" I ask, not lowering my weapon.

"No, Transcendent." He's still under my control? *Well, that's one less opponent to worry about.*

"Is Nolan gone?"

The fiend dips its head. Yes, I guess. But why is this fiend still obeying me and not the others? Did the Fiordans have something to do with it?

"What about the Fiordans. Did you see them?"

Another nod. *Oh, no.* "Where? Are they close?"

"To the divide."

My heart drops.

"There?" I point to the curtain of fire.

The fiend turns slowly and points to the right, further down the line. I suppose they haven't tracked down our camp yet. If that's even the target. *What the hell is their game?*

"What are they doing?"

A pause. The fiend makes some gesture I can't read. "Open."

Opening a gate.

"Shit," I whisper. "They're breaking through, all right. Can I ride?"

It's risky, but the other Pyros know what's coming. If I get to the gate first, maybe I can stop it opening.

Wishful thinking. But if there's anything I can do to stop them...

The fiend dips its head to let me climb onto its back. Strange how it doesn't obey the Fiordans. Maybe they don't know I had three of them under my control. They must have lost at least some of their army when Cas and I bombed them.

Cas.

I falter, half-on the fiend's back, as a phantom pain shoots up my left arm. Briefly, the image of flying flashes before my eyes. Flying over fire and smoke. The divide?

I blink and the image disappears. So much for spying on the Fiordans again. But I reckon if they're opening a gate, it'd be like a neon sign. I wouldn't be able to miss it.

The fiend takes off. I hold on tight, but fear pushes my discomfort aside as the ground passes by and there's no sign of the enemy. I don't let myself think going off alone is likely to run me into one of the Fiordans' traps until it's too late.

Until I spot the figure on the road below, walking towards a nearby town. This is much further from the divide than I expected, some miles north of what's left of Jared's place. It must have been totally destroyed, because I don't realise we've passed it by until I see the figure and recognise the road from where Ryan and I ran to confront the people under Jared's control. I'd forgotten there was supposed to be a town nearby.

The tall female figure approaches the gates. Like most towns that survived, it has high fences and padlocked gates. The few people with guns are the ones in charge. A shout rings from below. The woman wears the unmistakable red coat. My insides lurch, and I motion the fiend to touch down behind her, quietly as possible. There's no reason for Val to be here. Unless the Fiordans are messing with her.

"What do you want?" asks a voice from behind the fence.

"Entry," she says, her voice high, frightened, not like Val at all.

I feel sick. Is she fighting the Fiordans' control? *Come on.* The fiend's claws silently brush the ground and I quietly jump down, but she doesn't turn around.

The gate opens a fraction. And Val grabs a handful of fire and throws it inside.

No! A cry bursts from me and I sprint up to her, but the damage has already been done. Two guards are knocked aside, screaming in pain. Val kicks the gate the rest of the way open and walks inside.

I tackle her from behind, sending both of us sprawling. I barely choke out a warning to people approaching from the streets before she's flipped me over and has a hand tight around my neck.

No! I kick and squirm, but she holds me tight. She's much stronger than the last time we sparred.

Claws dig into my neck, and I scream.

The claws retract and I fall onto my side, the world swimming before my eyes. Coughing, my throat burning, I sit up.

"Leah, run!"

It takes a few agonised seconds to realise the voice, guttural and harsh, came from Val.

She's turning into one of them. Spikes protrude from her

back, turning into wings. One hand is already clawed, and fangs curl from her mouth.

I freeze, horror-stricken. *No. Not Val.*

Val dives at me. I barely dodge aside in time, knuckles scraping the ground, fighting the instinct to grab my weapon and call on the fire. Does my Pyro blood recognise her as an enemy?

"This isn't you, Val."

My words don't get through. Of course not. Her attention turns to the gate to the town again, which is now sealed. A hungry expression crosses her face.

"Val," I say warningly, placing myself between the town and her. I have to stop her. Quickly. The Fiordans are trying to distract me while they—I don't know what they're doing. But I can't let them hurt my friends.

Or Val. Damn. Fire curls around my hands without me consciously calling it. Red light flares from my right palm. "You don't want to challenge me," I say.

You know what Cas would say. Just like with him. I have to stop her.

Val dives, claws swiping. I curse and duck, wondering how long I can fight without my dagger. Its absence is a physical ache, one I really don't need right now. Her claw grabs for my arm but catches fire instead, and she withdraws, hissing.

It's impossible for me not to hurt her. It's in my blood, somehow, even though we have the *same* blood. And speaking of blood...

I give into the urge and ready my dagger as she dives again. This time, I slash across her arm, hoping I haven't misjudged. My own dried blood's still on the blade.

Val goes still.

My heart twists. I never wanted to do this, and it'd be cruel to let her live. I know, but...

"Can you hear me?"

A nod.

"I want you to keep still."

Swallowing, I move in, grabbing her left arm and exposing the tattoo—now jet-black in colour, and half-covering her clawed hand.

"Sorry, Val."

A mixture of what looks like ink and human blood spurts from the wound. I cut my own palm, too, and hesitate. Can I really condemn someone else to this?

I place my hand over hers. *Please let this work. Please undo the damage—*

Val pulls away, abject horror flashing through her eyes. "Leah."

She's still clawed, still fanged, but the expression on her face is human. And devastated.

Then her wings beat and she flies away, over the divide.

I stare after her, appalled. No. I didn't save her. I made things worse. Has she gone to join *them* now?

The other fiend reminds me of its presence. I can't stay here. The others need me.

Why would the Fiordans send her alone, if not just to torment me? Guilt bubbles up in my throat. Guilt, and also rage. She never asked for this. None of us did.

I'll make them pay.

Rage dampens the grief, and I manage to scramble onto the fiend's back, shaking all over.

Focus, Leah. The Fiordans. No sign of them. They can appear and disappear like ghosts, and leave chaos in their wake. Val could have been an asset to them. They just wanted to hurt me.

Tears fall, and I make no attempt to stop them. There's no time to mourn the dead, and I only hope the fiends don't kill her over there.

"Val, I'm sorry," I whisper.

I couldn't save her. Even as a Transcendent. If I'd moved faster...

Stop. I force myself to watch the divide instead as we fly, searching for any hint of trouble. The shimmering air above the gulf stretches as far as the eye can see. But the Fiordans can move fast on their winged fiends. So can Cas.

Oh, God, Cas. He's probably the Fiordans' next target.

I urge the fiend to fly faster, faster. Find the Fiordans. I kill them, and this ends. There can be no other outcome.

A screech draws my attention back to the divide. I squint, frowning. Nothing seems out of place on the other side.

I fly alongside the divide, and more screeching noises follow me all the way. More than one fiend. A flock.

An army. They appear like a flood of hornets on the other side.

"Up!" I shout to the fiend, just in time. The shimmering air above the divide appears to explode outwards, and I'm sent tumbling over, clinging desperately to the fiend, urging it to fly high, away from the energy blast. The fiend's entire body trembles, and so does the air. Cracks appear in the earth below. The fire roaring above the divide shatters and reforms into a blurred pattern. A familiar pattern.

Like a gate.

"No," I cry out, raising my hand, grabbing for the raw energy I used last time. But the air is electric with it, and rather than pushing back, I'm the one sent flying. The fiend screams, and horror jolts through me when I realise its stone-like body is disintegrating underneath me. That was an energy blast, all right. We barely escaped.

My vision flickers and for an instant, I'm flying high over a different view, winged fiends to either side of me as far as the eye can see. I raise my hand and send a rippling pulse of energy towards the divide. On my right, another human-shaped figure does the same. The divide shakes, ripping open wider, the air trembling with the force of the recurring energy blasts.

I slam back into my own body when another energy blast shakes the air. Gasping for breath. Both Fiordans are using energy blasts at once, and that's apparently too much even for my Transcendent powers to counter.

The fiends approach like a swarm of locusts, and as one, pass through the divide.

"No!" I scream, and the dagger in my hand lights up. In the face of so many enemies, I might as well be waving a stick.

Find the Fiordans. End this. I shout a command to the fiend, but it's flagging. Damn. I need a new ride. I order the fiend to fly higher, and before I can contemplate the suicidal reck-lessness of my plan, I shout one last order and throw myself off its back.

For a heart-stopping instant, I'm falling, tumbling head over heels in the air, the dagger melded to my hand. I slam down onto the back of another fiend. The beast snarls, trying to buck me off, but I cut my palm on my dagger then run the blade along one of its wings. Another fiend swipes at me and I have to dodge to the side, holding on with my dagger hand as I transfer my blood over to the cut in the fiend's wing.

"You obey me!" I scream.

Two more fiends set upon me, claws slashing. I grab the fiend's back with my weaponless hand and swipe my dagger through the air, cutting anything that gets too close. There are too many for me to hold back on my own. But I need to draw the attention of my target.

I reach for the fire and let it flow to my fingertips. "Come and get me," I scream. The Fiordans must be somewhere amongst the army. My blood burns in my veins, reacting to their presence. Reminding me of what I am. Yet I feel less like the Transcendent, the supposed hero, than ever.

The rest of the group can't hope to stand against these numbers. Every attempt I make to push on the energy current rippling above the divide meets with resistance. The gates are opening along the divide, and I can't do a thing.

They did it again. The fiends tore our world apart and flooded it with their poison. A searing anger runs through my veins, and the edge of my weapon ignites.

"Come and get me!" I yell.

Several fiends try to dive-bomb me, but I hit them with a blast of energy from up in the air. The fiend I'm flying on cries in pain. Oh, crap. The fire's a bit too effective, and if I'm not careful, I'll lose my ride.

A laugh sounds behind me, and I spin around, holding onto the fiend's back with only my legs.

"Get here and face me," I snarl at the oncoming fiends. There's no sign of the Fiordan, but my blood burns under my skin. They're close. Hiding amongst the enemies.

I reach for the fire and knock the attacking fiends away with another wave of energy. It's getting easier, but there are too many of them. The gate remains open.

A clawed hand reaches and closes over my dagger. I jerk back, expecting the hand to burn and let go any second—but it doesn't. The winged fiend facing me grins as it yanks at my weapon. I'm not prepared for its strength, which almost pulls me off the other fiend's back.

That's no ordinary fiend. Only the Fiordans can touch a Pyro's weapon and not burn.

Which means the Fiordans are masquerading as ordinary fiends.

Hell. I send more flames down my dagger, but from the fiend—Fiordan's—reaction, I might have done nothing at all. Its smile remains in place.

Damn. It's stronger than anything I've faced before. I thought the dagger would burn right through its hand.

Leaning forward on the fiend's back, I push, like I did when I closed the divide the last time. But the Fiordan's clawed hand lets go of my dagger and pushes at the air, and the fiend I sit on screams in pain. I'm barely given a second's warning before the fiend crumples, wings splintering, skin breaking apart.

The Fiordan killed one of its own. Guess I shouldn't be surprised.

I can survive any fall, but I panic at the thought of the Fiordan getting away and grab for the nearest fiend's clawed foot.

The Fiordan drops down to my level, half-transformed into the skinless beast I faced on the ground, but winged. Its claw lashes out, and the air ripples with the force of a small energy blast. It doesn't hurt me, but the fiend I grabbed for disintegrates into rock-like fragments in the time it takes to fall another metre. The wind roars in my ears, and the ground appears distorted, bucking and breaking open.

I stop falling, abruptly, when a claw snags my foot. The Fiordan's not done with me yet.

"Fight me, you cowardly scum," I snarl, the blood rushing to my head. "You know I can survive anything. Just fight me face to face." I hang upside-down, a roaring in my ears drowning the sounds of the other fiends in flight.

"Now isn't the time for making demands," hisses the Fiordan, letting go of my foot only to catch me again seconds later. It's toying with me.

"Coward," I spit.

The Fiordan's other hand reaches out, latching onto my dagger again. The blade immediately lights up, but has no effect on the enemy.

"You'll regret taunting me," hisses the Fiordan, and its hand clenches over my weapon.

A wrenching sensation travels up my arm, so sudden and unexpected, I fall several metres again. My hand burns like I've put it into a live flame and I recoil—*I thought fire couldn't burn me!*

This can't be happening.

But it is. The Fiordan's hand clenches, and my dagger explodes in a burst of fire.

A choked scream escapes. The Fiordan's teeth are bared in a grin as it lets me go, sending me plummeting towards the ground.

15

The shock of losing my weapon obliterates all thought. For a moment, I watch blurred images of the fiends flying away to war before I slam into my own body. An explosion of pain whites out my vision again and I curl into it, not sure if I'm screaming aloud, just in my head. Some sensible part of me telling me my injuries are healing, that I'm on the ground. I fell, but survived.

My weapon didn't.

I gasp for breath, a tingling sensation in my chest telling me broken ribs have just healed.

I reach feebly for the fire, but it's gone out.

Tears prick my eyes. My weapon's gone, and I feel its absence like a severed limb. How can I fight without it? It was Val who told me a Pyro bonds to one blade, and I suspect that goes double for a Transcendent. Without it, I can't save the others.

If I'm not too late already.

I stumble over the cracked ground, wishing I could unleash the scream building inside me.

Seconds blur together and I don't realise I've reached camp until I stumble over the first body.

Oh. God. No.

Dead Pyros lie scattered, bodies marked with terrible wounds. Garry is amongst them. And Ryan, a Pyro I spoke to once.

I drop to my knees, shaking all over.

They're dead. A sob rises in my chest. I'm too late to save anyone. I can't even bring myself to look down at the bodies at first, can't even lift my head to see the nightmare the fiends have turned our world into.

They're dead.

"Leah!"

I look up blearily. Now I'm imagining Poppy's voice. As if it wasn't cruel enough that they had to die once.

"Leah!"

Crap. There really are people approaching from the divide.

I shuffle to the nearest body, pushing back the nausea, and grab the weapon from the Pyro's hand. I don't get the same surge of energy as I would with my own blade, but it'll have to do.

"You stay away from them," I shout, my voice cracking.

"Leah, it's really us!" says Poppy. Tyler's beside her. And behind, two other Pyros. Three of them.

There are only two Fiordans. I stop, lowering the weapon. "You're really..."

"Murray helped us over the divide when it opened," says Poppy. "We had to shelter in the hideout. What's his name, Declan, he helped us."

I blink stupidly at them. "You hid out with the others? But the Fiordans—"

"They were too focused on invading Earth to come near

the others," says Poppy. "I think the Fiordans gave them directions. They're like…"

"Blood control," says Tyler. "They all move at the same time."

"And they're here on Earth." I swallow, staring out at the wreckage. "How many did we lose?"

"Fifteen," says Poppy, her eyes bright. "Murray said to leave the bodies. We can't do anything about them now. You need to get to Declan. He has a plan."

"He does?" *Damn.* My mind spins. But she's right, I can't stick around here. The Fiordans are out there. If there's anything I can do to slow down their invasion, I have to.

But where in the world is the army? And the Fiordans?

To my absolute shock, there's no sign of any fiends on the other side of the divide. Now it's properly open, even humans might be able to cross safely. But that's no consolation now the fiends have once again invaded our world.

Several other Pyros wait at the rise leading to the Pyros' shelter.

"I don't understand," I whisper. "How did they not see you?"

"Because they weren't looking for us," says Ray, coming over to me with a tangle of wires in his hands. "We're booby-trapping every inch of the place for when those buggers come over." He points at the horizon, over to the right.

My heart sinks. Out of the corner of my eye, I thought it was a line of rolling hills. But they're moving.

The army. No wonder my brain thought it was hills. The enemy lines stretch easily the width of the mountain we used to call home.

"Crap," I whisper. "Is there anything I can do? My weapon broke." I swallow. "The Fiordan broke it. I don't know where they went, or the others…"

Hopelessness rises inside me. The Fiordans will seek me

out again, but without a weapon, I'm more of a liability to the others.

"We're rigging the ground," says Ray. "Some of us have volunteered to draw their attention, too—both over here and in our world. You know here the divide just goes on and on? Well, over in our world, it ends less than a mile from here in the middle of the ocean. If they cross the divide at that point, they'll fall into the water. I'll bet the fiends can't swim."

I blink. I never thought of that. "Maybe not, but they have wings."

"Some of them do," says Declan. "We'll blast them out of the air then lead them into our trap. It's not perfect, and there's a risk for the volunteers, of course, but it's our best chance. The fiends have no idea what's on the other side of the divide, right?"

"I guess not," I say. "But the Fiordans are leading them, and they're super-intelligent."

"So are we," says Ray, without a trace of modesty. "It's time they paid for underestimating us."

"But it's practically suicide," I protest. "Besides, the Fiordans are disguising themselves as winged fiends now. I don' think anything can harm them, aside from energy blasts." *And their own weapons.* But now they know I know that, I doubt they'll make it easy for me.

"Really?" Ray's eyes narrow. "Damn things."

"I'll help anyway, if I can," I say.

"Go to Declan," he says. "He's with Murray."

Oh, God. I have to tell the others what happened to Val.

The entrance to the hideout is wide open, but from the shouts inside, they're minutes from sealing it. Sounds like they're expecting the Fiordans to make another move. While I'm waiting to get through the door, I try to tap into whatever showed me the vision of the Fiordans before, but get nothing but white noise.

What use am I now? I have no weapon. My Transcendent powers couldn't close the divide.

And I couldn't save Cas.

Yet now's the worst possible time to break down. I don't want to be a burden. I *have* to fight, and worry about the consequences later.

My being here will draw the Fiordans' attention. If they don't already know we're here. Some of them *must* have seen us. They flew right overhead. But then, most of the invasion happened miles down the divide. Where they burst it open.

"Murray," I gasp, spotting him in conversation with Declan. "I need another weapon."

I don't have time to panic or grieve. Quickly, I explain what happened to Val, and how the Fiordans broke my weapon. And Cas. I have a horrible feeling they're preparing to use him against me next. Because they're worse than Jared, if that's even possible. They could trample the world flat if they wanted, but all they want is to torment me. Because I'm Transcendent. Because they're psychotic. I haven't a clue.

"I need to get back outside," I say. "I'm their target, and they'll mow us down to get to me."

"They can't," says Declan. "This place has survived even energy blasts."

"They'll kill everyone," I say with absolute certainty. "They'll do anything to draw me out. I need another weapon. This one's... I took it from one of the dead Pyros." I swallow. "I'm not sure it can stand up to another attack from the Fiordans."

"This way." Declan beckons me to follow him down the corridor, where other Pyros swarm about. No one gives me a second glance. I guess they really have been prepared for the war a long time. The Pyros from Murray's group are easy to pick out—dust-covered and haunted-looking.

This war isn't over unless I kill them.

"Here," says Declan, pushing open a door. "There should be some spare weapons in here."

Every wall in the room is covered in daggers—or it would be, but most of them have clearly been removed, judging by the number of empty hooks. But some are left behind. I move from one blade to the next, searching for one that brings the spark of fire to my hands. But none of them do.

Crap. I don't have time for this. I snatch up one dagger then another, tucking them into the holsters in my boots, on my legs, and inside my coat. I never made use of all the holsters for weapons on my uniform before, because I thought I didn't need them when I had my Transcendent weapon.

It's too late for regret. By now, the Pyros are organised into some kind of order, and Declan returns to giving directions. Some people volunteer to go aboveground and create diversions, others are set on backup. I ask to go to the surface, but Murray refuses.

"Leah, they don't know you're here, and they can't break in. We'll fight to the last to defend this place, whatever it takes."

You're more use to us off the field, is what I hear. My fist clenches. I need to fight, but if the Fiordans show up and they take me out, that's it for everyone else. If I'm the only one who can close the divide.

"Right," I say, hollowly. "It'd help if I knew how to use whatever power I used to close the first divide, because it seems to operate at total random. That's really not helpful in the middle of a war."

"It does?" Declan blinks at me. "Ask Ray, if you want to know about energy blasts. He knows more than I do."

Luckily, Ray's back underground by now, hurrying around talking to people carrying wired devices. Bombs, I'd guess, or some kind of other weaponry.

"Ray, can I talk to you a moment?" I have to ask twice before he hears me. Urgency presses down on us. We don't have long. But there's no one else I can ask.

"Sure, Leah," he says, taking me aside.

I quickly explain my problem. I closed the first divide, but either I depleted all my energy or I'm doing something wrong. Or this gate is stronger.

"Maybe it depends on skin contact," says Ray. "Or blade contact. Good question. You know, they don't use tattoos on their fiends like Jared did? We caught one earlier. I checked."

I stare at him. "You caught one? And… killed it?"

"No. It mentioned the Transcendent. I remember you gave one orders."

Hell. "Where is it?" The fiend can only be the one I jumped from. I'm assuming it obeyed, even as the other Pyros were dying.

"It flew off," says Ray. "But it's true, there were no markings anywhere on it."

I shake my head. "That can't be right. They use blood control…" And all fiends share Fiordan blood. But how else could the Fiordans control all of them at once?

"We don't know all their tricks. But the energy blast often acts as a chain effect. You light a fuse, the spark travels down the wire. Maybe it's more like a fire spreading than a concentrated blast."

"That's… seriously confusing."

And yet I didn't close the first divide with one energy blast. It spread, like a ripple effect. Maybe there's something to that—maybe I just need to find a critical point, where it first opened, and close it from there. Maybe I'm the spark.

I don't know whether to laugh or cry. I'm losing it, right before the battle for the end of the Earth.

A shout rings out. "Everyone inside!"

"What's happening?" The corridor becomes thick with people running in barely-contained panic.

Declan rushes past. "The fiends. They know we're here. They're faster than I thought."

"Crap," I say. "Are the Fiordans with them?"

"I didn't see."

Shit. The Fiordans must know I'm here, which means they'll do anything to smoke me out. I'm not sure even this place could stand up to one of their energy blasts, whatever Ray and Declan say.

Another tremble, but the ceiling doesn't split. It just shakes, over and over. Particles of dust rain down on us.

"They're not marching above us, are they?" I ask.

"Not the giants. They're too slow." Declan looks up, his face pale. "But it's too soon for us to set up all the traps."

More shaking. I clench my fists. "What happens if they bring the ceiling down?"

"They won't," says Declan, but with considerably less confidence than before. "But we do have other exits, also blood-protected." He points to two tunnels. "We dug them out ourselves, in case anything happened to the front door. Not that we've had occasion to go outside, but just in case."

"Good." I nod, then wince as the ceiling shakes again. Another group of Pyros leaves through the front door, armed heavily, faces set.

I fidget, my hand twitching on my own weapon. I'm carrying half an armoury, and yet I might as well be as vulnerable as when I was alone in the wilderness, naked and hunted by the fiends. The Pyro uniform is as resilient as ever, totally unmarked by the fighting, the energy blasts, and my fall to the ground. I absently shake dust out of my hood.

"Can't I pretend to be one of the others?" I ask Declan. "The fiends won't know me if I keep my hood down, not now I don't have my Transcendent weapon. I can move fast."

"I'm aware of that," says Declan. "But the Fiordans—"

"You said yourself they aren't out there." *Yet.* "If I just—"

"Let her leave," says Murray, wearily. "I'm going out to fight myself. Maybe I'll draw the Fiordans' attention, but they're looking for me anyway."

"Exactly," I say. "We're Transcendent. Or close to." Even without a weapon, I'm a force to be reckoned with. Designed to kill the fiends.

"Your call, Murray," says Declan, as the ceiling gives another shake. "Good luck."

We hurry down a side tunnel. The ceiling continues to tremble, as does the floor. I wish I could believe this place was safe, but the Fiordans have destroyed so much already.

We run around another corner, past another gap in the ground. Blood control. *Human blood is dominant here,* I think. That's the one thing the Fiordans and the fiends alike don't have.

The one thing *I* don't have. But I must have some left in me, if I can get through the blood barrier.

The thought gives me an odd feeling, like I'm missing part of a puzzle, but there's no time to think about it. A door waits ahead, open. I nod to Murray, and we sprint out onto the fiends' world.

A shelf of rock overhead gives me the clue we're under a cliff. The fiends can't see us. Murray closes the door behind us, not that the fiends can get past the blood-defence anyway.

The ground shudders. I move slowly at first, knowing there are traps underground. Murray leads the way. Fiends wheel overhead, fewer than I expected. They must be on the ground.

How did they move so quickly? They were miles away. But if the Fiordans give an order, the fiends have to obey, at whatever cost.

An explosion rips through the air, sending both of us flying. I sit up, struggling to catch my breath. Dust covers my vision, but the sound of fiends screaming fills my ears.

I get to my feet and grab for the nearest hand-hold on the cliff. I climb, Murray behind me, hoping and hoping the explosion was one of Ray's. Because if not, there could only have been one source.

The dust clears as we reach the cliff's top, revealing chaos. Red-clad figures run everywhere, bursts of fire lighting up the sky as they attack the fiends soaring past. But most of the attackers must have walked across the ground, judging by the crumbled, rock-like remains scattered around. Debris covers the cracked soil, and one patch of ground is burned black. The bomb must have gone off there. Looks like the Pyros won this round.

Then I see the giant.

16

War in real life doesn't look like the movies. There aren't two clearly defined sides facing off. Just confusion and panic, like we're caught in a bubble where everything happens in slow-motion yet doesn't last longer than a few seconds.

A lumbering shape approaches on the distant horizon, like a hill come to life. My heart sinks. I fought one of those gigantic super-fiends before, but alone. They're hard to bring down, and I had to use my Transcendent powers the last time.

I can't count on them anymore.

A thunderous roar hits me like a blow to the head, and the world tilts under my feet. The air is thick with flying fiends, slamming into one another, grappling amongst themselves in an attempt to get out of the way. On the ground, most of the monsters are running in all directions. There's no sign of the Fiordans—or Cas.

But the giant rock-like creature running at us leaves no room for anything else in my head. *I have to lead it away from the base.*

"Get the others away!" I yell back at Murray, before running forward.

But the Pyros have other ideas. Shouts ring out, an older Pyro giving directions and sending a group of them running west of here.

"Watch your step, guys!" someone shouts. "If the bombs fail, get it to the divide. Distract it."

Crap. There are more bombs underfoot. But could even they bring down a giant?

The monster moves so fast, the ground rattles with every step. It's hard to keep my footing, but I take off after the others, swiping at a fiend that dives at me. My hood's pulled down, but keeps slipping back, and I have to slow down to make sure I don't trigger any traps. Before we know it, the giant's on us.

It's massive, the size of a garden shed at least. Its giant arms bulge with muscle, and it holds a three-foot-long piece of red rock like a club.

"Run," someone hisses, and we sprint across the open ground as one. The giant can't see one easy target, and it lumbers after all of us at once. We angle towards the divide, running in a zigzag, avoiding the chain of explosives.

Please let them work.

The giant swipes at the nearest Pyro, who panics and rushes forward. Someone curses, and there's a distinct metal noise—then a blast rocks the earth.

We dive forward, clinging to solid ground, as the giant is engulfed in what looks like magma. One of the Fiordans' explosives, I'd guess. So much dust clogs the air, it's hard to make out what's happening.

A giant hand swipes at my feet. I curse, jumping back out of reach. *We didn't kill it. We just really, really pissed it off.*

The monster bellows, the ground shaking as it stomps a giant foot. I roll underneath its legs and stab with my dagger, catching the back of its knee. If I can bring it down, it'll be easier to deliver a fatal blow.

Wielding two daggers, I slash again and again, playing for time. The giant's granite skin cracks as I deliver twin cuts to its feet. It stomps and bellows but it's too slow to catch me. I'm a blur of fire. The others have cleared out the way, probably figuring it's not a good idea to get too close.

The club slams down, and I strike out to meet it, sending a surge of power to the blade as I do so.

The dagger shakes in my hand. It's all I can do to hold it steady, but when the club strikes, rippling fire transfers from my weapon and pieces of it start to break away, forcing me to duck and roll. Roaring, the giant thunders towards me.

My dagger chooses that moment to break. I swear, dropping the fragments and reaching into my boot for another. If regular Pyros' weapons can't withstand the heat of Transcendent fire, there's no way they can stand an energy blast.

I need a better weapon.

But I can kill the giant. My other dagger swings, stabbing into its leg. Light flares from the wound, burning filling the air. My hand comes detached from the weapon, but not before I've channelled a wave of energy with every ounce of fury I possess.

The fiend's leg disintegrates even as it falls, its body crumbling like a stone statue.

I roll back to my feet as the giant collapses in a ton of rock-like fragments. I step back, eyes already roving across the sky, but there's no sign of any other fiends, or Fiordans.

Sobbing reaches my ears. *Oh, God. Not everyone made it.* Of course not. More red-cloaked bodies lie on the ground. I don't recognise any of them, but despair rises to choke me all the same.

The battle is over. We return to the shelter in silence with the bodies. This might be a temporary reprieve, but the others don't want to leave their dead outside for the fiends.

We're up against an unstoppable force. The loss sits on my heart like a weight, like the loss of Val and all the others who sacrificed themselves.

Nobody's in Ray's room, so I slump down in a chair, fighting tears. *This is too much.* I can't protect anyone.

Where the hell are the Fiordans? Their absence bothers me than I would've thought possible, because I *know* they could have come and killed us if they wanted. What the hell are they doing?

Back underground, we gather in what I guess is the hall the Pyros here use for meetings. I try to listen to Declan's explanation of various strategies, but worry makes me restless. If they're not here, the Fiordans must be scheming something else. They must have some kind of strategy, even if it's impossible for us to tell what it is.

Where in the world is Cas?

"Is it true?" Declan's voice snaps me to my senses.

"Is what true?" I ask hoarsely.

"Cas."

"I don't want to talk about him." Part of me knows I shouldn't take it out on him, but I can't help it. Even knocking out that giant can't quell the feeling I let everyone down.

"I understand." A pause. "I felt the same when Murray and the others were left behind. We didn't know if they were alive or dead."

It's not the same, I want to say. But that's unfair. Some of his people—Pyros—died today, too.

The door opens again. I half groan. I came here to get some peace. But it's Murray.

"We're having a quiet ceremony for the dead," he says,

swallowing. "If you want to…" An unspoken question is in his eyes. *Do you want to talk about Cas?*

I shake my head. "Cas isn't dead." The words come out flat. Like there isn't a storm happening in my head and heart.

"Leah…" Murray stifles a sigh, running a hand through his hair. His eyes are red. "He'd want you to accept it."

"Yeah, but I was never good at following his orders." I blink furiously. "He accepted I was going to die, yeah, but this… it's different."

"He didn't accept it," says Murray. "I've never seen him as agitated as he was when he brought you back from here, unconscious. And I've known him a long time."

I look away. Like *that* matters.

"It wasn't your fault. Cas wouldn't want you to—"

"I don't know what he'd want, and thanks to the Fiordans, I never will." The words explode from me before I can stop them. "He was right. I was stupid to talk about after the war like it'll ever happen."

"It *will* happen," Murray says quietly. "We'll survive and rebuild."

I rub my eyes. "On what? Most of Earth is dead. And you guys are stuck here…" I trail off. "I'm sorry," I say to Declan.

"Don't worry, I'm more of a stubborn optimist than this guy." Declan gives me a weary smile. "I already have a plan to get everyone back to Earth in the event that the divide opens to everyone like it did before. Earth's *our* territory, and we'll fight to defend it." He pauses. "Besides, I need to teach the rest of your group to see sense and accept Murray as leader again."

Murray turns to him, surprise flashing across his expression, and in that moment, I know why he didn't tell anyone about Cas. He's had one miracle already, and found two hundred people who were supposed to be dead. Maybe it's easier to believe in miracles when something like that happens.

I leave the two of them and return to my own room. I could say I've never had a miracle, but that'd be a lie. I found the Pyros. I came back from the *dead.* Maybe I'm out of second chances. But the Pyros, like the rest of humanity, have survived by believing it's possible for us to win the war. It's more than day-to-day survival. It's making a world worth surviving in.

Maybe I can help do that. Whether Cas survives or not, I'm not the person I was when I joined the Pyros. There's more to living than not dying.

———

I'm sitting in a dark room, a wide room with a high, arched ceiling. Plush carpets under my feet. Fancy paintings on the walls. Like a rich family's house, in the time before.

Cas stands against the opposite wall. Beside him, a red-cloaked woman. It's too dark to make out any of their features, but I'd know Cas anywhere.

"She's not coming," he says, his tone flat. "She is devoted to her fellow Pyros. She knows you plan to lure her out again. She's intelligent."

"She will come." The male voice comes from me. The other Fiordan.

Where are they?

"She can't bear to see you suffer," says the woman, with a grin. "You know that."

Cas says nothing.

"Did you tell the girl every time you use your healing powers brings you one step closer to death?" whispers the female Fiordan. "You chose to keep silent until we took you. I find that... cowardly."

Cas doesn't reply. Of course not. He can only speak with permission.

"We saw Jared's research, when we raided your lab. You were a coincidence, were you not? The others died so that you could live. You were a risk. I'll bet they told you it was worth it. They lied. Now they've given us the means to annihilate the girl. How you must have envied her. She has our blood, but not obedience. An anomaly."

Again, no response.

"She deserves to die." The female Fiordan's teeth gleam in the dark. "But in the proper way, surrounded by those she's powerless to save. Even if she lets you go, Cas, we have another incentive." She beckons to someone out of sight.

Two winged fiends shuffle into view, dragging a small, human figure between them.

Elle.

The shock jolts me back into my own body, where I dozed off against the wall after sitting for hours. Waiting. I'm sweating all over, gasping for breath. *No. Not her. They wouldn't.*

They would.

They knew how to break me. Somehow…

Before I can consider what I'm doing, I jump to my feet and run outside into the corridor, searching, searching—

"Murray!" I gasp. "They're on Earth, they're attacking a town. Elle's there."

At the sound of his daughter's name, every drop of blood drains from Murray's face.

"No," he whispers. "They can't be."

"They're doing it to torture us." My eyes burn with useless tears. "Cas is there, and he has Elle. It's a trap. For the both of us."

Murray's hand goes to the sword at his waist. "I'm not leaving her. Declan!"

Confused shouts echo around us. Some of the Pyros will see this as a betrayal. But I've made up my mind. The Fiordans think they can break me by killing the people I care about right in front of me. But if I stay away now, it's proof I'm broken. It's proof that losing my sister, that living in the wilderness, that being Jared's pet, did too much damage ever to recover from. But I'll fight for the others to my last breath, and I refuse to see it as a weakness.

"You can't go out there," Declan protests.

"They know we're here," I say. "I'm sure of it. Besides, his winged fiends are on Earth. In the town, with—with humans."

"Damn," says Declan.

"The Fiordans are behind all this," I say. "We kill them, we take out the army. They're using blood control, of some kind. Once they're dead, I'll be able to close the divide unchallenged." *I think.*

"Right," says Declan. "If that's the case, then we'll set up some last traps along the divide. You two go ahead, with whoever wants to help out. I'll spread the word."

"About what?" Poppy and Tyler appear, amongst several other Pyros from Murray's group. "What's happening?"

"The Fiordans have Elle," I say. "They've taken over the town, and their fiends are there. I have to kill them."

"Then we're coming with you."

I start to protest, then stop. No matter what happens, this is our last stand. We're all Pyros. This is our mission: to do everything we can to rid the Earth of the fiends.

"Right," I say. "Can you tell everyone who wants to come with us that if you find yourself up against a Fiordan, you can kill them with their own blades if you disarm them? Their own weapons are their weakness."

"Really?" Tyler blinks at me.

"Yeah. Tell the others, just in case. The Fiordans are

messing with us. I don't know what we'll find there, but Murray and I are going to go ahead and see what's happening."

"Okay," says Poppy.

Murray pushes through the crowd to me. "What did you see in the vision, exactly?"

I tell him, while we walk to the weapons room. Murray says my description sounds like the mayor's house, the central building in the town. I hope he's right, because we don't have a lot of time. My heart hammers, my pulse races, and with every second that passes, the Fiordans could be torturing Elle.

"Go ahead," says Murray. "You're faster, Leah. I wouldn't ask you to go ahead if I didn't know you'd do it anyway."

I manage a faint smile. "You know me."

He does. Even some of the other Pyros do. I won't die alone, not really.

The thought's enough to keep me going as I arm myself with as many weapons as possible, even cramming my pockets with small explosives Ray hands me. They probably won't do much harm to me if I'm caught in the blast, though I'm more concerned about the humans. I should have known the Fiordans would pull a dirty trick like this.

They're toying with me. They *let* me see that vision to torture me. We have to be prepared for anything. The rage inside me is like a living thing, a twisting ball of fire. I'm not at the height of my power. I'm as good as weaponless. The Fiordans can inflict torture on me or one of the others in a heartbeat. But sometimes you have to run towards the fire rather than shrinking away in the shadows, when the alternative's much, much worse. I know that now.

And I will suffer anything to save my friends.

Murray and I walk outside, turn to the divide, and break into a sprint. I overtake him, feet pounding the air, until I'm suspended over the divide. My heartbeat kicks up again, and the blood in my veins races like a fever. Close. I'm close to the end. Maybe the end of my life.

Maybe the end of Cas's.

Even when I was Jared's captive, I always imagined I'd walk into battle at the head of an army to defend our world from the monsters. Not sneak in alone, too late to save anyone. Too late to save Cas.

It hurts, so much, but the truth of it keeps me walking forwards. Because despite everything, I'm *capable* of caring about another person—even someone like him, who's never been loved in his whole life. Whether he felt the same about me is irrelevant now.

The best thing to do… is to stop him.

17

B ack to Earth. As we touch down, the shimmering fire of the divide fades away, replaced by the scene of horror we left on Earth. There's no point going back in the direction of camp.

Nothing's left now except bodies and ashes.

Murray points the way, and I run along the dirt road. One side is a Burned Spot, but patches of trees are visible in the distance. The latest energy blasts didn't wipe out anything.

Maybe there's a place to hide. *We have to get everyone out of the town. If they even know what's happening in there.*

The town itself is surrounded by a fence, making it hard to see, but the smell of burning is clear enough. Flames leap up to the sky, and roaring and screams hit the ears in a cacophony. My chest tightens, but I hurry on, legs burning, leaving Murray behind. *No. I can't be too late.*

A sick sensation rushes through my veins.

I'm walking through a street, flames on every side, but they can't hurt me, even though screaming, blackened figures collapse around me... one runs at me, arms wrapping around my legs, screaming at me to spare them. I flick my blade casually and his head rolls away to the side—

No—I'm Leah, and I'm outside the town, knees stinging where I hit the ground. I shake my head fiercely. This is how they plan to torment me next. I can't afford to be distracted. But do they already know I'm here, somehow, maybe through our linked blood...?

I don't need to find the gate. A massive part of the fence has been ripped away, torn and tossed aside. It was made of wire anyway. Fiends have skin like granite, but I guess this was the best defence they could make.

Then I see a man's body tangled up in the fence, feebly twitching. Sparks jolt from the twisted remains, and the body convulses.

Electric fence. I walk over to the man and slice through the remaining ends of wire with one of my knives. The man shudders and goes still. I can't tell if he's breathing. But at that moment, the ground trembles again, and a tremendous crash from somewhere amongst the houses makes me raise my head.

Past the fence, the smell of burning drifts with clouds of smoke. As I watch, one building collapses sideways, bricks crumbling as if something's knocked the foundation out from underneath them. The trembling under my feet tells me the likely cause. Screaming comes from the ruins, but muted somehow.

Several batlike shapes soar over the ruins, jumping at the people climbing through the wreckage. I leap the fence, running at it with my dagger held high.

"HEY!" I shout.

It works. The fiend turns to face me, baring its fangs. The woman drags herself over the ground, leaving a trail of blood.

I hold up my weapon, which gleams with fire, and throw

myself into the fight. Everything else disappears in a flare of light. Using my Transcendent powers in such a confined space is a bad idea—especially if the Fiordans are running around somewhere nearby. The fiend howls, on the defensive now, as I slash repeatedly, breaking its stone-like skin with bursts of fire.

I'm barely out of breath when the beast collapses, but the smell of smoke reminds me of the danger. Crap—there are people in the town, trapped by the fire and the destruction. The adrenaline fades, replaced by hopelessness. More dead. People—innocent, helpless people, with no tricks up their sleeves, nothing that can save them from the monsters.

I hurry out of the alley and into another street, searching around wildly for more of the fiends. I find a family struggling to pull their father from the wreckage of their collapsed door. They give my red coat suspicious looks and flinch away when I come near them.

"Please let me help," I say, and even put my dagger into my pocket. Not that there's anywhere they can run to anyway, I think as I easily pull the wooden frame away.

"Hide somewhere," I tell them. "There's a gap in the fence that way—there's a bunch of trees outside. I can't promise more of them won't come, but I have a feeling they're planning to burn this place down."

"That's what I said," says the father, nodding at me gratefully. The family hurry off, fast as they can, and I really, really hope they make it.

Others aren't so lucky. I find a pile of mutilated bodies two streets later, limbs pulled off and tossed in the road. The fiends are killing indiscriminately.

This isn't war. This is slaughter.

I make for the direction the nearest noise comes from. A street lined with what used to be shops is filled with corpses, sprawled in the roads and in doorways. Blood streaks the tarmac, and at the end of the road, a bigger building, possibly a bank, has been pummelled to the ground. Harsh screams echo from inside it. Cursing, I run for it, wondering how in the world I'm going to get anyone out of there. Children run every which way, crying, screaming something about going back to get their parents, but from the growls and roars coming from inside the collapsed brick walls, they have bigger problems.

"Everyone, get out!" I yell. "Aim for the gap in the fence. Don't stop, just *run!*"

The message gets through to at least some of them. Now I need to do something about that building. I kick at the pile of rubble blocking the door. Several fiends surge towards me, climbing out of the gloom, kicking corpses aside. Rage makes the fire ignite around me, like I'm a human torch. Which is fine by me. *Let them come.*

The fiends' stone-like bodies crumble at my touch, and the light sends some of them cringing away. A few break away from the confused tangle of bodies and run at the far wall, causing an avalanche of brick and dust. I curse, realising the ominous creaking from above means the ceiling's about to collapse on us.

Looking wildly around, I try to see if anyone's still alive. Doesn't look like it. The monsters already killed everyone. With a snarl, I send a jolt of power into a spare dagger pulled from my boot, and hurl it at one of the fleeing fiends. The knife spins in the air, sinking into the fiend's shoulder. It howls and drops to its knees, causing several of the others to stumble over and around it. Leaving their comrade behind. They feel no kinship to each other.

And yet… I get a brief mental image of stone houses in a deserted street. Whipping posts. A platform to hang the doomed. They're not under their own power. If I controlled them…

No. The fiends might have been close to sympathetic once, but they're monsters now. I can't afford sympathy. I have to kill the Fiordans. Nothing else matters.

A huge body drops from the ceiling to land directly in front of me. A car-sized specimen with vast, muscular legs and curled tusks. Spotting me, the fiend lets out a triumphant roar, and charges.

I raise my dagger, sending energy pumping into it. The fiend runs right into the blade, which sinks up to the hilt in its thigh. Flames burst into life, and white light pours from my hand out as the fiend dissolves. So does my dagger, breaking into pieces in my hand, but I draw another one quickly, blinking the glare from my eyes.

Crap—that was brighter than I expected. Bright enough to send a beacon right up to the sky. I have to find the Fiordans, and stop this.

I clamber out of the ruined building, cutting down two fiends which were too slow and clumsy to get out of the way. Outside, a fire burns—not because of me, but a genuine blaze, engulfing an entire row of houses. *Hell.* Did some people start that to try to defend themselves? The fiends don't need to set something ablaze to kill.

Of course, there's another possibility. The one I least want to consider, even though it's most likely true—that Cas is here. Life doesn't give either of us a freaking break.

Cursing, I run in the direction of the shouts and screams, coming from beyond the houses, and emerge into what must be the town centre, judging by the battered shop fronts and shattered glass windows. It's a bloodbath—almost literally. The glass fragments are stained red, and broken bodies lie amongst it. For an instant, I hesitate, horror clawing at me as each image imprints itself on my mind. *Focus, Leah. The Fiordans. Stop the Fiordans.*

Schoolchildren, trapped behind their own gate, hands

reaching between the bars desperately as monsters tear their way through the building behind them.

Men, women and children of all ages being ripped apart in the street.

Red staining the road and shop fronts.

Monsters, tearing into anything that moves, stomping on limbs, punching bodies that are long-dead.

And I'm running, screaming a hoarse war cry, and light's blazing from my dagger. If there was any doubt anyone could see me before, I know they can now.

The air crackles, the ground shakes. I'm on the verge of losing control and sending my own energy wave of destruction through the town. But there's no way I'm doing that. I'm not one of the monsters. I'm Transcendent.

Energy flows along the edge of my dagger and I point it at the nearest fiends, who've looked up from tearing into a group of humans. As I run at them, their tusked, ugly faces twist, either in confusion or fear—I can't tell. And I don't care.

I stab my dagger into the nearest monster and send a blast of energy along with it. The fiend's skin cracks open, but I've already pulled out the blade and stabbed another. Realising the danger, some of the others start to run. The road breaks open as the earth buckles, and it takes a second to conclude I'm not causing it—there's something big approaching.

One of the gigantic fiends tramples through the row of shops in front of me, kicking at everything in its path, its feet leaving huge dents in the road as it aims for the few remaining fleeing humans. *Shit.* The monster must have got past the explosives, over the divide.

"Over here!" I scream, and the fiend looks directly at me, its great ugly mouth stretched in a frown as it tries to figure out why I'm running towards it rather than away.

I'm close enough to brush its brutish leg, and send a jolt of energy sizzling from my hand. The giant roars with a noise like thunder, and I roll onto the ground, hands pressed to my ears. A second later, I realise I've made a mistake when the rocks start falling. Pieces of the fallen monster. Cursing myself, I sprint across the street and run in a zigzag pattern to avoid being hit, but several small rocks strike me on the back and shoulders. I keep running, the bruises already healing.

"Guys, get *out!*" I scream, pointing wildly in the direction of the fence. "Hide in the trees!"

That won't stop the winged fiends. But I'm a blazing beacon, and if anyone's going to draw attention, it's me. Sure enough, another fiend dives at me, claws splayed out. I duck, refusing to make the mistake of killing it while it's literally on top of me. My dagger brushes the underside of its claw, while it's blazing, and the fiend shrieks.

Wait. I didn't even pierce the skin—I'm not even sure I *touched* the fiend. Can I really harm them from a distance? I've only ever tried that with energy blasts, and I didn't really know what I was doing. The fire's not part of my weapon. It can't be, because these daggers break under pressure.

When another fiend dives at me, I send fire to my blade— and up, knocking the fiend out of the air before it can get close enough to strike. The distraction is enough to let a few people escape from nearby houses, and I quickly point them in the direction of the fence before striking the fiend again. But it's already fallen, crumbling on the roadside.

Whoa. At least I'm back at full fighting power. I just hope it lasts. I run wildly from one street to another, bellowing directions until my throat stings. I have no idea how many people are going to follow my advice, but I want to clear as many people out of the way as possible.

Soon the streets are full of people fleeing. Whenever I see

a fiend, brandishing my dagger either sends them scurrying away or provoke them to attack. I'm surrounded by a halo of fire, and one touch evaporates any fiend to dust.

Why didn't this happen before? Or did it? Come to think of it, fights are usually over too fast for me to pay much attention. I always relied on my weapon.

I can fight without it. The realisation stuns me, almost stops me in my tracks. *I can kill the Fiordans like this.*

"Come and get me," I cry out, climbing on top of a parked car. It doesn't look like it's been in use for some time, but it gets me a high vantage point to see over the collapsed buildings on one side. The fleeing humans run towards the gap in the fence. Amongst them are several red-clad figures. Pyros. Murray said some of the injured were here, and the Pyros too young or old to fight a war.

Pride blossoms in my chest, despite myself, at the sight of them helping to defend the survivors. I can't sense the Fiordans, but they *must* be here.

Unless it was another town. Unless this is a decoy. They move fast.

No. I can't afford to doubt myself now. I know what I saw in that vision. Elle was here.

Where are they?

I've searched every street on this side, so I jump down from the car and take a side street, finding myself in a wild tangle of ramshackle houses. Like a slum. Looks like this town was welcoming to outsiders off the road, unlike many others. Deja-vu strikes me, of all the times my old group ran up to a town begging to be let in only to be tossed aside. Not all humans have lost faith in humanity. Even now.

"That way!" I shout at another group. "Follow the people wearing red. They'll get you out."

I hear a little boy ask, "Why's that girl set herself on fire?" as I round a corner, then skid to a halt. A large manor house lies before me, more like a fortress than anything, surrounded by a deep trench filled with sharpened wooden spikes, and another fence behind that. The building itself is brick but the walls have been reinforced with metal, as have the doors. It looks impenetrable. Who on earth lives in a place like that? I guess that's what Murray meant when he said this place was secure.

For some people. Who, the leaders? Again, an image flashes into my head. The fiends' world was the same. No idea how these people organised it, but obviously the ones voted as most important got all the security.

Pacing around the outside, I spot a fiend that's managed to crawl through the spiked moat. With a shout, I brandish my dagger, drawing its attention. The stupid monster can't resist easy prey, and starts to crawl towards me. Fire blazes around me, fanning out, and the fiend yelps as it's caught in the blaze. It's falling before I even touch it. As the beast crumbles to pieces, a shout rings out from behind. Murray sprints towards me, wielding his twin swords, and strikes down another fiend.

Crap. I turn back to the mansion. There are people inside, even if it's probably the safest place in the town…

An image flashes through my mind. Two fiends dragging Elle into a high-ceilinged room. *Oh, hell.* The other houses are far too small. The Fiordans can't be in here… can they?

One way to find out. Silence rings out in the wake of the battle, and a prickling on the back of my neck tells me I'm being watched. But there are no faces in the windows. Most have been shattered. Most houses are deserted.

This whole area is a dead zone. Did I imagine that child's cry?

A high scream. A girl's.

"Elle," Murray says in a choked voice, and before I can

warn him, he's jumped the fence and sprinted up to the doors. "Elle!" he shouts.

No response. But if the Fiordans are inside, they'll know we're here. *Crap.*

I can't sense them, but everything's felt muted since I lost my weapon. Drawing in a deep breath, I pace behind Murray, looking out for more fiends. But the chaotic noise has almost faded entirely.

What happened? We didn't kill all the fiends. A chill creeps across my back. Somehow, I know the Fiordans are watching from inside.

A screeching noise tears through the sky, and I look up. Fiends rise between the houses, from the wreckage of collapsed buildings—too many to count. My throat dries up. They move in exact unison, which means the Fiordans must have given them an order. *Who's their target?*

The answer becomes clear as all the Fiordans turns as one to face the direction we came into the town by. Though the buildings make it impossible to make out the divide beyond, I know what else is there: the gap in the fence, and the forest.

They're attacking the people outside.

rap. Oh, crap. If I run to help, Murray will have to face both Fiordans alone, at the risk of Elle's life. But there's at least a hundred people out there in that forest, some fleeing. The Pyros protecting them can't fend off more than a handful of fiends.

Damn. I turn to Murray, who strikes at the door with both his swords, slicing through the reinforced metal easily.

"I have to help them," I say. "I'll be fast."

I have to be. Calling on the fire once again, I light up, running through the street, but no matter how bright the fire, the fiends don't look at me. Because they've been given an order.

The Fiordans did this on purpose, to split us up.

Cursing, I clamber through the wreckage of a house, climbing to a high point, and use it to jump at the nearest fiend. Fire arcs from my blazing dagger as I throw it, hitting the fiend between the shoulder blades more out of luck than anything. Even with the screams of their dying companion, the other fiends don't turn around. I vault over the remains of the building and run into a debris-strewn street.

A line of red-cloaked figures blocks the road, some standing on collapsed roofs, all holding weapons. My heart lifts, then sinks. The fiends are flying too high to reach. Pyro fire can't reach that high, can it? I've never tried. But I hit that fiend out of the sky before.

And I have explosives in my pockets. I can't risk hitting the Pyros, but some of the fiends flying from the east are above an area I already cleared. There are no people there.

I turn that way, grabbing one of the devices from my pocket and trying to recall Ray's instructions. A spark of Pyro fire is enough to set it off, and I'm already ablaze.

I just hope my aim is right.

"Duck, everyone!" I shout. The other Pyros aren't close enough to get hit, but I'm never completely sure how far the effects of my powers will spread.

Raising my arm, I throw the explosive high, over the wrecked houses and deserted streets. The device sparks before it leaves my hands, flies right into the middle of a thick group of winged fiends—and explodes.

Shattered pieces of rock rain down. The fiends crash into one another in a maelstrom of confusion, bodies falling out of the sky. Several red-cloaked figures run to intercept them, before I can shout a warning.

Wait. They're not the same Pyros as before. They must have followed Murray. Which means reinforcements have arrived.

Thank God. I can't risk using any more explosives, but I only have three, and I might need them later. I run to join the other Pyros, climbing over other wrecked houses, glass cutting my bare hands even as the fire streaming from my palms melts everything I touch.

Climbing to a high point, I shout, "Guys, there are people in the forest, hiding. Get the fiends away from them!"

"That's the plan!"

I look for the speaker and spot Poppy and Tyler clambering onto the collapsed roof. They stand back to back, jumping and stabbing at the fiends flying overhead. I rush over to them, climbing up to the highest point, and leap to tackle one of the fiends. The surprise knocks it out of the air, me slamming down on top of it. *Slow them down.* I stab its claw, then let blood drip from my still-bleeding hand into the wound.

"Attack the others!" I shout at it. "Stop them reaching the forest—take out their wings!"

I can't hope to stop all of them, but if I can slow them down, anything will help. By the looks of things, some of the Pyros have reached the forest already. The fiends are at a clear disadvantage with all the branches in the way, especially with backup arriving. But most of the people hiding have no way to defend themselves.

Murray's back there. And Elle. A tugging sensation pulls at my arm, more under my skin than on the surface. From behind me. I turn around.

"Leah?" Poppy appears beside me.

"I have to go back," I say. "Murray's going after the two Fiordans alone. They have—"

An explosion knocks all three of us flying. One second we're precariously crouched on the roof, the next, the air is thick with debris. I scream as sharp pain slices through my hands, and throw my arms over my head to protect my eyes from the dust and glass.

My back slams down on concrete, knocking the wind from my lungs. I lie gasping, the world spinning around me.

A scream from nearby. Poppy.

Oh, no. Coughing, I let my arms fall to my sides. The sky boils red as blood. I sit up gingerly, biting my teeth together to keep from crying out. Broken ribs, I think. But I forget all about the pain when I see Poppy crouched over a still, unmoving body.

Tyler.

No. God, no. A moan escapes my lips, but I push to my feet all the same. *No. Not him.*

Poppy turns to me, her face tear-streaked. Tyler lies still, a foot-long shard of glass embedded in his chest.

"He's not breathing," she chokes, shuddering all over. "He —he's not…"

"He died quickly," I say. "He won't have been in pain for long."

But that's no consolation to either of us. Where did the explosion even come from? It definitely wasn't one of mine. The fiends? Or is the Fiordan watching us?

I look wildly around, but the entire area is cleared. Further down the road, however, fiends and Pyros clash. Seems like the fiend I hijacked knocked at least some of them out of the air, ready for the Pyros to attack. But not enough.

I crawl over the wreckage, wincing at every movement. My ribs will heal. Tyler won't.

"I'm sorry." My throat tightens, eyes burning, as the adrenaline wears off and reality sinks in. The fire's gone out around me, burned out. Poppy's face is streaked with tears, but her expression hardens when her gaze lands on something behind me. One of the fiends. It stands still, eyes blank.

"Wait. I'm controlling that one." I cough, eyes watering, chest tight and painful.

"Those bastards killed Tyler," Poppy snarls. "They all deserve to die."

"That's why I'm turning them against each other."

If I can. If I could do what the Fiordans do, and control all of them at once. I share their blood, but that's where the similarities end. At any other time I'd be glad of it, but now…

I stumble over to the fiend. "Why can I control you? Is it just my blood?"

No answer, of course. I don't expect intelligent conversation from a fiend, and its shoulder moves in an odd movement that might be a shrug. I feel like screaming in frustration and grief. Only the sharp pains in my chest stop me doing exactly that.

"Right," I croak. "You, bring me another fiend. Then another one. Keep doing it. Fast."

My head's fuzzy. I'm not thinking this plan over at all, but when I glance at Poppy, she's left the fiend alone and started to climb down the roof, dragging Tyler's body.

"Leave him," I say, hating myself for it.

"I won't let the fiends have him," she says, the last word ending on a sob. "I won't let them."

My chest goes hollow. "Let me help."

Between us, we quickly carry Tyler down to ground level. This street is deserted, the fight now outside the gates. *Right near the woods.*

On cue, the fiend lands beside me, carrying another squirming fiend in its clawed hands. My own are covered in blood, so it's easy for me to transfer the blood control effect. I do the same to two others as Poppy and I pick our way through the devastation the explosion caused.

"Did you see what exploded?" My voice cracks, but I can breathe easier now. The broken ribs healed.

"It—it was under the roof. Someone planted it there."

"The Fiordans," I say, with growing certainty. "They're setting us up. Somehow. Bastards."

"They won't get away with this," says Poppy, through clenched teeth. "I'm gonna kill every last one of them."

"Kill the fiends," I say. As the fiend I'm controlling lands in front of me again, depositing a struggling winged monster on the road, I hurry over. *There has to be a more practical way of doing this.*

Wait. Rather than applying the blood control, I slice open my palm and let my hand light up, gleaming with blood. With energy, and light.

"I control you," I snarl.

The fiend stops struggling against its partner. The other fiend lets go, to my astonishment, and makes an odd gesture I can't understand. A circling motion, I think, but it's hard to tell with those claws.

"Around… what?" I ask, confused. I have no idea what it's attempting to say.

"Leah, the fiends are over there!" yells Poppy.

Dammit. I can't stick around and figure out what the fiend's trying to tell me. "Cause as much disruption as possible," I say, then run after Poppy.

She's stopped dead, staring at the chaos of the street ahead. Fiends and Pyros collide in a devastating mass. My hands are alight, and somehow, so are the fiends, though it might be my blurred eyesight.

No. Not again.

But a vision doesn't come. The world remains distorted, flames outlining the fiends, and the Pyros. No, not flames. Shields. All around. Like… energy.

Is that what the fiend meant? I can't figure it out. The cuts on my hands have healed already.

Poppy lays Tyler's body down carefully. She pulls out two daggers, and I see her hands shaking. She's been trained for this for years, but I know how she feels. *I'm sorry, Tyler.*

"Let's go and kill every one of those blasted fiends," I say to her.

She nods, and we run.

Before I can reach the battle, an explosive noise comes from behind me, a shattering combined with the crackle of flames. I whirl around. Another building's caught fire. *Did the Fiordans booby trap the place?* This street was already deserted, the buildings collapsed. A sinking feeling descends. The Pyros are fighting far too close together.

"Draw them outside the town!" I shout, but the aftershock of the explosion makes the words muffled to my own ears. I rush up to Poppy. "I think the Fiordans might have planted more bombs. Can you try to get everyone out? I have to find the Fiordans."

I wait for her to nod, so I'm sure she understood me. I have to end this. Find Murray. Kill the fiends' leaders. Make sure Elle's safe.

It seems like an impossible task, even for me. How many of those explosives have they set up? I can't warn all the Pyros when they're in the middle of fighting a war. Cursing, I jump down to ground level, sprinting up the street as fast as I can with the debris in the way. Following the tugging sensation under my skin. I'm not imagining it. The Fiordans.

My vision breaks, showing me trees, far below, as I'm flying—

Stop. The Fiordans are trying to break my concentration again.

I won't let them. Shaking my head fiercely, I kick up speed until I'm knocking huge chunks of debris aside which would have crushed me had I not been Transcendent. Nothing stops me.

Murray.

Elle.

Cas.

Oh, God.

I skid to a halt in the area outside the house. The doors hang off the hinges, but there's no sign of Murray, though the marks of his swords remain on the door.

Silence reigns.

Swallowing my unease, I walk towards the house.

An image flashes—*red sky, above a thick forest. My own arm outstretched, throwing vivid fire down on screaming red-cloaked figures. Laughter comes from my own mouth as they scatter and run amongst the trees. They can't reach me up here—*

I blink back to the present. Was that real? The Fiordans—were they even here, or did they leave the house long before I arrived? No way. They wouldn't be showing me this if they didn't want to distract me.

I can't afford to let them. Checking for traps, I make my way over to the door and climb through the ruins. The hallway's dark, quiet. My feet sink into the carpet.

The faint smell of burning lingers, but I can't tell where it's coming from.

Screw it. "Murray?" I call out. If the Fiordans are here, they'll already know *I* am.

No answer. A burning sensation under my skin pulls me onwards, but it's too quiet. Except for a faint dripping.

A chill races across my spine. I push open the nearest door.

Several bodies hang from the ceiling, mutilated beyond all recognition. I clap a hand to my mouth to keep from screaming, before realising Elle and Murray aren't amongst them. They don't wear Pyro uniform. Humans.

Gagging, I let the door close. No Fiordans or fiends. No reason for them to have killed those people for sport. And to torment me.

No one in the next room. My heart races, the smell of blood from the first room mingling with the ever-growing smell of burning.

Another room. A kitchen. Two more bodies, these burned. *The uniform's fireproof,* I tell myself. *It'll have survived, and so will they.*

Thud.

I look up. *No, they're not upstairs, are they?*

Oh, no.

Somehow, I don't think the Fiordans sent that vision. Because if I went after them, I wouldn't be here.

I wouldn't have run into their trap.

Two more bodies drop from the ceiling to land in front of me. Fiends, winged and baring teeth. They shuffle forwards, claws stained with blood. My stomach lurches. *The Fiordans made them kill the humans.* Rage and guilt churn inside me. I know beyond doubt the Fiordans are responsible for every life lost.

I back away down the hallway. I'm not about to get boxed into an enclosed space.

Crack.

Flames leap up behind me, but I'm already falling back. Luckily, the fire has no effect on me, but the panic of the flames rising makes me stumble over the doorway and fall flat on my back. The Transcendents move forward—and a blast of heat sends me tumbling head over heels.

Again, I'm deafened, choked with dust, and raging mad. I push to my feet, ignoring my body's protests, and stare. The house lies at a crooked angle, and half of it's *gone*, taken out by the explosion.

"You'll have to do better than that," I say, aloud. "Did you forget I can't die from energy blasts?"

A growl. The two fiends stumble from the ruins, dripping blood anywhere. One of them's lost an arm, and both look too shaken to be on their feet. But they're following orders. They'll walk until they die.

Dammit. I run to intercept them, but they stop dead as a figure runs out of an alleyway.

An achingly familiar figure, cloaked in red. Even the fiends turn to look in his direction.

Oh, God, Cas.

There's no recognition in his eyes as his gaze sweeps over me. The Fiordans gave him an order.

I have to stop him.

He's not my ally anymore. He's my enemy.

Cas's blade flicks out, decapitating both fiends. He advances on me, no recognition in his eyes, no remorse. No doubt.

I run at Cas, weapon raised to kill, ignoring the knife twisting in my own chest.

19

C as's expressionless eyes meet mine as I run at him. This is it. If he doesn't move, I'll take him out. No going back.

My feet kick up dust and I launch myself off the ground at the same time as he does, colliding in a clang of metal. I catch a glimpse of his blank expression and know Cas is gone, leaving a stranger behind. His expression doesn't change even as we land back on the edge of the pavement, blades locked together.

'Wake up,' I say. 'Snap the hell out of it. Don't let that bastard win.'

But it's no use. The Fiordan is controlling his very blood. There's no way I can stop that unless I kill the Fiordan—both of them. And I've no idea where they're hiding.

Cas moves suddenly, sword swishing in a motion that comes within an inch of disarming me. A line of fire sears my arm, and blood drips to the ground. Crap—he's fast. Of course he is. I've seen him fight countless times, and he's as close to Transcendent as it's possible for a human to be.

And he's really trying to kill me.

I move my weapon to intercept another strike, sending a mild jolt of energy into his blade through mine. He barely flinches. It's like battling a robot—a robot in the shape and form of someone I once hated, argued with, came to care about, and now—

Stop being sentimental! I tell myself as my moment of hesitation nearly costs me my arm. Swinging the dagger around, I'm aware that my shorter knife puts me at a disadvantage. As does the fact that the one power that could bring him down will also kill him, and I…

Can I do it?

Stupid question, I think, blocking another strike. Of course I *can*, but whether I could ever live with that is another thing entirely. Not that I'm going to live long anyway the way things are going.

Wait a minute. If the tattoo's working, can he see the same visions as I can? Our link was stronger than Jared's mark—at least, I thought it was. Back at the lab, he suffered the same injury when I stabbed my own arm, and he saw at least one of the glimpses I did. Maybe…

Stop getting your hopes up! yells the more pragmatic voice. Sweat's running down my face, and he's slowly driving me back with his strikes. Cas's sword is little more than a blur. He's giving everything he has. I'm facing the Pyros' best swordsman at his strongest, with only a short dagger and not even my own weapon. I'm stuck on the defensive, driven back inch by inch, while the fiends try to break their way into the building behind us.

My breath comes out in gasps. Blood streams down my arm from sharp cuts where I'm not fast enough to block him. Heat pours from the dagger, and I have to focus all my energy on keeping the fire burning. Cas's own sword gleams bright, sweeping through the air, majestic and deadly.

Breaking through my defences.

The metal goes right through my chest. Pain flares through my whole body and I scream. The sword's *inside* me, sharp and raw. I crumple to the ground, my body spasming with pain again as Cas withdraws the blade. I cry as it slides out of my skin, scream and scream, my throat torn ragged. Blood soaks through my clothes, seeping onto the ground.

Flashes of pain, not my own. A man trapped behind a mask, watching his own body stride towards me with his sword poised for the kill. Trapped, screaming, beating at the walls of a cage, and yet unable to do a thing.

Cas knows what he's doing, and he can't stop it.

I gasp. Pulling on strength, God knows where from, I drag my body away, feebly raising my dagger. My eyes lock with Cas's blank ones.

"Please," I mouth, coughing on blood.

He carries on. The blade comes down in a wide arc, and I just about get my dagger in the way before he slices off my arm. The edges of the blades strain against each other, and I push him back, the hole in my chest healing, the pain receding. Not quick enough.

Out of the corners of my eyes, I'm aware the fiends are watching us now. They know a real fight when they see one. But they'll be back to slaughtering soon, and there are thousands more out there.

I have to end this.

Only one way to do that—kill him. Or incapacitate him so that he can't recover. But he's invincible, as far as it's possible to be. There's nothing he can't heal from.

Jared would know. The irony of that burns in my blood. Of course I wouldn't have asked for his weakness. Even when I thought he might be Jared's for life, I stubbornly clung to the belief that we'd always be on the same side. Damn, was I ever wrong.

Sentimental idiot, Leah.

The knife vibrates in my hand. Power pulses under my skin, demanding to be let out. I let some of it flow into the dagger and the fire leaps into life again. I fight back, matching blow for blow, letting anger and pain drive me forward. He thrusts the blade up in a vicious strike but I've already whirled around his back, and thrown one of my spare daggers at him. It sinks into his shoulder. But he takes another swing at me, apparently unaffected by the pain, with a vicious cut across my left arm. He knocks me back, and I send another jolt of energy into the blade. This time he slows, the pressure loosening as he lets go of the sword hilt with one hand. The left hand, covered in black marks from Jared's tattoo. The one that's controlling him.

I snarl and push back with the dagger, letting the fire feed into it. As he moves to strike, I whip out another dagger and lunge forward, catching his wrist. Our blades clash again, giving me the chance to stab wildly at his left hand. It's not a precise strike, but blood spurts everywhere, blackened by the tattoo ink. Or rather, Fiordan blood.

With everything I have, I project an image of the fiends dragging Elle between them. The Fiordans almost killing me.

"You want to kill them, Cas," I snarl. "They're your enemies. Not me. You're stronger than that."

Pain lances through my chest again as Cas takes advantage of my distraction to strike with his blade. I'm flung back into a ruined shop, stained with the blood of humans. Bits of brick shower me as I slam into the ground. I groan. The wound's shallow this time, but long, a crimson line down my chest.

Already, I feel it healing. I pull another dagger out of my shoe. My hand's slick with blood, but I slice my palm again on the blade's edge all the same. I'm not well-trained in fighting with two weapons at once. I'm not well-trained at all, really, certainly not on Cas's level. It'd be a joke pairing us up against one another. We're equal in strength and endurance, but not skill.

All I have, as usual, is the element of surprise.

I climb the wreckage of the house, scaling the collapsing walls like a cliff. Cas approaches slowly, suspecting a trap, I guess. Or maybe he has a plan of his own. The remainder of the roof sags inwards and swings precariously as I climb onto it. I have seconds.

I jump, a flying leap that carries me directly over Cas, and I strike out with the spare blade as I do. His sword meets the weaker weapon, and its crumble to pieces in my hand.

But I've already stabbed my other knife into his lower arm.

Moved it down, right onto that awful tattoo.

And pressed, hard, sending energy shooting into the blade.

Into his blood.

Cas's entire arm lights up in fiery orange-white, like the sun. I screw my eyes up against the blaze, and wetness spreads over my face. Tears.

Pain ignites my left side. I collapse, my knees buckling beneath me.

More wetness soaks my skin. Blood. His or mine—can't tell. The world dissolves into a reddish-black haze. Every heartbeat hurts.

He cut me deep. Very deep. My limbs have turned to lead.

Leah, you have to move.

Spots dance before my eyes.

Come on...

My eyes fly open. Everything's confusing and bright and jagged edges—red sky, fallen buildings, and fiends coming at me from every direction.

I need to run. They'll take me to pieces otherwise. But

mind and body feel disconnected, and I can't move. Can't defend myself.

A shadowy figure steps in front of me. Cas. No. He's on his feet. Then he'll be the one to finish me off, not the fiends. I should have guessed.

If I was capable of one last action, I'd make some witty comment about the irony of it all, seeing as he's wanted me dead from the moment we met. I guess it is kind of fitting. And I'd rather he killed me than the monsters.

He turns his back on me to face the oncoming fiends, sword held high.

Oh my God.

The first fiend leaps. Cas swings the blade in an arc, blood flies, and sweet relief seeps through me.

I pass out.

20

I'm flying over the barren red ground, screaming with laughter as red-cloaked figures run around like ants below us.

And every part of the ground is swarming with monsters. Fiends of all sizes, warped and winged and twisted. Amongst them, giant monsters trample everything in their path. And as I fly lower, I see other figures, much smaller... people.

Red-cloaked people. They're outnumbered. A small group is rallied in a circle surrounded by spiked metal instruments forming a kind of fence. Throwing small objects at the fiends. Bombs.

Outside their small circle, chaos reigns. Fiends grapple with each other, giants crush their own kin.

And now I know this isn't a flashback. It's happening right now.

"Get up."

I groan.

"Get up." Louder. Not a voice in my head.

I open my eyes. Cas stands across from me, in shadow, though I can tell he's spattered with blood from head to toe. We're in what looks like an alleyway, crumbling buildings on either side of us. Agony burns my chest and arms, but the manageable kind of pain that tells me I'm healing rapidly.

"Dammit, Leah, get up before they find us."

I struggle to focus. Blood soaks my clothes, too, but I'm no longer bleeding to death. Slowly, I sit up, and Cas moves out of the shadows. I gasp, seeing open wounds healing on his arms.

"Oh my God, Cas."

"You're not much to look at yourself either, you know."

I choke on a relieved laugh. "Sorry."

He's alive. He's really alive.

Pain dampens the relief and I wince.

"I almost killed you, and you're apologising to *me?*" Cas shakes his head. "Let's get out of this damned alley before more fiends find come along."

"The Fiordans," I say. "They set us up. That was a trap for me. No idea where they went."

One of them was flying, in the vision. But where's Murray? And Elle?

Damn them.

"I think they Fiordans are back in their own world," I say. "Back where Declan and the others are."

"You saw it." Not a question.

"I did. But when I saw them in the house, Murray broke in, but that wasn't long ago at all. I think they'd gone by the time we'd arrived."

"So they set you up?"

"I guess so." *Except I saw them flying, just before I reached the house.* "I'm not completely sure though. I thought the Fiordans knew I could see them, but I saw them fighting on the fiends' world…"

"And if that's another trap?"

I rub my head, wishing it would stop aching. I've pushed my body to its limits, even for a Transcendent. "I didn't see

Murray or Elle, but it makes no sense for them to take those two back to their own world, when half the Pyros are there. I think the other Fiordan must have them."

"And did you see *them?*"

"No. I think the visions are selective."

"And useless."

"Thanks," I shoot at him, then inwardly wince. I didn't save his life to start arguing again. Glancing at him, I see his mouth's pulled down, blood streaking his face. He looks tired, for the first time since I've known him. "You know, I didn't sign up for this." I almost got killed in that house. If I hadn't followed the vision, I might have been able to help…

"I know you didn't," he says. "Sorry."

I half gape at him. "Did you just apologise to me?"

"Apparently." And he actually reaches to help me to my feet.

Surprise sets in, but then I take his hand, pulling myself upright and staggering forward a few steps. "I have to get to the others. They're fighting in the forest."

Now I focus, I can hear the distant sounds of fiends screeching. More distant than I expected.

Something's changed.

"They are?" Cas's eyes narrow. "I don't remember anything. They blocked it out."

"What… the Fiordans?"

A nod. "Yeah. I saw some of it, but blurred."

"They made you forget. I guess they have some kind of control through the tattoo."

And I'm still missing a piece. Can the Fiordans see what *I'm* doing? Does it work both ways?

Hell. Is that how they knew the others were in the fiends' world? But maybe… maybe they didn't intend me to spy on them after all. And if they didn't, could I do it again, on my own?

"They controlled me," says Cas quietly. "Total will domination, but not memory. I think what you saw must have been real, but they left the house before you could get here."

"Right." That makes sense. But it doesn't leave us any closer to finding out where they are. *They can't have gone far.* But then again, I have no idea what happened to the rest of their army.

"Come on." He beckons me, and it strikes me he could have left whenever he liked, but stuck around. Why, to make sure I woke up? Or guilt over nearly killing me?

"When will this end?" I whisper, shaking my head as we step out of the alleyway into yet another scene of carnage.

"Never. We can drive them from our world, but humans always find a way to kill each other anyway. I'll bet whoever was in charge of this place ran as soon as the Fiordans came. Those weren't the leaders in that house."

"They weren't?"

He shakes his head. "Must have cleared out."

"Or been taken," I say. "You forget we don't know *when* the Fiordans got here. Or… do you remember?"

Another head-shake. Anger is etched on his face. "I wish I could. It's like they blanked out everything."

"Did you see where they went?"

"Can't you sense them?"

I blink. "What, me? No. I've never been able to." But now I think about it, there was that odd tugging sense warning me away from the mansion, maybe towards the Fiordans. I frown, trying to remember what it felt like.

Wait. *Fire,* I think. I lost my weapon at some point in the fight, but I have several left in the various holsters in my uniform. Even the explosions didn't shake them all loose.

"What in the world are you doing?"

"An experiment."

Cas's eyes narrow at the word, then widen as light flares

around my outstretched hand. I can feel… something. In the air. A thrumming sense, like energy. Like the energy blast?

"If you're trying to draw their attention, there are better ways," says Cas. "Come on." He moves down the road, and I follow, my hand blazing. I think of how I used fire at a distance. I can do the same with energy blasts. Is that somehow tied in with the Fiordans' other abilities, or have I got it completely wrong? *The fiends don't have tattoos…*

"The other fiends are fighting the Pyros." The fiends were probably outnumbered if all our backup arrived, but they had hundreds of terrified humans to target. I let the fire drop. That won't help. "Poppy's there somewhere. Tyler got killed by one of the Fiordans' bombs."

Oh God. What if she's dead, too?

"They set them up on every roof on this side of town," he says. "I remember that part."

"So… not that side?"

I point to the left, the direction of the gap in the fence and the world outside. He shakes his head. "Are you sure you want to go into battle? If you're still having visions—"

"Of course," I say, before it registers Cas actually noticed.

"Since when did you care?"

He blinks at me. "Since I know you're gonna run headlong into danger anyway."

"You can talk," I say. "I almost cut your arm off back there."

"Yeah. You did." But there's nothing accusing in his eyes. "You really should have killed me."

"None of that." I cross my arms, refusing to let him guilt-trip me. "Guess you're in my debt."

"Maybe." He backs away, gaze drifting over the houses. "We should go. See what's happening out there."

Yeah. I'm shaking, covered in blood, but the pain of my injuries has faded entirely.

We both break into a run, swift footsteps kicking up dirt and debris. My stomach twists as I see the bodies in the road where the Pyros once stood guard. Not Poppy.

She's okay. She has to be. The fight must have moved outside the town. Maybe people realised the houses were booby-trapped. But that also brings them closer to the forest, where the others hide.

The same place I saw in the vision.

My hands clench. "I'm going to kill both those damn Fiordans."

"Don't you think I've earned that right?" Cas says. "The things the bastard made me do… I'd almost have preferred Jared's torture." He's masking his feelings again, but I can see them beneath. He's hurting. Badly.

"They'll pay for it," I say. "I'll find them."

"If they wanted to be found…" He stops. "We've fallen into one of their traps already."

"What are you saying? I thought you wanted to kill them."

"You think I don't?" His eyes narrow. "They're playing us, Leah. That's why they set me against you. If they're confident in taking down a Transcendent *and* an artificial warrior even when they know we could kill them as easily as we killed the other one, I'd say there's some major drawback we're missing."

I stare at him defiantly. "You think? They have Elle. Murray's gone. I'm not about to run out of here now."

"The war's on the other side," he says. "We'll be playing into their hands by chasing them now."

I blink at him. It's beyond me to tell what's going through his head right now.

"I thought it was about revenge on the Fiordans. You changed your mind pretty quickly."

"It's been coming on for a while," he says quietly. "You don't understand just how long I've been angry—furious, at the world in general, and especially at Jared. How many years I dreamed of slaughtering him, killing him in the most brutal way, inflicting something barely close to the pain he inflicted on me. That's why I went after him before, and got you caught, too. I won't let it happen again. Better to draw them to us and risk death than walk into a trap for the sake of revenge."

A pause. My throat closes up. Tears sting my eyes. Both choices mean leaving, losing people.

"Then we'll draw them away." I swallow. "But I can't let anyone else die because of me. And if I kill the Fiordan, too, I can end the war. That's all I really want to do. I totally respect if you want to go off alone and join the other fighters. They broke my weapon. I don't even know if I can close the divide without it. But I'm going to try. You can go alone. If I can't stop them, they've probably got bombs planted under this whole town. You need to get out."

A pause, while he stares at me longer than ever before. Kind of unnerving. "What?"

Cas shakes his head. "If you die, I die, too. I should by rights be dead already."

Sharp darts pierce my heart. "None of that," I say. "You deserve to get out alive."

"How can you say that, after what you've seen—after what *I* did?"

"Maybe it's because I'm human?"

His expression hardens. Oh, crap. He thinks I meant *he's* not human.

"You're more human than I am," I say. "According to the Fiordans, anyway. You know what? I don't give a crap, because if being Fiordan means wanting to torch whole planets, I'm pretty sure that makes me their opposite. And you."

"No, it makes you a strong person. I don't think most people could have done that in the same position."

My heart skips forwards. *A strong person?* Cas doesn't hand out compliments.

"And you're not strong? Give me a break. The fact that you're still alive and sane after what you went through says it all. So don't give me that bullcrap about giving up."

"Fine." The merest hint of a smile curls his lip. "Guess we'll just have to stick to being the most fucked-up sort-of-humans in this world."

Before I can stop myself, I throw my arms around him. This stolen moment might not come again, and I'm beyond caring. Here, in the middle of this ravaged town, in the middle of a freaking war, I hug him and he hugs me back and it's okay.

Neither of us need to say a word. By mutual assent, we leave the street, heading towards the faint sounds of fighting. It seems too quiet, and when we reach the gap in the fence, I see why.

There's *no* fighting near the forest. Bodies lie in the streets, but the town ends on a boundary circling the patch of woodland. Must be a last defence. In fact, now I move between the trees, there's some kind of reinforced building in a clearing ahead, like the house...

No. They can't be in there.

I glance up. No fiends hover nearby, but distant shapes fly towards the divide.

"Dammit. I'm going to see if I can sense where they are."

I should have tried this before, but the fiends have always sought me out. I've never had reason to track them down on my own. I let the blade in my hands slice across my palm, barely feeling the sting of pain. I breathe slowly, try to slip into that state when I'm not in my own head anymore. *Focus, Leah.* Like falling asleep, or... or calling on the fire.

An electric tug under my skin makes me jump back. Suddenly, I have the horrible suspicion I'm not alone in my own head, in my own body. The tug pulls me in a thousand directions at once. I focus on the closest. Somewhere behind me...

"Leah," Cas hisses, pointing at a fiend that's crawled out of a nearby alley. One wing is broken, but its blank expression latches onto me. It must be one of the fiends I gave orders to.

I had to speak to give it orders. The Fiordans don't. If I can sense the fiends, there must be a way I can direct them by thought, or blood—something.

I raise my bloodstained hand, and an odd trail of white light stretches between me and the fiend. It's bleeding. Our blood *glows*, a beam connecting us. Energy. Not blood, but energy.

It was never about my blood. *Energy conduits,* Jared called Cas and me. The first time I saw the energy blaze like this was when I faced the first Fiordan.

The moment that thought hits me, a small red-cloaked body tackles the fiend from the side.

"Get away from them, you bastard!"

"Poppy?" I quickly move to intervene. "It's okay. I was controlling that one."

"Leah." She looks at me, eyes wide. "You're both okay? Cas isn't..."

"Cas is himself again." Poppy's eyes widen. "And we're trying to find the Fiordans. What happened over at the forest anyway? Where are the others? Did they get out okay?" *Please, no more deaths.* Anxiety over Elle and Murray rises within me again. I assume Murray's okay, because he has enough Transcendent power to heal from most injuries—but Elle's vulnerable, not to mention the Fiordans have control over her tattoo. *Bastards.*

"The fiends just... went," says Poppy. "They stopped

fighting and left. A lot of them died in the fighting anyway. Some of them turned on one another, and a bunch got knocked out of the sky and killed by the Pyros. And then they left. The others ran after them, because the divide's still open, but…" She trails off.

"The divide." I need to close the damn thing, but as long as the Fiordans are here, Earth's in as much danger as ever. "And the fiends. If I could stop them—all of them."

"Impossible," says Cas, flatly. "They'll always keep killing. It's in their blood."

"No, it's in the *Fiordans'* blood," I say. "They're controlling every fiend, all the time."

And I don't see why I can't do it, too. We're the *same*, if I believe what that Fiordan told me. But I don't want to freak Poppy out, and besides, we really need to find the others.

"They're here," I say quietly. "They're hiding somewhere else. They never were in that house. It was a setup. Is there another house that looks similar to that one?"

"With those defences?" Cas shakes his head.

"Not necessarily," I say. "They must have been fairly confident we'd walk into that one. Just one that hasn't been booby-trapped. Away from the fighting. So it has to be…"

"It'd make sense for them to hide somewhere they can watch us," says Cas, scanning the houses.

"High up?" That's about the least appealing idea right now.

Poppy watches us, a nervous expression on her face. Blood stains her hands, but she doesn't appear to be injured. Was she really the only person to stay behind?

I turn to Cas, sudden foreboding washing over me. No. They wouldn't have.

"Poppy," I say, slowly. "Whereabouts is Tyler?"

She blinks at me. It's a slight hesitation, but her reaction doesn't match someone who just lost their best friend.

Cas steps forward, weapon in hand. He's picked up on the same thing. *They were hiding here all along.*

"Show yourself, Fiordan," I say, pulling two knives of my own.

Poppy, or the Fiordan, grins. "I was starting to think you'd never show up, Leah."

21

"Bastard," I say, through clenched teeth. "How long have you been mimicking her?" It couldn't have been earlier. Which means either Poppy left with the others, or she's—

Anger and grief swirl within me, the fire coming to the surface almost without me consciously calling on it. Fire— and a line of white light, like an energy beam, connecting us.

Connecting me to the monster.

Poppy's—no, the Fiordan's—eyes go wide. "What are you doing?"

It doesn't know? Then again, neither do I. It's not blood control, but energy. I can see the beam connecting our blood. Does that mean I can control the *Fiordan?*

I don't hesitate. Forcing myself to look away from Poppy's face, I say, "Draw your weapon."

A pause. The Fiordan smiles at me. "You're expecting a fair fight?"

No. It didn't work. Idiot. That's all I have time to think before the air explodes in white light again. My back slams into a wall, glass cutting my hands again, ears ringing with a familiar buzz. Lights burst before my eyes and it takes a few seconds before I realise it's streaming from my own hands. Light surrounds the healing cuts.

Not light. Energy. I've never seen that when I healed before… but I've never paid attention, especially when close to death. For some reason, that book Cas and I found in the Fiordans' city flashes before my eyes. *Stages of Transcendence…*

The light goes out. I look wildly around for Cas, but the road ends abruptly where we were just standing, a gaping hole torn into the tarmac, smoke obscuring the houses opposite.

Those explosives. The Fiordan knows exactly where they're planted. This is a game. Stupid of me to think I might be able to control the *Fiordan* like I did the fiends. That streaming energy, though… it wasn't there before. Energy connecting me and the fiends, and the Fiordans. The first time I saw it was when I fought that Fiordan on the bridge. When my weapon touched it. Or maybe when I killed it?

I shake my head to clear the ringing, willing my vision to stop blurring. Shifting between here, and a red sky, and a battlefield. Red-cloaked figures battle fiends of all sizes, fiends beyond counting swarming over the verge.

The other Fiordan. I'm sure they're flying over a battle-field. Back on their own world. But am I really supposed to be able to see this? I shake my head again, staggering forward. Cas half-lies against a parked car, his expression livid, blood streaming from a cut on his cheek.

"Bastard gave us the slip."

"For God's sake. It's playing a game with us." With explosives under our feet. But the Fiordans know full well Cas and I can heal ourselves. What's their game this time? To distract us from the real war, happening over the other side? Maybe Cas was right, and the best thing to do is to join the others and make the Fiordans come to us…

But they took Elle. She wasn't in the vision. If there's the slightest chance she's here, I have to—no, *we* have to find her. I glance at Cas, who scans the houses. "I can't tell where they hid their explosives," he says. "There are no signs, not like with ours. They're under the ground, I guess, if we can't see them."

"Hmm." I stare around, wishing my vision would stop flickering. Light flashes in the corners of my eyes. Light, like energy. What does it mean? "Can you see that?"

"See what?"

I shake my head, frustrated. "I've been seeing these flashes of light, on and off. I can't tell if it's because of the visions, or my own powers, or something to do with—them."

"The Fiordans?" Cas frowns. "*Where, exactly?*"

"Everywhere." I point to both sides. "When I turn that way, it disappears."

"Try using your powers, like you did before."

I never thought of that. The fire comes without conscious thought, again more like white energy than actual flames. Like an energy blast. Like a...

Hidden bomb.

I stop dead, gaping at the road. A line of white trails through the wreckage, travelling through the middle of the tarmac. Through the whole town. Both ways. White light.

Oh my God. I can see the bombs.

It's energy, of some sort. The Fiordans can manipulate it easily. Of course they can. We're literally standing on a bomb.

And how close are the others?

I breathe fast, trying to keep from panicking. "Cas," I say, my voice slightly high. "Step to the left. Away from that... line." But he can't see it. Somehow, my senses have shifted. Maybe it's because of what I did with the energy, closing the divide. Now I concentrate, more tugging sensations pull under my skin. I thought it was my skin healing from all the injuries today. But maybe it's telling me something. Or a warning?

The line of energy has to lead somewhere. Both ways. But one way leads outside the town, into no-man's-land. The other, to the town's heart. And probably where the Fiordan hides. *I think.*

"This is going to sound crazy," I say to Cas, "but I think I can see their bombs."

I expect a derisive comment, but he waits for me to continue. *Huh?*

"There are lines of like... white light. I've seen it before whenever they've used explosions, or energy blasts. They're under the roads, the buildings, everything." I trace them in the air with my fingers. "It's like a thread. But we were standing on it when that last explosion went off." *And the one that killed Tyler on the roof. Damn. I hope all the others got out.*

"You absolutely sure?"

"Yeah, of course." I clench my fists. "Elle's in here somewhere."

"Was she in the vision?"

"No." I focus again, trying to slip out of my head. Flashes of the battlefield crop up, but I run headlong into a mental block. "That was odd. I couldn't see clearly that time."

"You're not supposed to be able to see it at all, are you?" says Cas. "Hold on. You say there's a line?"

"Yeah, but if we follow it, there might be a trap at the other end. Or Elle. Murray won't have given up. He'd be going after her even though the Fiordans weren't in that house."

"Or he's dead."

"No way." He's Transcendent. "If he is, we *have* to find her. Well, I do."

"Fine. Tell me where the line goes. It's our only clue, unless your fiend tracker's working."

I take my dagger in hand again. It glows faintly around the edges. I've lost count of how many I broke, but I have at least three left. *I need one of* their *weapons, ideally. To replace mine.*

The dagger's glow lingers in my vision. White light streaming down the road. White light... tugging under my skin.

"C'mon."

Ninety percent of me knows this is a bad idea, but if the whole town's a trap, at least we aren't condemning Elle to her death. We walk quickly, as far from the line as possible in case the whole thing blows up, severing the street down the middle like...

I stop again, and Cas makes an impatient noise. "What?"

"The divide," I say. "Oh my God." I trace the line in the air with my fingertips again. "That's how they must have opened it. The energy blast is a *bomb*. Their bomb. They used it..."

"Shit," says Cas, the colour draining from his face. "The others are sheltering right next to this—no way they're far away enough to be out of range."

Out of range. I clench my fists, nails biting into my palms in an attempt to block the flow of images.

"What are the Fiordans waiting for?" I ask, as quietly as possible. "This is obviously a setup."

"What do you think?" says a cold, female voice. "We're waiting for you."

Val steps out onto the road in front of us, splays her hands, and a blast of energy sends me staggering back. I push against it like I'm shoving a closing door, but despite the effort, it drives me closer to the line, step by step.

"It's always more fun when your enemy knows the real

consequences of their actions," she says with a cold grin, nothing like Val at all.

"Use your own face, you ugly bitch," I shoot at her, and push on the energy so hard, my dagger cracks into pieces in my hand. I push anyway, the pieces somehow held together in mid-air. Connected by energy.

It's all energy. The bombs, the blood control—all of it. I'm as strong as a Fiordan, and they're scared of me.

I push back, the white light flaring brighter and brighter, threads of energy connecting us like miniature sunbeams.

Our blood is the same.

My vision flickers, and for an instant, I see myself from the outside, haloed in white light.

And I'm afraid, terrified of the creature in front of me.

Then I'm Leah again.

"You felt that," I say, raising my voice. "I can break you."

I let go of the energy and send the Fiordan flying back down the street into the ruins of a building. Away from the line of the bomb, but not far enough. Grabbing wildly for another weapon, I jump at the Fiordan, who no longer looks remotely like Val. She—it, whatever—changes into Jared.

"That one's old," I say, too wary of the bomb underground to risk using the energy blast again. But I knocked the Fiordan back without my weapon.

I can win.

Jared's face turns to me, with the same menacing fury I've seen on it before. "You're going to pay for that, Leah."

"Enough of this crap." I jump, weapon out, but someone slams into me from behind, sending me sprawling. A small figure. For a heart-stopping second I think it's Poppy again. But it's not.

It's Elle.

Fury flares to life inside me again as Elle stares me out in a horrible blank expression not like her at all.

"Are you out of ideas?" I snap.

The Fiordan's mouth twists in a smile. "Why change our plan when it works so well?"

Elle. The livid red mark on her hand. Her blanked-out eyes. Familiar, just as horrible as when Jared controlled her.

"So what did you do to Murray?" I ask, my heart sinking already.

"The old man? Killed him, of course."

No. He can't be dead. He's Transcendent.

The Fiordan smiles at me. "So you see why you can't win this, Leah. If you can't bring yourself to kill her, she'll destroy you... and him."

Cas. Not again.

Jared grins at me.

"I stopped you already," I snarl. "This is between you and me, anyway. Not Cas, nor any of the others. Or are you too scared to fight me yourself?"

Elle advances on me.

"You're the one who's afraid, Leah," says the Fiordan.

I call the fire once more, light flaring around my hands, around everything. And I see it. More than the beams of light under the road—I see the light connecting the Fiordan to Elle. Linked not by blood, but energy.

I reach for the link, and pull. Elle turns sharply towards me, as does the Fiordan. Breathing quickly, aware the Fiordan's perilously close to Elle, I step towards her, look her in the eyes.

"You're not under his control anymore. You're free."

"You can't do that," snarls the Fiordan. "That's not how it works—"

Cas jumps forward, whipping out his blade, and spears the Fiordan through the spine.

Jared's face twists in a grimace, a harsh scream escaping. "You can't!"

"I can," says Cas, yanking the sword free. "Your idiotic tricks won't work on us. Leah?"

Unbelievable. He's going to let me kill the Fiordan. Wait. Its weapon. The Fiordan never got the chance to attack. It relied on the energy beam. And speaking of…

I reach for the threads between myself and the Fiordan, looking into Jared's eyes as they turn flat black. "You're going to hand me your weapon."

There's resistance again, like pushing at an invisible barrier. But slowly, the Fiordan reaches for his belt and pulls out an arm-length knife. My blood sings as I take it. Fiordan blood. My blood.

I point the blade directly at the Fiordan's heart.

22

B efore I can move, pressure wraps around my throat, choking the breath from me. My vision swims.

How? The Fiordan didn't touch me. The monster remains bleeding on the roadside, but grins at me as if I'm the one on the ground.

Elle darts up and grabs my arm. "Leah?"

I can't breathe, I want to say, but I can't.

The Fiordan shifts, blood welling from the wound in its chest. "I have… one weapon left, Transcendent. I can crush the energy from you… with my life. My brother will take the Earth."

I can't respond. Cas makes a hissing sound, but he's held back by the wall of energy that's crushing me. Like a vacuum. Over and over, my throat is crushed, even as I feel it healing itself each time.

There's a limit, a voice whispers in my ear. A limit on my healing powers. The Fiordan's using the little strength it has left to trap me, until my healing power runs out and I die.

I black out the pain, desperately pushing back. *I know how to win this. I know.*

My body feels heavy, the muscles locking in place. The energy, whatever it is, presses against me all over, literally crushing the life from me. I can't suck in a breath for relief, and even though I can survive without breathing, my Transcendent body still thinks it's human.

I'm dying.

Then it stops, the pressure loosening from my throat. I gasp, blinking frantically. At first, I think my rescuer is Cas. But he remains behind the barrier of energy the Fiordan used to push me back. Another figure steps right through it, behind the Fiordan, soaked in so much blood I can't make out their features.

The Fiordan twists around, eyes bulging. "You can't be alive. I killed you."

"I thought you wouldn't recognise another Transcendent, even staring you in the face." Murray regards him coldly. He's barely on his feet, missing a hand, but the Transcendent healing powers kept him alive, even against impossible odds.

"Dad!" Elle cries out, behind me.

Murray grabs the Fiordan by the throat with his remaining hand.

"You'll die," croaks the Fiordan. "The pressure will crush both of us."

White light folds around them, like the lines that pressed against me. But I can breathe again, Cas and I can move freely—and so can Elle. Cas grabs the back of her coat to stop her running after Murray.

"He knows what he's doing," Cas tells her quietly.

"He'll *die*," she gasps.

The Fiordan and Murray break apart, dropping onto the concrete. Murray falls onto his side, and forsaking caution, I hurry up to him with Elle, who ignores the twitching body of the Fiordan and wraps her arms around her father. Murray lies still, blood staining one side of his face.

"No," she moans. "No, Dad, no…"

The Fiordan coughs. "It's too late for—all of you, Transcendent."

Cas kicks it aside, viciously, and this time, it doesn't get up. But just in case, I push down my revulsion, raise the weapon I took, and stab the Fiordan through its heart with its own dagger.

"Done," Cas says, tonelessly. "Leah—the bomb. Is it active?"

My heart wrenches at the sight of Elle sobbing over her father, but he's right. The threads of energy… they're disappearing. Only now do I see they connect directly with the Fiordan's hands.

"It was controlling them all along," I whisper. My voice comes out in a croak, weakened by the near-strangling. "So, when they opened the divide… they must have done something similar." But does that mean the divide covers the whole planet? There's no way to tell, and it's irrelevant as long as the fiends keep invading.

I need to close the divide.

But first…

Murray shifts in Elle's arms. "Leah," he gasps. "Take her to the safe house. Please."

My chest tightens in a vice grip. "I will."

"You… your blood, Leah. Not yours. Take mine…"

His head falls back, his eyes open, unseeing. Elle's cry tears at my chest, and tears spill from my own eyes before I can stop them. "I'm sorry, Murray," I whisper, backing away to let Elle hug her father's body.

There's no time for grieving. We need to get to the fiends' world and end this fight. Kill the last Fiordan. I've no idea what Murray meant by his last words. But we can't stop and puzzle it out. He's dead.

And we need to get Elle to safety. I turn to Cas,

wondering when I started trusting him like this. Trusting him with my life.

"All right," he says. "Are you *sure* the other Fiordan isn't here?"

What—oh, the visions. I slip almost easily into the between-state now, enough to get a glimpse of the fiends' world, a battlefield, and then slip back. "If it's not a trick, they're fighting on the other side of the divide." I look at Cas. "We have to get back."

"Right," he says. "Elle..."

"I'm not leaving him." Her tear-streaked face is determined. "I'm not letting my dad get eaten by those monsters. He'd want—" She chokes off, sobbing again.

"I'll carry him," says Cas. "But we need to move. The last Fiordan's still out there."

We walk silently but quickly, leaving the dead Fiordan behind. I pause to check he's definitely dead, and find he no longer has Jared's face. In death, the Fiordan has shrunk to its real, child-sized monster form.

I can kill the other. End this. And yet as Elle clings to my arm, sobbing quietly, I just wish I'd been able to finish them sooner. *If I'd known how the power worked... the energy...*

That has to be the key to closing the divide. This time, there's no going back.

Through the gap in the fence, into the forest. I check there aren't any fiends around, but all that remains are crumbling corpses. The Pyros took care of them. But why did the Fiordan make the army take off like that?

The reinforced building remains shut, and there's no way to get the door open—of course. I reach to tap on the sealed metal door and fire leaps up, circling the whole building. The Pyros put up a defence, one even the fiends couldn't get through.

Maybe that's why they left. But did they all go back over

the divide, along with the Pyros? No way can I leave Elle out there with her father's body, unprotected...

A figure steps out from behind the building's side. I instantly tense, but it's a red-cloaked girl...

"Poppy?" I don't move, watching her carefully. I don't trust the Fiordans not to pull another trick.

"Leah?" She doesn't move, either. Her eyes latch onto Murray's body, in Cas's arms. "No. No, he can't be dead." Her voice cracks. "Elle, I'm sorry!"

She turns and steps right through the fire to the door, rapping on the metal. *It's her,* I think, relief melting away my doubt.

"Poppy." I surprise myself by rushing up and hugging her. "You're alive. I thought they killed you."

"I knew you'd be alive." She hugs me tight. "I was so scared—you were *them.*"

"It's dead," I say. "One of them, anyway. We need to get over the divide."

"I thought so." She draws back, blinking tears from her eyes. "I stayed, and so did a few of the others. I wanted to make sure you were alive. The fiends just *left.* I thought they were planning something, but fireworks started going off near the divide, and..."

The door opens. "Who's this?" says an elderly man. Pyro. He wears the uniform. *So the other people who couldn't fight are here. They made this place safe.*

"Murray's dead," I croak. "Elle needs somewhere to stay."

"Yes, we need to *move,*" Cas says impatiently.

Poppy glares at him, but sighs. "I know. I wish... oh, Elle, I'm sorry."

The two hug, both sobbing. We've lost so many people already.

I'll do everything I can to stop it happening again.

"I'm going," I say. "I'll kill the last Fiordan and close the divide. Then we'll come back. That's a promise."

The old man nods. I don't think we've even spoken before. But we're Pyros. Human or not, I'm one of them.

Elle wraps her arms around me. "I think I know what my dad meant," she whispers. "Your blood—it doesn't make you a monster. But the divide's made of Fiordan blood. He meant you could undo it, I think."

"I—" Undo it?

"Leah." Cas appears beside me, having handed Murray's body over to some of the others so they can—I've no idea. Cremate him, maybe. It's how the Pyros usually treat their dead. Use their ashes to build weapons.

"I'll come back," I say one last time, to Elle.

We join Poppy in the forest again. A few other Pyros have gathered, too, back from combing the woods for more fiends. *Why did they leave?*

I slip into the Fiordan's mind again, but it looks the same as before—a battlefield from above. Fiends and Pyros clashing, energy blasts engulfing everything in their path.

I try to envision the streams of energy again, too, but draw a blank. Is it because the Fiordans are too far away, or something else? The other Transcendent could do it, supposedly. *She lit up whenever the fiends were near. She could track them.*

I puzzle it over, but soon enough, familiar sounds of battle reach us, and we pick up speed, heading for the line that cuts the world in two for the last time. I take the lead, the ground flying away.

I hear Cas running behind me as I leap at the divide, and once again, into the fiends' barren world.

23

Light flares out from the dagger I took from the Fiordan. *My* dagger. Dust immediately clouds over my vision when my feet touch the ground. An energy blast must have gone off recently. Or a bomb. I'm hoping it's the latter.

Declan. Ray. Please let them still be alive. Sure, they have a hideout here, but they won't win the war from in there. And where the hell is the Fiordan?

Again, I slip out of my body and into the sky. Damn thing must have hitched a ride again.

Unless it's pretending to be one of the fiends, like when the other one broke my weapon.

Cas touches down beside me. "Any clues?"

"I think the other Fiordan's hiding somewhere with the army," I say. "It was there all along, disguised as a regular fiend."

"Why would it do that?" Cas steps forward, checking the ground for traps. Smoke obscures the air, while fiends dart in and out of the sky like spectres. "If it wanted to kill us, it'd have a better chance on the ground."

"Not necessarily," I say. "But yeah, we're missing something for sure."

Like why the fiends abandoned Earth. There weren't *that* many of them left after the fight, and the Pyros were safe, but if the Fiordan really wanted to destroy everyone I cared about, I'd expect it to do a more thorough job.

Unless the plan was to lure us here.

The other Pyros are behind me. As of now, all our army's on this side. No sign of Declan or Ray or any of the others, but the red-cloaked figures are lost in the general chaos. The smoke clears somewhat, revealing the hunched shapes of fiends fighting on the ground, their winged counterparts diving in and out of the fray in groups. Jumping into the middle of the fight would get the others killed.

I need to find the Fiordan. Squinting, I jump when Cas's knife flares to life next to me. *The fire.* It might draw attention, but I *want* the Fiordan to come to me.

As I light up, the strands of energy become visible, fanning out from the divide, and darker lines connecting the fiends. If I follow them, I can find the leader, hiding amongst them.

Of course, the lines lead right up into the sky, amongst the flock of winged fiends blotting out the low sun. The Fiordan's too much of a coward to fight.

It's waiting for me.

"Come and face me," I mutter, pacing along the divide's front. More lines of energy appear, snaking along the ground. "Shit. Guys, watch out!" I turn back to make sure Poppy and the others can hear me. "There are bombs under the ground here."

No. There are bombs everywhere, just like in the town. The Fiordan was waiting for me to come back before it activated them.

I pause, my heartbeat frantic, letting the fire die down. If I draw the Fiordan's attention, it might activate the bombs. I'd be a fool to think the Fiordan wouldn't sacrifice the other fiends to get rid of me. They're collateral damage. The threads of energy are countless, like they're built into the earth itself. Of course they are. The Fiordans are part of everything here.

Oh, shit. The underground shelter's part of the earth, too, even if it's protected. But the others won't get there in time. The Fiordan might already know I'm here.

"Guys," I say quickly. "Watch where you tread. The bombs are under our feet. You either need to get into the shelter, or get back over the divide, before the Fiordan realises we're here."

Muttering breaks out, but thankfully, quiet. The racket of the battle is too loud anyway. As the fog clears a bit, the cause becomes obvious—a massive crater's been blasted into the ground not ten metres to our left. One of Ray's bombs.

I hope the victims were fiends.

Right now, I'm more of a danger to the others if I stick with them. Worse, even though I've let the fire go out, the white light fanning from my fingertips edges my whole body, and I've no idea how to turn it off. Fine white lines surround me, like the lines connecting the fiends.

And the winged beast that lands behind me, claws digging into the ground. Poppy jumps forward immediately, but I hold up a hand. "This one's mine." Its wing's torn, but it looks at me with an expectant expression that throws me off for a second. "Uh. Can you fly?"

The fiend dips its head.

"Right. Guys, you—just get somewhere safe. Please. I'm going to draw the Fiordan's attention and end this."

Two more fiends land behind it. Others I brought under my control.

"Good timing," says Cas.

I gape at him. "You *want* to hitch a ride this time?"

"You need backup."

I open my mouth to protest. But then—he has a point. Anyone can kill the Fiordans if they get hold of a weapon.

"Someone needs to warn the others," I say to Poppy. "The bombs—there's no way for everyone to get out of range. If I walk out there, the Fiordan will spot me, and... look, I have to get away."

No one argues. Another blast of energy somewhere far off to the right engulfs us in dust. That one was closer. We don't have much time.

Poppy hugs me briefly. "I get it, Leah. Kick them into the next world."

"Will do." I glance back over the divide, but I know better than to persuade her to leave. We'll fight as Pyros to the end.

"Come on," I say to Cas. Hoping the others will be safe.

Hoping I can pull this off.

I climb onto the fiend's back. Almost immediately, we're in the air, and flying high. Just like in the vision—climbing above the smoke, above the fighting, searching for the one target to end the war...

A flock of fiends circles above the battlefield. *The Fiordan has to be there.* They might look identical, but the energy beams all converge at one point, at the fiend in the middle of the group. *Clever.* It has to be close enough to give all the fiends orders from the battlefield, I'd guess. That makes a lot of sense. If control relies on energy manipulation, not some kind of psychic link, all I need to do is distract the Fiordan's attention and there's no reason I can't stop the fighting.

I regret the thought in an instant. Energy crackles across the ground in spider-webbing lines as the flock of fiends changes direction. Towards me.

I stop mid-flight and send an energy wave of my own at the fiends, almost without thinking. The central fiend raises a clawed hand to block my attack. *So you're the one.* I push back fiercely, trying to knock the fiend off-balance or at least away from the battlefield. The other fiends move in unison around it. Like they've been ordered to.

White light flares around my hand, around the weapon I took from the other Fiordan. I have maybe seconds before the fiend I'm riding breaks from the pressure. But the other fiends are vulnerable, and the Fiordan must have ordered them to keep following. It can't give other orders while we're locked in a stalemate. The threads of energy connecting them and the one the Fiordan attacks me with are part of the same thing.

I push as hard as I can, and aim at the other fiends rather than the Fiordan. As the fire ripples through the air, their bodies crash into one another like dominoes, knocking into the Fiordan. It might be stronger, but there are more of them.

The fiends fall in a tangle of limbs. I resume my attack, holding onto the energy beams. "You obey me!" I shout at the fiends, and tug, hard. The Fiordan's no longer visible under the weight of the other fiends, and they're falling fast. I follow, dropping steadily in the air. A quick glance behind me to make sure the others are out of harm's way, and I drop towards the Fiordan. I have to take it out before it can activate the bombs. The visible white lines tell me that's not happening yet, but I have no doubt the Fiordan will push the other fiends out the way to get at me.

They crash into the ground in a cloud of dust, fire flaring as the Fiordan pushes to the surface, kicking its fellow fiends aside until the area around it is undisturbed. Fiends scramble over one another in an attempt to get out of the way. The Fiordan's no longer bothering to control them. Its attention's all on me.

As I planned.

"Give up," I shout, weapon held high. "You're as good as dead."

"You killed all of our kind," hisses the Fiordan. "You hunted us into extinction."

"You brought it on yourselves," I say, loudly. "You invaded our world and killed most of the population. You enslaved the fiends and used them as cannon fodder. No one will forgive you for this, so don't expect me to."

I touch down on the ground, on a level with the Fiordan. Ready to call the fire one last time and end this.

Sudden pain flares through my bones and I grit my teeth against a scream. *What the hell is it doing?* My vision goes white, the lines of energy blurring together.

"You won't win this, Transcendent," the Fiordan hisses, and pain sparks up my hand. Jared's face flashes before my eyes, the way he once inflicted horrible pain on me just by touch.

I can hardly see through the pain, and when Jared's face pops up again, I think I'm hallucinating.

No. The Fiordan walks up close, wearing Jared's face again.

A gasp of pain behind me. Cas.

"I know how to break you both. You shouldn't have brought him with you."

The Fiordan gestures, and one of the tangled beams of energy flicks like a whip, knocking me to the ground. Another flick, and a fiend launches itself at me. I barely gather myself to strike, only to be knocked down by a wave of pain. The fiend's claws stab downwards, and I barely roll out of the way in time. I collide with Cas, who fights his own fiend. They're not under my control any longer.

Before the Fiordan can strike me again, I grab onto the nearest energy beam myself, mimicking the same gesture the Fiordan used. Ignoring the voice telling me it's too late, I don't know what I'm doing, I'm far outclassed. I was a fool to think I could bluff my way through. Even being Transcendent.

But I'll never forgive myself if Cas dies for my mistake.

The beam whips forward, knocking the Fiordan back the same way it did to me. The Fiordan pushes back, hands splayed, fire flaring outwards. The other fiends fall over one another in an attempt to get out of the way. But under their feet, ribbons of white light move. From here, I can see where they end up—not at the Fiordan's hands, but at the divide itself.

They're not bombs. But what are they?

The Fiordan flicks another light beam at me, lashing me across the chest. Blood instantly rises, startling me. Jared's face grins, a reminder the Fiordan has more tricks up its sleeve, and despite those damned useless visions, I've no idea what it's thinking.

Cas's opponent falls to the ground, crumbling. But we're backed up against the divide. I didn't realise we'd moved so close. The fiends scramble around us in total confusion, no longer under anyone's control. The Fiordan knocks me back with another energy wave, and my feet stumble on the edge of the divide itself. Blood drips to the parched earth, mingling with the white light.

The divide ignites with a flare of red. Quickly, I grab onto another beam of energy and manage to stop myself falling. But the Fiordan doesn't try to push me. It stands there—and laughs.

The wound in my chest has already healed. Fresh fire rises to the surface, but the beams of white light continue to move on the ground. The Fiordan's hand flexes, and a miniature explosion sparks above the divide.

"Perfect." The voice is nothing like Jared's, but low and gravelly.

"What the hell was that?" I demand. "What did you do?"

Something with my blood. And energy. The divide.

"The divide is closed on this side," hisses the Fiordan. "You humans are trapped. There are no Pyros left on Earth, and the ones here will be dead within a minute."

Oh, no.

That was their plan—to lure every single one of us over here, and trap us. That way, we can't save Earth. Can't save the people left behind. Even without the Fiordans, the fiends' killing instincts can't be tamed. And more divides can open, more invasions.

Both worlds will be at the monsters' mercy.

"This whole world will die," he says, grinning. "It's outlived its usefulness to me and to everyone else. All your people are on this side. Who will save the humans on the other side now? If we die, so do you."

"You'd sacrifice your own life? You won't live forever, will you?" I'm grasping at straws now. "You have no one left. The other Fiordans are dead."

"My blood lives on," hisses the Fiordan. "We'll rise again, as we have every time you people have destroyed us."

"You've lost," Cas snarls. "Give up."

"We've all lost," snarls the Fiordan. "But I can still bring your death." The white beams flick, and the winged fiends move to surround us.

Except one, human-shaped despite the wings.

It's Nolan.

24

*N*olan. *Impossible. He's dead.*

A chill runs through me. His skin is cracked and red as the burned ground, his wings black and batlike, one arm severed at the wrist. But his glare is directed at the Fiordan… who isn't looking at him.

I don't dare move or speak. He's not under the Fiordan's control. And he carries a weapon.

The Fiordan spins, knife lashing in a swirl of energy. Nolan falls with a yell of pain, sprawling to the ground near the divide's edge.

I gape at both of them. Before I can recover from the shock and attack, the Fiordan pushes me back with the same energy wave.

"You," it snarls at Nolan, not keeping its eyes off me. "You should be dead."

"I'm not," says Nolan. "I was too far away for you to control me."

No way. The Fiordans can only control the fiends within range? No wonder the Fiordans all left Earth when the other one died.

Nolan steps back, away from the Fiordan. "I saw what you did. You want everyone to die along with you. But they won't." His blade flashes against the stump of his own wrist. "Only Fiordan blood can pass through the divide. But you're forgetting Jared stole all your ideas. We've been using a version of blood control to protect our headquarters for years. *Human blood,* not Fiordan. And I know how to do the same."

Before any of us can move, Nolan steps over the divide. A spurt of blood, and he vanishes.

The world remains suspended for a heartbeat.

The Fiordan shouts, "Kill them. Kill all the Pyros!"

I snap to my senses and yell at Cas, "Get the others. Now!"

Nolan reversed the divide's blood control barrier. Now, instead of Fiordan blood restricting access to Transcendents, *humans* can pass through. But the bombs are still under our feet. The Fiordan's already reaching for the energy, but a new surge of power runs through me. I pull the fiends' energy streams and yell, "Attack him! Stop him!"

And they do. The fiends move between the Fiordan and the energy rippling under the ground. *They can stop it?* But they had no will of their own, even if they had power. The Fiordan dominated them.

My power is more than a blood weapon, more even than the fire. Pure energy, controlled and wielded by me alone. In my skin. In every part of me. In the fiends. The Fiordans took power from their fellow species and enslaved them.

I reach for the fire and it spreads across my hand. I'm in control. I won't let it explode outwards and destroy everything in its path. Not even the other fiends.

This time, I know how to control it.

This time, I'm going to use it to kill the Fiordan.

Jared's eyes widen as he realises I'm not going to stop,

that I'm in control. But it's too late for him to do anything to stop me.

The blast of energy roars from my fingertips and slams into his arm. For a brief instant, Jared's illuminated in white, as the fire spreads over his body, covering every inch of him. Tiny orange flames burning to pure white, like the old sky on a day where the sun beamed from behind clouds.

Then, he comes apart. Like a hollow mannequin shattering, breaking into tiny particles which blow away instantly. Ashes.

And then I pull the blast back with me, back through my fingertips. My dagger trembles in my other hand, gleaming in the afterglow. It's *energy*—like an energy blast, but on a smaller scale. A mental rather than a physical thing, like Jared's pain tattoos. And unlike the tattoos, it doesn't require a physical mark. The fiends are all linked genetically. Linked to *me*.

I send a surge of fire into the dagger, which lights up like a beacon.

"I'm your leader now," I call to the fiends. "I'm your leader. I have your blood. You're free."

I turn to Cas, breathing heavily. "We have to make sure the others get back."

A nod. He looks dazed, as though he can't quite believe what just happened. That we won.

I'm not sure I believe it either.

A winged figure touches down in front of me. I recoil back, dread closing around my heart. It's Val—her face is hers, even if her body's more like the fiends'.

"Val. I'm sorry." I have to make myself stand still and not back away. She's under her own power, not the Fiordans', but...

"Don't be." She half smiles at me. "What you did... saved my life, Leah."

I swallow. "What do you mean?"

She holds up her left hand, where Jared's mark remains, except red rather than black. "You broke the Fiordans' control. I… I saw them, during the fight. I understand how they work." She looks around at the fiends' army, or what's left of it—with no one to give them orders, most of the fiends are shuffling around with blank expressions on their faces.

"I… don't understand," I say. "You mean you saw through the Fiordans' eyes, right?"

She holds up a hand, which shimmers with a faint skein of energy.

No way. "You can use it, too?"

"A little. I can draw the fiends away from here. Leave you in peace."

"What? You mean *you* aren't coming back?" Impossible.

"I'm hardly Pyro anymore." Val looks ruefully down at her deformed fiend claw-hand. "But here… maybe I can help."

I shake my head, feeling dazed. Sure, the remaining fiends have a hell of a lot of rebuilding to do if they ever want their world to function again… but Val's Pyro. Human.

A shout draws my attention. Declan's marching through the Pyros, ordering them to step away from the fiends, who've simply stopped fighting back.

"Oh, crap," I say. "I guess I should… order them away. Back to the city." The image of those labs comes to mind. "Hmm. If I were them, I wouldn't want to go back there."

"Maybe not," says Val, "but this world has the tools for rebuilding."

"You aren't seriously thinking of…" I can't wrap my head around this at all. But another aggressive shout comes from a group of Pyros who surround a fiend. It doesn't retaliate against their taunting.

"Hey," I say. "It's over! The Fiordans are dead." I look at the fiend. "You can leave. You can all go home."

If the fiends even *have* a home. But one command from me sends them fleeing from the battlefield. Val takes over, getting them into position away from the Pyros.

Now for the tricky bit. The battle might have broken down, but coaxing everyone out the shelter seems to take an inordinately long time. I can't rid myself of the sense of danger, the fire burning under my skin. I don't even know what to say to Cas.

Thoughts bubble below the surface, unspoken.

The Pyros assemble, Declan at the head. Many of the others break down crying when I tell them about Murray. I wish we could talk for longer. Wish I could have more than a few moments with my friends. But they need to go home. And I...

"What's the problem?" Cas, of all people, finally asks. "You're free. The war's over. Why are you acting like we're still at the mercy of those creatures?"

"Isn't it obvious?" I draw in a breath. "I have to stay behind. My blood isn't human anymore."

"You *what?*"

"Nolan fixed the barrier of the divide so humans can pass through it," I say. "Humans, not Fiordans. And I need to close it for good, but last time... I don't think I destroyed it. I— directed energy from that divide to this one."

"And?"

"And my blood isn't human. I can't pass through. You guys need to get back, and then... I guess Val and I stay here. She's already organising the fiends over there."

"That's total bullshit, Leah. It's just blood. None of us are pure human by any measure."

"But I don't have any human blood left in me at all," I say. "It's true. I'm pure Transcendent. Isn't that the whole point in being Transcendent? I have to close the divide. This is *the* divide. The other one closed easily because there were two. I

—saw the energy absorbed into this one. I don't know what the Fiordans did but it's all under the ground here. We can't stay for long. I have to close it."

"You don't have to stay," says Cas. "It was a mistake, what the other Transcendent did. She thought sacrificing her life would close the divide, but it didn't. She climbed right into the middle of the divide, and that's where Jared attacked her."

"So she never got to complete her task," I say. "I get it."

The other Pyros are already crossing, led by Declan. Nobody wants to stick around here in this desolate waste-land. They're going home.

They think I'm going with them.

The feeling's a punch to the gut. I never meant to hurt anyone. But I'm more certain than ever my blood binds me to this place. I'm not human anymore.

Cas's hand closes around mine, startling me. He's never voluntarily touched me before.

I turn to stare, heart beating fast.

"You don't have to do this alone."

I blink at him, completely disarmed.

"Who are you and what did you do with Cas?"

No response. Great. "I'm not gonna let you give up your life just because you feel guilty about the last Transcendent," I say.

"You think this is about her?" His eyes are wide, searching my face. "It's not. You don't have to give up your life.'

'Hark who's talking?' I say. 'You've been doing your damned best to get yourself killed for years.'

'Because I thought I had nothing to live for,' he says. "You were right. I've never thought about after the war. Ever."

"And?" I prompt him.

"Until a really annoying girl showed up and started asking probing questions." He looks away. "You can't stay."

"It's not really a choice," I say. "It's in my blood."

"Blood means nothing. I wish I'd known that sooner."

My head's spinning, my eyes are burning, and half of me wants to scream at him to leave just so I can get this over with.

The other half wants to hold onto him and not let go.

The thought hits me like a sucker-punch. I can't believe it's taken me so long to realise I...

Declan walks up to me before I can even begin to assemble my thoughts.

"You were right. The Fiordans had them under total control. Will the same happen to the fiends on Earth?" he asks me.

"I don't know," I say honestly. "They sometimes attacked us in the wilderness, but maybe that was the Fiordans, too. But we're more than a match for them."

"Either way, we won. Murray would be proud of you," Declan tells me. "I'll... I don't know if you'll have me as a leader, but I'll do my best to rebuild the Pyros. Undo any damage Jared did."

I swallow, tears welling. "I—" I glance around at the others, and drop my voice. "All that's left to do is close the divide. But there's a chance I might get trapped here, or die. The other Transcendent did."

"Because Jared attacked her when she jumped into the breach," says Cas. "You'll survive."

"It's because the divide's fixed so only humans can pass through it," I say quickly. "But my blood—it's Transcendent."

Understanding passes over Declan's face. "I'd never ask you to sacrifice yourself, Leah, but this divide..."

"It's sucking the life out of Earth," I say. "The fiends can rebuild here, now the Fiordans are gone, but the divide needs to close. I'll risk anything for that. Val's staying. I used my blood to stop the visions breaking her down when the Fiordans had control of her."

And it's my fault. But I'm too burned out for more guilt. I'll apologise to her later. If I survive this.

Cas turns to me. "You did?"

"Yeah." I glance over my shoulder, and to my surprise, see her standing with two people. Humans? I squint at them, frowning.

"Those are the Transcendents," says Cas, also frowning. "They don't look like Jared anymore."

I thought they looked familiar. She approaches us, and nods to Cas.

"I found them," she explains, jerking her head over her shoulder. "They were in a bad way, but... there were Fiordan blood samples in the city."

"You went there?" Cas frowns at her. Then his eyebrows lift as batlike wings extend from Val's shoulders.

"It'll take some getting used to," says Val, with a rueful smile. "But... well. I'm glad to be alive."

Cas's expression is incredulous. "You want to stay *here?*"

"Not permanently," says Val, her smile fading. "But... I can't explain the feeling. It's like my blood's drawn to this place. I'm not sure if I'll be able to pass through the worlds like the Fiordans did before the divide or not, but someone has to help the fiends rebuild. Without the Fiordans."

I expect Cas to make a disparaging comment, but he just nods. "All right."

Energy spikes under my skin. I'm surer than ever that I need to close the divide *now*. As soon as possible. Earth's being poisoned by the link, and it wouldn't surprise me if that's one of the reasons *this* world has never recovered, either.

"I don't want to drag out the goodbye," I whisper, watching the others cross back to Earth in groups. Mostly Declan's lot. Some all but run across the divide, and I guess I can't blame them. They thought they'd never get home.

Cas shoots me an angry look that's more sadness than real rage. My tears spill over, and I don't care that he can see them.

Poppy catches my arm. "You're staying, aren't you?"

I don't ask how she knows. "I'm closing the divide."

"And you think you won't make it?"

I just hug her. A long goodbye will make it doubly hard for her, for the others. At least I know I'm capable of caring again. At least I know.

We walk, after the others. Sorrow wells up in my chest, for those lost in the fight, for those left behind.

But hope. There's always hope.

I want to hug Cas, but if I do, I'll never let go.

"You don't have to do this." Cas holds back even as Declan beckons the others on. "Leah, what you said about *after*—"

"Stop." I can't bear to hear it. "You're making this worse."

"Sorry." He looks away from me. A pause, while the others cross the divide. "You were right about me. I never saw myself as anything other than a Pyro. I forgot about the human part. And—you're not Resa. I never had chance to say goodbye to her."

I swallow. "Goodbyes are messy and stupid. Let's just say I might see you on the other side."

"Maybe."

I look up at him then, see the sadness stark in his expression, but he turns his back and walks away. Not in an unfriendly way, more like someone who's resigned himself to the inevitable.

I can relate.

My heart's pounding too fast, my limbs locking. I need to run before I lose my nerve.

I walk two steps, then sprint, spreading my arms and calling on the fire.

I'm suspended in the air above the divide, a rippling tide

below me. Strands of energy flow between me and the ground, as I'm blocked from Earth by the blood-shield Nolan created. But this line shouldn't be here.

Earth should be free.

This time, I don't even have to wait before the fiery light comes, like an old friend. Arcing down from the sky, it radiates outwards. The air before me ripples as the energy blast reaches it—but this time, I'm in control. I'm focused, holding onto that one thought, and somehow, I'm directing the waves.

I can see both sides of the divide, shimmering and wavering. The fire spreads out over the gate, covering the rippling wall. My eyesight blurs with the flicker of flames, and I can no longer tell which world I'm looking at.

"Close," I tell the gateway.

I send a wave of energy rippling out from my body, flooding the divide. I give everything, leaving nothing. I'm a human energy blast, a focus point. A gate.

Close.

The energy slams into me. Once again, I feel more than see the gears turning, the doors closing. Closing on me. I scream. White light blinds me. A clicking reverberates in my head, like a door closing.

Everything fades to black.

————

I don't expect to wake up. It's like a shock of cold water when eye-watering, horrible, burning pain ignites all over my body. I yell, twisting and writhing.

"Keep still!"

Cas's voice. I stop moving, instantly. Will my eyes to open.

Above is a terrifying, alien blackness, dark as far as the eyes can see, save for a few white pinpricks.

Stars.

The sky.

Cas holding his own bleeding hand over my body. I'm still healing, but I'm alive, *alive.*

"You bloody fool."

I half-laugh. "So I'm not dreaming."

"You nearly got cut in two," says Cas. "The divide slammed together, and you fell. You were unconscious."

I blink. "Seriously?"

"Don't move!" Poppy shrieks, and it hits me that I'm lying... under the sky. The *old* sky, black and dotted with stars.

"Where am I?"

"A field near—where the divide used to be," says Poppy. Tears streak her face. "We'll probably set up a new headquarters, but we couldn't move you in that state. I thought... you died."

"This state?" Holy crap, I'm covered in so much blood. Just the sight makes me dizzy. I close my eyes. "So I—I survived."

"I told you you didn't have to die," says Cas, and I think I'm the only person who catches the profound relief in his voice. "You had enough human blood left, you fool. Thought you did your damned best to lose it all."

"I'll get Declan," says Poppy. "And Elle—she's frantic."

Soft footsteps tell me she's leaving, but I'm too weak to sit up.

"The sky," says Cas, after a pause. "I'd forgotten what it looked like."

"Me, too," I say softly. "I thought it had gone for good."

"Apparently, we get a miracle after all." But he's looking at me. Not at the sky.

I manage to prop myself up on my elbows. "Never thought I'd hear that coming from you."

"No. I guess not." He's never looked at me this intently.

"Do you really think I'm annoying?" I ask to fill the silence.

"The most annoying."

"Same to you." I rest my head on the ground. "You really pulled me out of the fire?"

"Of course I did. I wasn't about to let you martyr yourself."

"And you wouldn't do the same?"

"I'm not the Transcendent, am I?"

I sit up again, this time managing to do it properly. I can't decide what's more surreal—the star-studded black sky or the fact that Cas is *smiling* at me.

"No, you're clearly an alien imposter," I say. "What's that odd expression on your face?"

The smile fades. "What? Shouldn't I be glad you're alive?"

"Never said that." I grin up at him, absurdly happy. I'm alive, and I've absolutely no clue what Cas's thinking—but I don't even care right now. "But I'm kind of confused. Does this mean you aren't going to be a dick to everyone?"

"I can't make any promises. Declan's ordering everyone around already, and he and Ray keep arguing about whether to set up a new base."

"I'd say yes," I say, "seeing as a mountain's not really the most practical place. Unless you can fly."

"Thankfully not," says Cas, looking up at the sky, frowning. "But someone can." He tenses, and I notice the sword lying on the rock as he snatches it up—it's the first time I've seen him not carrying his weapon. But he points it at the fiend as it lands.

Not it. She. Val.

"What…?"

"Leah." Val still has fiend wings and one clawed hand, but is otherwise human-looking. "I hoped you lived. I just came back to check…"

"You *just* came back?" I gape at her. "I thought the fiends' world was closed."

"You forget I'm part Transcendent." White energy flares around her, and she half-vanishes, then appears again. "Looks like I can shift over. So I can update you guys on what's happening over there…"

"Seriously?" Cas's incredulous expression matches my own. "You can shift over."

"I might be able to *shape*-shift, too," says Val. "I've not tried yet, but I've time enough." She grins at us. "I'll catch you later."

And she vanishes, leaving me gawping in disbelief.

"Did that just happen?"

"Apparently." Cas turns to me again. "What she said— we've time enough now. It's true."

"Yeah." I slump back on the ground, and Cas sits alongside me, close enough that I find myself unconsciously leaning on him. "We've time enough to…" Find out what Cas and I have. I can't deny that being here, being this close to him, makes me happier than I've felt in a long time. Longer than I can remember.

"Our world is ours again."

I nod. Society may be almost finished, billions dead—and yet, some of us lived.

Maybe it's futile to believe we won't be our own undoing, that we won't raze our own world to the ground the way the Fiordans did to theirs. But they won't interfere any longer. Our future is ours to build.

I don't know what will happen. But we've time enough to find out.

"Yeah," I say, reaching my hand out to clasp his. "It's ours."

ABOUT THE AUTHOR

Emma is the New York Times and USA Today Bestselling author of the Changeling Chronicles urban fantasy series.

Emma spent her childhood creating imaginary worlds to compensate for a disappointingly average reality, so it was probably inevitable that she ended up writing fantasy novels. When she's not immersed in her own fictional universes, Emma can be found with her head in a book or wandering around the world in search of adventure.

Find out more about Emma's books at www.emmaladams.com.